SPIES IN SILK

SPIES
IN
SILK

Piers Falconer

First published in Great Britain in 1992 by
Nexus
338 Ladbroke Grove
London W10 5AH

Typeset by TW Typesetting, Plymouth, Devon
Printed and bound in Great Britain by
Cox & Wyman Ltd, Reading, Berkshire

ISBN 0 352 32819 3

A catalogue record for this title is available from the
British Library

CONTENTS

PART ONE

Tanya, Comtesse de Beccelone	3
Madeleine	17
Sylvia	38
Ingrid	62
Jeanne	84
Christine	102
Meik	123
Jacqui	139

PART TWO

London	165
Liverpool	188
Paris	207
Marseilles	227
Washington	244
Epilogue	261

CONTENT

PART ONE

Tanya, Comtesse de Beccelonne

Lord Chomsmy dined at the Ritz. The country had been at war for ten months, and he was very conscious of being one of the few men out of uniform in the dining room. However, it had been a successful day. The selection board had done well; seven attractive young ladies had been chosen. He smiled. It seemed that he could look forward to a good war after all. It was an ill wind indeed. They were all fiercely patriotic young women, eager to take their place beside the men to fight the war. He was giving them that chance, and they were grateful. Each one had sworn at her interview that she would be prepared to use any means to help defeat the enemy.

Thinking of the women, and his plans for them, made him randy. It was a moonlight night, and he decided to walk to Curzon Street. He wondered how long it would be before Hitler unleashed his Luftwaffe upon the peaceful streets of London. The girls around Shepherd's Market were already on the streets, and the way they flashed their torches to illuminate themselves in the blackout brought a great rising in his trousers. He pondered whether to engage the services of a statuesque brunette who spoke to him in a lilting Irish accent, as there was always a chance Tanya wouldn't be at home. He should have telephoned from the Ritz.

He walked up the steps to be let into a luxurious apartment by an elderly butler. The exertion of climbing the stairs had done nothing to quieten the monster straining at his fly. He expected the buttons to fly off at any second. An antidote must be found quickly.

'Tell the Comtesse Tanya I have urgent need of her, and will be waiting in the small anteroom.'

The butler disappeared. Lord Chomsmy walked into the small room, used as a waiting room, at the side of the entrance hall. He hadn't long to wait for her arrival. She closed the door behind her, and smiled at him. She was a tall elegant woman; the perfect shape of her breasts and curve of her thighs emphasised the exquisite femininity of her body. An almost regal face, beautifully proportioned, gazed out from beneath a mane of chestnut hair that highlighted her extraordinary apple-green eyes. She glided to him, clothed in a clinging emerald-green evening gown that must have cost a fortune. She smiled, an intimate expression of devotion rather than love. He made no effort to disguise the bulge in his trousers; his stance tended to emphasise it. She stood facing him.

'You are in a state, George,' she grinned.

She fell to her knees. Her fingers expertly unbuttoned his flies, allowing his rampant weapon to spring forward as if powered by elastic. She eased the stiffened prong completely free of the restraining material and, bending forward, gently licked the helmet with the tip of her delightful pink tongue. The great prick seemed to swell until it quivered like a tuning fork. With an expertise born of experience, she took it into her warm, wet mouth, gliding her red lips tantalisingly down the long shaft until the knob had reached the back of her throat. He groaned, pushing his thighs forward as if he

4

wanted her to swallow his whole cock deep down into her stomach. She held back her long chestnut hair with her fingers to stop it cascading forward and hiding her face from his downward glance. She knew he loved to see his prick encircled by her pouting red lips, to watch her suck and lick along the whole shaft with flickering teasing tongue. She gave immense delight, and appeared to derive a great deal of pleasure from her task, like a greedy girl gorging herself on a long stick of chocolate. Her sensitive lips warned her that his climax was nearby; she felt an incredible stiffening, and it seemed his penis must burst. She gulped, allowing his sperm as far down into her throat as was possible without choking her, sucking the explosion of cream into her mouth until the last drops had been drained from his balls. She looked up at him, and allowed his limp member to slip from her lips. She raised her face, her eyes smiled wickedly, and then slowly, deliberately, she swallowed.

'Thank you, Tanya,' he breathed. 'You get better and better.'

They had known each other a long time, he being the only man to whom the Comtesse de Beccelonne bent her knee. In the winter of 1917, she had been a thirteen-year-old Parisienne schoolgirl, and he a handsome Guards major. He had met the half-starved waif while on leave from the trenches, and she had given him her virginity in return for the generosity he had shown her family. He promised to return if he survived the war.

Three years later Paris had become the hub of 1920s society, the intellectual playground of the civilised world. He returned, and took her as his mistress. In 1924 his father died, leaving him the family title and wealth. His riches were enough to support him in a life of debauchery, and his name was soon respected in gaming houses and brothels throughout the world.

Tanya married the impoverished and ailing Comte de Beccelonne, and on his death travelled to London to become a courtesan of impeccable reputation. She learned to lead the good life, to mix with aristocrats and to be accepted by them. Her discretion was renowned, and never once had she been involved in scandal. Her rooms in Curzon Street were the haunt of the rich and the powerful, and an invitation was much sought after. Only he knew her background, and together they smiled at the high-born men who fawned upon her.

'I have important news, Tanya. Order a bottle of claret for us to share, and I will tell you.'

'George, I'm sorry. I have company. We are just going to sit down.'

'Excuse yourself, bring the claret and join me; you won't be sorry.'

He had buttoned his flies, but she knew by his tone that he would soon be hot for her to unbutton them again. He would never change while he had lead in that huge pencil. She had never found true love, and George was the nearest she had ever got to a grand passion. She liked him, probably because they were so alike. She excused herself from the dinner and, armed with a good claret, returned to find him in her private sitting room.

He poured the wine while her nimble fingers began to undress him. The room was warm, and soon he was lying naked on the long comfortable sofa. She sipped the wine, her eyes smiling knavishly over the rim of the glass. She stood sheathed in the evening gown of heavy silk, expertly fashioned to cling to the curves of her magnificent body. In what appeared to be one smooth movement, she removed the gown rather in the same manner as she might have peeled off a glove. It was her one item of clothing, and now she stood as naked as the day she was born.

He looked up at her, drinking in the beauty of her nudity. She was as beautiful as ever; it was a different, more mature beauty, but still enough to make a man of any age gasp in admiration. He knew men who had paid a king's ransom to possess her, and men she'd driven crazy by refusing.

She mounted him astride, lowering her thighs until her soft bush tickled his sleeping member. She gently rubbed the moistened lips of her simmering crack along his wakening phallus until her juices leaked from her and he was as upright as a barber's pole. She sat above him like a frog turned into a beautiful princess and, easing her labia apart with her fingers, she lowered herself until the tip of his knob found her clitoris. Wantonly, she massaged herself. He watched the expression of sensual concentration etched on her face, the far-off look of delight in her eyes. He saw the cascading mane of chestnut hair, half hiding the gentle swaying of her perfect ivory breasts. She sank on to him, so very slowly, moving inch by inch down his throbbing shaft until she had him completely imprisoned within her.

'Now,' she breathed, 'tell me your news.'

He marvelled at her expertise. More than ever he was convinced that she was the only woman who could play the part he had in mind.

'I've been given my commission back. I'm soon to be a serving officer on the General List.'

'What rank, my darling?'

'Lieutenant colonel.'

7

She moved her thighs sensuously, squeezing her vaginal muscles so that his throbbing penis jerked inside her. She recognised his expression of acute ecstasy, and bent forward to kiss him.

'Will I have to salute you, Colonel?'

'You'll have to do better than that, woman.'

She grinned and allowed the hardened nipples of her swinging bubbies to brush against his chest.

'Tell me more.'

'I have been given the task of training selected young women who have volunteered to become secret agents in occupied Europe.'

'Train them in what?'

'Seduction.'

'Great heavens!'

'It's true.'

'You old goat,' she laughed. 'How did you manage that?'

'You'll have heard that after Dunkirk, Churchill commanded a secret army be formed to "set Europe alight". I suggested a spy school for female agents, who would use their God-given charms to extract information from the enemy.'

'A team of Mata Haris?'

'If you like, but it has to be confidential. If the House of Commons or the press gets to hear, there'll be the devil of a hullabaloo.'

'So you are serious. However did you persuade the War Office to give you free rein over a bevy of virgins? My God, you are the last person on earth they should trust.'

He raised himself up and landed a resounding slap on her backside. She squealed.

'I've loaned Holmsley Manor to the War Office for the training centre. There'll be seven girls, so they can

8

have a bedroom each. Their military espionage training will be done at the army camp some two miles away. Their evenings will be spent with us, learning the many devious ways of seduction.'

'Us?'

'Yes, my dear. I have put your name forward as my assistant.'

'Why should I want to bury myself in the country?'

'Seven eager young girls to be whipped into shape. Don't tell me that doesn't appeal to you.'

'Why, should it?'

He raised his hand again. The slap that landed on the bare flesh of her plump rear echoed like a gunshot throughout the room.

'You beast,' she shrieked.

'I know you've always fancied yourself as a madam. You will be able to teach these girls your whole extensive repertoire, and who knows, after the war they might join you in the bawdiest house in Europe!'

'My God, George. Between us we can thoroughly debauch these innocents. Is that what the War Office wants?'

'It's not quite what they have in mind. The War Office appears to believe a theoretical training would be sufficient for the girls to carry out their missions successfully.'

'But you, being a practical man, disagree?'

'Exactly.'

'Shall I have to move into Holmsley Manor?'

'I've asked that you be given an emergency commission in one of the women's services, and you'll be stationed there, under my command.'

'It's got to be the WRNS,' she squealed excitedly. 'Imagine the Comtesse de Beccelonne, an officer in the British Navy. I was worrying how I'd survive the war without being thought a useless parasite. Thanks, George, you really are marvellous.'

She bent forward and kissed him, slipping her tongue into his open mouth, and sucking his lips with hers. She was still astride him, and all through their conversation she had held him tight inside her. Now, sitting upright above him, she began to manoeuvre her thighs to a position to give them mutual pleasure. She raised herself, sliding slowly up his pole until the pink swollen lips of her twat rested upon the very tip of his knob. For one brief moment she held herself still, gripping the helmet of his throbbing shaft between the slippery outer lips of her zealous quim. He found it agonising to wait for her to lower herself down on to his anxious pego. At last she slid down on to him, millimetre by millimetre, the elasticity of her tunnel walls gripping him as if she had him enclosed within a velvet glove. Gradually she raised the tempo until her thighs moved like a steam piston, each stroke measuring the whole length of his penis. Suddenly her stroke faltered, her body tensed, her breathing quickened and she began to moan. He reached up and grabbed her swinging orbs, like soft ripe melons, to squeeze them in his hands. She gasped, and collapsed on to him, her body trembling as if in a convulsion, her juices trickling down on to his balls.

He was still hard inside her, and he knew she would be ready to meet his challenge the instant he moved inside her. But he had a yen for the secret passage she guarded so zealously. She wouldn't like it, but she wouldn't refuse him, not at this time. He rolled her off him on to the thick piled carpet, where he manoeuvred her on to her hands and knees with the plump white spheres of her arse prettily raised before him.

'You will be able to write a book about your part in

the war,' he said, 'and how you helped your beloved France. It will enhance your reputation, and calls for a special celebration. Don't you agree, comtesse?'

He sat balanced on the very edge of the sofa, his prong hard and quivering, about an inch distant from her comely posterior. He poured himself a glass of claret, smacking his lips as he drank.

'So I claim a reward.'

'You don't improve, m'lord,' she giggled. 'You were ever a greedy pig. Haven't I been generous enough already? What more can I offer?'

He held the glass above her curved backside, and allowed the claret to spill and trickle down the cleft between the cheeks of her haunches.

'Your derrière, dear Tanya. My stallion itches to travel that dark passage tonight.'

He eased apart the soft cheeks to reveal the nut-brown orifice she guarded so well, and presented the tip of his swollen member to the puckered entrance, which quivered beneath his touch.

'No, George, not that way. Please, no. You know I grant no man that favour.'

It was true. He had taken her that way several times, the first on her seventeenth birthday when she had become his mistress. She liked it well enough, but felt that by offering her fundament she was no longer in control. When a man corked her there he was calling the tune, and she was his slave. Tanya liked to believe she was always in control, both of herself and the man who was mounting her. She had allowed one other man access – the American millionaire from whom she'd inherited the apartments in Curzon Street – but George had no knowledge of that.

'Please, George, there are my guests. I have left them too long already.'

11

'True, my beauty, but I shall have my way later.'

'So be it.' She smiled gently.

'We will celebrate. We will have a night as we did on the Silver Jubilee. What say you, Tanya?'

'I say you're depraved, Lord George.'

'Do you remember it?'

'Well enough, and I still blush at the thought.'

'And when you blush, is it the cheeks of your face, or the cheeks of your pretty bum?'

'George, you embarrass me.'

They dressed, and joined the comtesse's guests – a single banker, and two politicians with their paramours – who were still dining. A wife rarely crossed the threshold of Curzon Street, certainly never a wife with her husband. The conversation was of the war, the evacuation at Dunkirk and the probability of an invasion before the winter.

It was well past midnight before the last couple left and Tanya and Lord Chomsmy were at last alone. He summoned the old butler who knew he had been impatient for the guests to leave.

'Yes, m'lord?' enquired the old chap, who had come with the apartments, and now knew the comtesse's ways, and was discretion itself. He knew she adored Lord Chomsmy, a frequent visitor. He knew of Lord C.'s reputation as a roué and a lecher, and of his sometime nickname Lord George Spanker, given to him because of his liking for warming the ladies' bottoms.

'We are retiring, James. Bring us a magnum of champagne, please, and a stout strap for your mistress's bottom.'

The comtesse blushed prettily, but willingly took Lord Chomsmy's arm as they trod the stairs to her boudoir. He stood in his shirt sleeves fingering the strap James had brought as she flounced off to the bathroom. She looked exquisitely feminine adorned in a full-skirted negligée, her heavy breasts plainly visible through the thin material. His sense of anticipation was heightened by the champagne, and the blood raced through his veins. She rested her hands on his shoulders and, very deliberately, she kissed him.

'I'm ready. You may take your pleasure of me.'

'And what would please you?'

'Whatever you do to me, I shall enjoy.'

He undid the top button of her negligée, and it billowed away from her gorgeous body leaving her ravishingly naked. Her perfect body never failed to arouse him: no woman possessed such earthy beauty, such mundane sensuality. It wasn't the beauty of a goddess to be worshipped, but of a woman to be fucked. He dragged three pillows from the head of the bed, and threw them into the middle. He pointed sternly to the bed.

'On your belly, woman, with the pillows under your thighs.'

She lay, holding the rail at the head of the bed, her head on the one remaining pillow, her luscious backside raised by the other three.

He fingered the strap, which was of three-inch leather divided into two flat thongs. The leather was smooth and pliable, shaped lovingly for a lady's bottom. He looked at her naked outstretched body, and his chest muscles tightened; a band of steel crushed his ribs. She presented a mouthwatering picture of feminine submission and obedience. Her rump was presented to him exposed and unprotected. He raised the strap, and gently lashed her firm white buttocks. The rounded globes quivered under the pliable leather, the tender flesh reddened as the strap stroked across

13

her plump nates. She gasped, squealed and whimpered.

'Stop, please, no more. It stings. Stop, my bum's on fire!'

In answer he increased the tempo. She screamed obscenities, bucked and twisted, and kicked her legs. Tears coursed down her face, her thick chestnut hair tangled about her shoulders. He took her arm, helping her from the bed, and forced her down on to her hands and knees.

'My bottom's on fire. Feel it, George.'

She had allowed herself to be spanked many times – she enjoyed it as a prelude to sex – but she'd been thrashed only twice before, and each time by him. She wouldn't be able to sit comfortably for days, and would regret it; but he knew that the masochist in her revelled in the soreness of her behind. It satisfied a dark facet of her character. He cupped her reddened cheeks in the palms of his hand. The flesh was quite hot, and that heat warming his hands spread to his loins, turning his desire for her into an urgent lust.

'Is it very red?' she asked, as if to ascertain whether he had done his work properly.

He jerked down his trousers, clearing the decks for his big gun to spring into action.

'It's red hot,' he replied, reaching for the champagne bottle. 'But before I take the plunge into the fiery furnace, I'll cool it a little.'

He shook the bottle and allowed the bubbling liquor to squirt over her hindquarters. She squeaked with surprise and delight, but then felt his fingers sliding into the valley between her twin moons, his anxious charger demanding entrance to her back gate. Grasping her hips, he pressed forward; the tip of his knob crushed against her forbidden orifice. She yelped and winced in pain as her sphincter parted, and he bur-rowed deep into her. She gasped. His big tool was already buried far into her rectum. She stayed silent as he possessed her, moaning when he removed his cock only to plunge it back time and time again. He fumbled for her boobs, swinging like huge peaches on a tree, and squeezed them spitefully in his hands as he bellowed like a wild boar and shot his load into her.

They lay there, with him sprawled over her rump like a tamed bull, strangely relaxed as if they had been purged of a dark inhibition. He pulled her to her feet, and poured two glasses of champagne. She raised her glass.

'My God, George, you have exhausted me. I shall be sore for a week.'

He sat on the bed while she crossed to the long mirror to view her backside. He smiled. It was strange how all females needed to know how much the skin had reddened after a spanking. Perhaps they were checking to see the job was well done, or perhaps the discolouring excited them. She appeared to be satisfied with what she saw. The flesh would bruise, but the skin was unbroken.

'Who else is to help us, in this spy school of yours?'

'My nephew, Nigel.'

'Great heavens! Why?' He's a lout, and he's not yet twenty-one.'

'He might be young, but he's hung like a bull elephant,' he replied. 'On his fifteenth birthday I paid a whore to entertain him. Break him in, so to speak. Afterwards she told me it was him who exhausted her. It was like having a buffalo between her legs.'

'When must I take up residence at Holmsley Manor?'

'We will proceed there in about a month. The girls

are to be enlisted into the women's services, and have to suffer four weeks initial military training. I see no real point in it, but the powers that be insist.'

'Where do these girls come from?'

'Special Intelligence put the word out, and we were swamped with volunteers. We finally selected seven attractive young women of differing nationalities and backgrounds, all fluent in two or more languages.'

'That must have been difficult.'

'Not really, from the number we had to choose from,' he replied. 'What was difficult was finding ways to hint that their task would be to seduce, rather than fight, the enemy.'

'I can imagine,' she grinned.

'Our innuendos went over the heads of most, and we could see others would be disgusted by the whole concept. Of the remainder, most just weren't sexy enough; but we did finally find seven real beauties who would fit the bill. You'll love 'em, Tanya, and by the time we've finished we'll have eight sirens to lure the unsuspecting Nazis on to the rocks.'

'Eight?'

'You will take your natural place, as their leader.'

'I wasn't interviewed.'

'We didn't think that was necessary.'

'We?' she said sharply. 'Who else was on that interview board?'

'Vice-Admiral Lord Pymph, and Major-General Spotty Spaunder.'

'Both of whom have been in my bed.'

'Exactly!'

'Pour me another champagne, colonel,' she grinned impishly, 'and then you may take me to bed. We'll make this a night to remember before we sally forth to play our lecherous part in the winning of the war.'

Madeleine

An old piano was tinkling the haunting melody of 'Unforgettable', and a young woman crooned the lyric, slipping between French and English as she sang. Her voice was thin but pleasant enough, and seemed to delight the crowd of half-drunken men. She exuded a sexual magnetism that enabled her to keep her audience spellbound, yet she possessed an aloofness that kept them at bay. Everybody said she was too good for the Blue Parrot, a dimly lit, smoke-filled nightclub which was little more than a bawdy house. But she was happy there, and everybody wanted her to stay. She was certainly attractive, and her looks held up in the daylight when the other girls looked like scrubbers. A petite brunette barely five feet tall, with a vivacious smile and alert brown eyes, she had all the essentials of a pocket Venus.

She'd worked at the Blue Parrot for nearly a year since she first arrived one night on the arm of a big spender from Brussels. He had belted her once too often, and she'd knifed him. A dozen witnesses swore he'd been stabbed by a drunk from out of town who'd escaped in the confusion, so she'd stayed on and become a firm favourite. She was as willing as any of the girls to accompany a customer to the back rooms, but she was too pricy for most of the locals. She probably wouldn't have stayed but for the war breaking out.

Her little Belgian town was soon swarming with soldiers of the British expeditionary force, who weren't millionaires but were full of good-natured fun. It was then she fell in love. A pug-ugly battery sergeant major, old enough to be her father, captured her heart. He did so without trying, for he couldn't have imagined such a lovely woman falling for him. She'd laughed when he'd told her how nervous he'd been inviting her to the back rooms for the first time. He'd been stationed near the town for six months, and they'd discussed marriage. He wanted her to marry him, and go to England. He was certain that the Nazi war machine would never be halted by the poorly armed British and French armies.

The song finished, and she bowed into the spotlight before it was switched off by the management, who hoped she'd made the audience thirsty enough to order more liquor or randy enough to herd the girls into the back rooms. She stepped down from the rickety stage into the arms of the stocky, balding BSM; and the crowd whistled and catcalled as the couple headed towards the back rooms. They stood by an old wooden-framed bed which sagged with age and hard usage, and he took her hand.

'There's something in the air,' he said. 'I can smell it. This phoney war's going to explode with the hell of a bang. See if I'm not right.'

'Please,' she pleaded, 'don't talk of it. Just make love to me.'

He eased the thin velvet straps of her long black evening gown down from her shoulders, so that the low-cut bodice slipped to reveal the delightful curve of her white breasts. Her boobs were small, but perfectly shaped like two delicious ripe peaches. He sat on the bed before her, and tongued each fleshy orb in turn, long, luxurious licks like a contented cat grooming its fur. The pliant mounds moved like blancmange under his insistent tongue, until his lips closed over a pert nipple to suck the sweetness from it. He eased down the gown over her hips so it fell in a circle around her feet. She was naked beneath. Slowly he moved his tongue over her stomach, darting into her small inviting navel, tugging at her adorable pubic hair with his lips.

He fetched a bowl of water, and washed her feet, playing piggie with her toes and sucking each one in turn. She giggled happily, and felt like a child. No other man had so adored her. She was used to being treated as a whore. Yet this rugged professional soldier, veteran of a thousand brothels around the world, treated her like a lady.

She urged him on to the bed, and pushed him on to his back, mounting astride him to indulge in his favourite, *soixante-neuf*. Her face was directly above his crotch; she took his testicles, one at a time, into her warm sensual mouth, sucking like a schoolgirl with a gobstopper. She watched his dormant prick rise before her eyes, and she popped it into her mouth while, fondling his balls with expert fingers. She sucked like an angel, and he clutched her thighs, which were spread wide open an inch from his nose, and buried his lips into her gaping twat. He sucked at the soft fleshy outer lips of her slit, grinding the flesh between his lips while his tongue searched for her tiny, sensitive clitoris. Their oral union was complete as each sucked lustily at the other's genitalia; and when she came with a deep sigh he sipped her juices as if they were nectar. The thrill of her satisfaction urged him towards his own climax, and as she quickened the tempo of her sweet sucking, so he exploded into her willing mouth. They sucked each other dry, and she rolled beneath him in preparation to arouse John Thomas again for a bout of copulation.

It was not to be. A loud rap at the door disturbed them.

'They're screaming for another song, Madeleine,' a voice called.

'Let them scream,' he whispered.

'No, I must go. I will need this job when you go to war.'

The next morning Hitler's Panzers struck across the French and Belgian borders, and he was gone. As he forecast, rifles and bravery were no match for modern armour, and the Allies were soon in full retreat. Refugees flocked from the Belgian towns, but she wasn't among them. He arrived an hour ahead of the Nazis to lead her to safety. His battery had been destroyed, and he had heard rumours of an evacuation through Dunkirk. He dressed her in British army uniform, and she hid her long black hair under a steel helmet. Somehow he got her on to a waiting ship, only to get dive-bombed and sunk just outside the harbour. They swam together in the oily water until a passing boat picked them up, but as he helped her aboard he was killed by a machine-gun bullet.

She was distraught. In England she was accepted as a genuine refugee, but she was inconsolable. A naval officer took her under his wing, and she became his mistress. It was he who told her of Lord C.'s attempt to recruit multilingual females. It was a chance to take revenge for her man's death. She was accepted for interview, and described herself as a nightclub singer. They mustn't discover she was a prostitute; she'd never

20

be accepted for any kind of important work. The sanctimonious British were puritanical in their attitudes towards prostitution. However, Lord C. took an instant liking to the spunky little Belgian girl, and soon she was on her way to the ATS enlistment centre. Her war had begun in earnest.

Madeleine stood to attention. She was in trouble again. A sergeant sat behind the desk, bawling her out, and not for the first time. She hated the camp, detested the training and found the discipline unbearable. She knew she'd never make a servicewoman, but she was driven on by her thirst for revenge and her desire to return to Europe, and so she persevered. She was a week into the month's initial training that the seven girls were required to complete. Their first report was due, and the sergeant was telling her she had about as much chance of passing as a snowball in hell . . . unless. His tirade passed over her head, but she caught the meaning of that last word quickly enough.

'I must have a good report, sergeant,' she pleaded, 'whichever way I get it. Whatever you want me to do?'

He had no need to reply. They both knew a bargain had been struck. Madeleine's confidence blossomed. She was on home ground now. When the sergeant was being a military man he frightened her, but when he was being human, she could handle him. He walked around the desk towards her, keeping her standing at attention. She watched him kneel before her, felt his hands groping under her uniform skirt and sliding up the outside of her legs. She trembled as his fingers touched the bare flesh above her stocking tops.

'Keep still, Miss Madeleine,' he smiled sardonically. 'I've never thought much of women as soldiers, but women in uniform sure make me horny.'

The first few days at the camp had been hell, until the distinguished Lord C. had paid them a visit. He'd been dressed in the uniform of a colonel, and accompanied by a WRNS officer who looked more like a film star than a servicewoman. Her uniform had been tailored like a glove, and her hat had perched on her chestnut mane at a very precarious angle. When he asked whether there were any complaints, the girls had taken him seriously. They complained loud and long. They complained they had not volunteered to join the women's services to polish buttons, or to parade around a drill square. They had not expected to wear baggy uniforms and ludicrous underwear, to sleep in wooden cots in a bare barrack room. Lord C. had been flummoxed. It was the sergeant who had tried to explain they needed discipline to train for the sort of tasks they might be asked to undertake in occupied Europe. As a result of the visit they were allowed several privileges, including the wearing of ther own civilian lingerie.

The sergeant's fingers had discovered the elastic waistband of Madeleine's knickers, and she was acutely conscious of them being slipped down her legs until they circled her feet. One by one, he lifted her feet, and she watched him toss the intimate garment onto the desk. He stood facing her. Their eyes were level, his smiling, hers submissive.

'I don't like girls who wear knickers,' he growled. 'Remember that in future, Miss Madeleine.'

He stooped, took the bottom of her skirt and whipped it up until it circled her waist. She stood naked from the waist down.

'For a week you girls have tormented me, flaunting your sex so casually, leaving me with a permanent jack up to my eyebrows. Now, let's see if you can cure it, Miss Madeleine.'

He took her by the waist, and swung her up on to the desk like a doll, so that she was balanced on the very edge. Reaching down he took her ankles, and with a jerk lifted her legs high above her head. She toppled backwards, finding herself flat on her back with her legs in the air. He bent back her knees until they touched her chin. She could imagine the sight she presented, and almost blushed for herself. She was lying on her back on a desk cluttered with stationery: her skirt rucked up around her waist, her bare arse hanging over the edge and her knees behind her ears. The centrepiece of this fine display was her honeypot, completely exposed for him to see. She could sense him gazing between her legs, drinking in the delights of her delectable pussy; and then she felt the wet warmth of his lips as his mouth closed over her rich ripe fig. His frustration had been building up for a week, and now the storm was released. He settled on her rosebud like a swarm of bees, sucking the harvest of her glutinous juices, gorging her swollen vulva deep into his mouth as if he was searching for the food of the gods.

He had been certain from the beginning that Miss Madeleine would be the best bet: the other six looked too chaste. He decided they'd all need a bit of time and work, but Madeleine had that look about her, as if she knew what hung between a man's legs and wasn't averse to a bit of the action. He ceased his violent sucking to savour the juices that had begun to flow freely from inside her. He carefully parted her pudenda with his fingers, and ran his tongue over the red inner lips before beginning to suck at her darling little clitoris. He felt the small shivers that ran through her body as he teased her clit with his tongue and gently pulled at it with his teeth.

In all his army service he'd never had a posting

anything like this, supervising the initial training of seven girls from the three services. Seven girls in a Nissen hut which was supposed to house thirty. Seven girls who must be called Miss, and allowed to wear their hair long, and who were supplied with furniture from the officer's mess, and given curtains to slide around their bed space. But for the war he would have been out over a year ago. Now all he was worth was to mollycoddle women.

He buried his face in her soft curly muff: there were compensations. His nose snuffled among her furry bush like an inquisitive dog as his teeth sank into her piquant twat. Then, opening his mouth wider than a town crier, he sucked her whole scrumptious wet quim into his gob as if he were trying to eat her. She shoved her thighs forward, endeavouring to aid him in his desire to swallow her fig whole. Her breathing became shallow and she began to pant. She was about to orgasm. She grasped at his head between her legs, pushing him closer and closer into her crotch, and then, she screamed: a short sharp yelp which became a gurgle. He sucked at the gummy secretion that poured from the walls of her vagina until his mouth was full. He swallowed her love juice, and tongued between her thighs like a dog licking gravy from a plate.

He ordered her to her feet. She saw he was hard with excitement, and needed relief.

'Bend over,' he ordered.

'You're not going to beat me?'

'Don't give me ideas.'

She obeyed, her skirt still raised to her waist, her uniform jacket rumped and creased where it had bunched around her ribs.

'Open your legs, and grip your ankles.'

She positioned herself as she was told, and from

24

between her legs she glimpsed him unbuttoning his khaki trousers to release his rampant cock into the daylight. Her hands circled her ankles, which she grasped tightly when she felt him approach from behind. He positioned his anxious tool at her entrance. Her quim was wet with her juices and his saliva, allowing his pego to slip into her like a knife into butter. Her body shuddered, and such was the force of his thrusting inside her that she was afraid of toppling forward. He jabbed deep into her passage with long piston strokes, his balls slapping against her bum, invading her to the complete length of his weapon. She felt his stroke increase, and his pego swell, ready to discharge its load. At the very instant he came, as the hot sperm flooded her uterus, there came a knock and the door flew open.

Oh, my God, the shame. A young soldier appeared, his face so youthful, his cheeks so smooth that it was difficult to imagine he was old enough to serve his King and country. He froze, open-mouthed, looking aghast at the scene before him. An ATS girl, naked from the waist down, bent over double with his sergeant rooted up her like a boar up a sow. The look on the sergeant's face changed from ecstasy to surprise, to anger, as he barked,

'Wait outside, soldier.'

Madeleine sprang to her feet, automatically adjusting her skirt, her face scarlet with embarrassment. She couldn't remember the last time she had blushed. She had been caught in worse situations but it was the unexpected intrusion and the position she'd been forced to adopt that she found so mortifying. She could imagine herself bent double, grasping her ankles and being taken from behind. She didn't wonder she was embarrassed.

'The lad will spread it around like a forest fire,' he grunted, buttoning his fly, 'unless you stop him, Miss Madeleine.'

'How?'

'How do you think? The boy's probably a virgin.' He grinned at her. 'You can claim his cherry. You can have the office for an hour. No one will disturb you.'

She heard the sergeant talking to the young soldier, but couldn't make out what was said. The door opened and the boy came inside. His expression was one of anxiety, nervousness and anticipation, his smooth white cheeks were turning pink as he looked at her. Madeleine had already removed her jacket and now she stripped off the remainder of her clothes, slowly, tantalisingly, with a panache she'd learned over the years. She posed naked before the lad, thrusting out her full breasts for his admiration. She guessed he'd probably dreamed of such a scene, a beautiful woman stripping sexily for him while he masturbated.

'Do you like what you see, soldier?'

He stuttered a reply which she took for Yes.

'Do you want to fuck me?'

He nodded nervously.

'You promise to tell nobody about what you saw?'

'Yes,' he mumbled, 'the sarge'd kill me if I did.'

As he stood gawking at her naked body which she was flaunting so provocatively, she thought she glimpsed a look of wild excitement in his eyes. She sensed he wasn't far from orgasm. Swiftly she unfastened his fly, allowing his poor agitated willy its freedom. She quickly closed her hand around the shaft, massaging the foreskin, milking him with the expertise of a milkmaid and so jerking his explosion from him before it flooded out without human aid. She allowed his sperm to spatter over her bosom, as she had seen how

26

he admired it. He gave a gasp, followed by a low groan from way down inside him. Maybe it was the first time a female hand had brought him off. As he watched in astonishment she slowly massaged his spunk into her lovely breasts. She crossed to the small cubicle which served as a washroom and she saw the look on his young face. He thought she had finished with him, that she was going to leave him, that his premature ejaculation had robbed him of the opportunity to screw her.

'I'll be back,' she smiled. 'Undress and lie down on the rug.'

She returned to find him stretched out naked on the rug, looking like a lamb to the slaughter. She stood over him, her feet either side of his head, allowing him to peer up between her legs at the slightly parted lips of her sweet quim nestling in its bush of black curly hair.

'Have you seen a girl's pussy before?'

'No,' she heard him murmur.

She bent her knees and lowered herself into a crouching position, her rosebud almost touching his nose.

'Do you want to kiss it?'

She felt his lips gently brush the soft pubic hair and a nervous kiss land on the smooth folds. She knelt astride him, her superb breasts hanging like two ripening melons onto his face. She lowered herself until he could kiss them, first one and then the other. She manoeuvred herself so that her tiny erect nipples brushed his lips, and he reacted by sucking them both in turn until she felt herself aroused. She moved downwards and saw the blood was begining to pump back into his organ. He had a small dick compared with that of the sergeant, but it was thick enough to satisfy all but the loosest cunt. She lowered her soft bubbies on to it, massaging it with her twin globes until she could feel him erect and ready to go.

She slid beneath him, determined to allow him to seduce her. He must find his own way, his own style, to satisfy himself and his women. He supported himself on his elbows, gently stroking her dark hair. He kissed her without trying to part her lips, moving down her body, gently kissing her neck and shoulders and breasts. She knew he was anxious to be inside her. She parted and raised her legs and he moved between her thighs to fumble inexpertly at the opening of her love box. She guided him and in one anxious movement he slid to the hilt. She locked her legs around his thighs and felt him pumping desperately inside her willing vagina until he came with a rush, squirting his youthful seed into her. She tightened her quim to milk him of the last of his seed, and was rewarded by a groan of pure ecstasy. There had been no refinement, but he had fucked his first woman; she had claimed his cherry.

'Thank you, miss,' he smiled and was gone.

The following week Colonel Lord Chomsmy returned. He addressed the seven girls in the lecture room, and only the sergeant was allowed to be present.

'I'm sorry about this basic training you've been expected to attend. It wasn't my idea, but the War Office was adamant. If you are to be members of the women's services, then you must do some sort of training. I suppose it has helped you get fit, those of you who don't take part in any sport, and the discipline will do you no harm. There was no question, however, of any of you failing. I told the sergeant that at the beginning.'

Madeleine looked around sharply to where the sergeant was sitting. He grinned and shrugged.

'In a week or so, you'll come to Holmsley Manor,' continued the colonel, 'where you'll be under my command and where the real work of preparing you for Europe will be done.'

The weeks passed quickly enough, and before their posting to the manor they were given a seventy-two-hour pass to enable them to go home and show off their new uniforms. Madeleine was one of two girls who had been enlisted into the ATS and given the rank of sergeant. The other five were all upper-class, or well-educated young women, who were granted commissions into the WAAF or WRNS. The sergeant grumbled that it was typical of the British services, but it caused Madeleine no concern. She had no home or friends in England to visit, and he suggested they spent the day together. She knew what he had in mind, but was agreeable, as she had come to like him. He suggested they go out into the country to a spot where they could swim in the river.

He turned up with a motorbike he'd borrowed from the transport section and sandwiches he'd scrounged from the cookhouse. It was a warm summer day with not a cloud in the sky; the temperature must have been hitting ninety. The sergeant was wearing his uniform, but Madeleine had changed into civvies. She mounted the bike behind him, tucking her light summer dress around her legs as she wasn't wearing knickers. She had recalled his preference and decided it would do no harm to indulge him.

The bike trundled down the empty country lanes, deserted but for horse-drawn farm vehicles. After some twenty minutes he stopped in the gateway of an empty field. The copse that bordered the lane was deep in ferns, and he led her inside the lines of trees where they would be out of sight of any passers-by. She thought he was going to screw her, and didn't care for the spot he'd chosen. Instead, he pulled three smooth wooden balls from his inside pocket. They were joined by thin twine threaded through the centre of each. She wondered what they were, and why he'd stopped to show them to her. She was fairly certain there was some sexual reason. She was soon to find out she was correct.

'I'd like to try a little experiment,' he mused. 'I've often wondered what would be the result if a girl wore these on a motorbike.'

'How would she be wearing them?' she asked, and then she saw the answer to her question. 'You're a lecherous devil,' she said.

'I know, but would you like to try?'

'I wouldn't,' she retorted. 'Where'd you get them from? I've never seen anything like them before.'

'I brought them back from the Far East. The girls there pleasure themselves with them. Come on, have a go.'

'You make it sound like a game.'

'Well, it is, isn't it?'

He sounded like a petulant child who wanted his own way. She decided to please him. Well, why not? She'd spent half her life satisfying men. She flipped up the skirts of her summer dress and saw the smile on his face when he realised she was naked underneath. She stood with legs apart, ready to receive the wooden spheres. The idea of the smooth wooden balls being inserted into her slit suddenly made her feel sexy. She watched him kneel, felt him part her vulva, and then, gently but firmly, he steered the first of the spheres up into her moist tube. The second ball followed and then he moved around behind her.

'Bend over,' he commanded. 'The last one goes up your arse.'

She didn't like the idea, but there was no point arguing. In for a penny, in for a pound. As she bent over she heard him spit on his fingers and felt them gently circling the wrinkled muscle that guarded her anus. It wasn't unpleasant being explored; she anticipated the delight of his digit being forced into her tight little bum. The stab she felt caused a thrill in her sensitive back passage, and was followed by the pressure of the wooden ball being forced into her. The ring of muscle parted reluctantly as he pressed with his fingers until the sphere passed through her stretched opening and was gulped into her rectum.

The following motorbike ride was certainly different from anything she had previously experienced; with her legs astride the pillion and her crotch pushed into the leather saddle, the sensations inside her were excruciating. The continual movement of the motorbike coupled with the massage of the spheres against the walls of her vagina was indescribable. She pressed herelf into his back as the warmth in her crotch became an overbearing heat. It hurt, yet it was pleasant.

Eventually he drew to a halt, she dismounted and stood with legs apart so that her soaking vagina could expel the two balls. She watched him park the motorbike in a dell beside a slow moving river. She followed him, the two spheres dangling uncomfortably from her back passage; she felt a proper fool. She'd never fathom men's minds and the strange things they dreamed up in the name of sex. She lifted the back of her dress shamelessly to reveal what had happened. She heard him laugh, as he stooped down and pulled the third ball from her anus like a cork from a bottle.

'What was it like?'

'Different,' she muttered.

'Did it make you feel very sexy, all that bumping up

31

and down?' he enquired anxiously, as if the success of the rest of the day depended on it. 'Did you come?'

'I wouldn't want to do it again, but yes, I came.'

It was already noon; the sun was high overhead, and there was no wind to cool the hot summer air. The river looked cool and inviting; the sun reflected images on the ever-moving water. There wasn't a sound to be heard; even the birds were having a siesta. Madeleine stripped off her flimsy dress, kicked off her shoes, and ran joyously to the water's edge.

'Is it deep?' she squealed.

'Deep enough to dive in, if you can swim.'

'No, I can't swim,' she cried, taking a flying header from the bank into the deep silent water.

His heart lurched. Stupid woman, she'd drown. Then he saw her surface and strike away with a powerful crawl. He laughed and followed her into the water. His relief was such that he swam to her and grabbed her in his arms. She struggled free, laughing, and dived under him so easily, avoiding his grasp. She was at home in the water. It took her back to her carefree youth in Blankenberge, where she had lived until her father was killed and her mother died of a broken heart. She had such sweet memories of her childhood, but everything had gone wrong since those halcyon days. The sergeant flung his arms about her like a huge squid, and she took his face between her hands and kissed him. She was happy and that urgent sensation of lust was still between her thighs. She smiled. Those bloody balls and that motor bike had really got her going.

'You bastard,' she shouted suddenly, splashing the surface water at him in great spraying waves.

'What have I done?' he called.

He wasn't at ease in the water. She dived below him

and, reaching between his legs, grabbed his balls, fondling and gently squeezing them. She broke the surface in front of him, her back turned to him; he grabbed her breasts and pulled her close. She could feel his penis hard against her buttocks; she tried to turn, but he held her firmly by her boobies, squeezing the soft pliant globes.

'Let me turn round,' she spluttered. 'I want you.'

'Oh, oh,' he laughed, 'so my three balls did work wonders.'

'I didn't know you had three balls, you freak,' she squealed, struggling from his grip and turning to push him under the surface.

'I'll fuck you,' he gasped, his mouth spluttering water.

'That's the idea isn't it?' she giggled.

She loved the water; it gave her the upper hand. She took his ever-ready prong and guided it to her twat, parting the lips with her fingers and sliding him deep into her channel. Clinging to him like a limpet, she wrapped her legs around his thighs and her arms around his neck. Unfortunately he wasn't able to support her inert body, and kick as he might, they slowly sank beneath the surface. She freed herself and kicked them to the surface, giggling and watching him spit out water. His cock had slipped from her. She urged him up on to his back and lay above him, kicking her legs and moving her arms below the water. It worked; their heads stayed above the surface. She slid his prick back inside her, but once again they began to sink. Determined not to be defeated, she swam with him towards the bank, urging him to grasp an overhanging branch so that she was able to wind her legs around him without sinking. At last she could have her wicked way. She clung to him, her legs around his thighs, her arms gripping his back, her tube enveloping his nice hard dick. Moving her tongue inside his mouth and her backside to an easy rhythm, she brought herself to an orgasm, and her shout of pure ecstasy echoed in the silence that surrounded them.

Her climax over and her lust slaked, she saw the discomfort of his position, hanging like Tarzan, half in and half out of the water. It had all been so silly, but she hadn't been so happy since she left Belgium. She helped him out onto the bank and they lay side by side on the soft green grass to dry their bodies in the hot sun.

She rested her head on his stomach, blowing softly into his pubic hair and watching his prong very slowly rising like a tent pole. She continued blowing and began to tease his hanging scrotum with her agile fingers. Soon the large organ was pulsing with blood and she moved her face nearer, her nose touching it teasingly. Flirtatiously she put out her tongue. Moving her head upwards, she licked the whole shaft until she reached the tip of his knob. Grinning lecherously at him she slid the throbbing member between her lips and sucked so deliciously that he exploded with a cry into her mouth. She held his sperm on her tongue and opened her mouth so he could watch it slip down her throat.

The next day she travelled to Holmsley Manor. It meant she would arrive a day earlier than the other girls, but she had asked the sergeant to ring, and Lord C. had replied he would expect her late that afternoon. When she arrived she was shown into the library, where he sat garbed in velvet smoking jacket, reading Henry Miller. A tall, well-built man with a full head of pure white hair, he looked even more distinguished in the setting of his vast library.

'We won't be wearing uniform here,' he explained, 'only during the day when you go for your espionage training. Otherwise you are free to dress as you please. I'll have you shown to your room, and then perhaps you'd care to join me for tea?'

She thanked him and followed the elderly maid to the bedroom, which was most comfortably furnished. Tea had already been set out when she returned to the library. Lord Chomsmy poured and offered her a huge plate of cucumber sandwiches. She was surprised to see a whole cucumber lying beside the teapot and wondered vaguely why it was there.

'I'm proud of my crop of cucumbers this year,' he smiled, pointing to the prize specimen she'd been admiring. 'I asked the cook to send one in. Fine big fellow, isn't he?'

She sat puzzled. Was he an eccentric or really a keen gardener? She had no idea how to reply, so she sat and smiled.

'You may think me an old fool, but I was thinking how pleasant it would be to sit here peacefully and watch a pretty girl masturbate. It would make for an idyllic afternoon.'

He sat smiling innocently at her. There was no hint of suggestion in his voice, just casual conversation. She wondered if she'd heard him correctly. She realised she had when he picked up the prize cucumber and handed it to her. If it was a test, she couldn't afford to fail.

'Have I embarrassed you?' he asked sweetly.

'No,' she replied quietly. 'If it will give you pleasure, then I am happy to oblige.'

She moved herself forward in the big armchair until she was balanced on the very edge of the seat. With swift movements she bunched up her skirts, unbuttoned her camiknickers at the crotch, and tucked up all the material clear of her thighs. She saw his gaze fasten between her wide-open legs, beaming in on her shell-like haven nestling in its fleecy surround. She held the tip of the cucumber against her sweet pudenda, gently rocking herself until her passage was lubricated and she was able slowly to slide it up into her channel. He watched enthralled. She raised her backside off the chair to give him a full view of his prize vegetable circled by her gaping twat.

'You are the Belgian girl, are you not?' he enquired casually.

'That's correct.'

'Where was it you worked?'

'In a nightclub, sir.'

'I suspect it was a bawdy house.'

'No, sir,' she protested vehemently.

'You don't have to lie, young woman,' he smiled condescendingly. 'It makes no difference to me, and don't stop please; you make a delightful picture.'

She felt relieved and became aware of the flood of mucous that flowed from her honeypot on to the substitute phallus. She ceased manipulation and gritting her teeth, eased the cucumber up inside her body until it would go no farther. Then she deliberately presented herself to him, the picture of pure debauchery: her legs wide, the end of the cucumber protruding from her gash, and her fingers busily massaging her clitoris. She shut her eyes, whimpering, as she orgasmed, and then she slowly expelled the glistening vegetable.

Lord Chomsmy clapped approval.

'Bravo!' he grinned. 'You must dine with us tonight. Remember you are assured of your place on our first mission. You have only to do your utmost to persuade the other girls to participate in my practical sex lessons.'

It was a small price to pay – butter wouldn't melt in the mouth of most of them and she'd enjoy seeing them made to turn a trick.

At dinner she met Nigel, Lord C.'s nephew, a tall gangling youth with stooping shoulders and receding chin, clad in the dress uniform of a second lieutenant. His uncle had tried to wangle him a commission in the Guards but Nigel had had to be satisfied with the RASC. She thought he was the prototype of the weak upper-class English twit. Later she was to learn he harboured a deformity which established him as macho.

Lord C. was a brilliant conversationalist, and Madeleine was thrilled listening to him as she ignored Nigel's idiotic asides. It was an enjoyable meal and she was glad she'd come a day early.

'What's for dessert?' asked Nigel loudly.

'I thought Madeleine, served in the comfort of the lounge?'

'Super-dooper,' guffawed Nigel.

She had learned enough about Lord C. to know he wasn't joking. She was escorted into the adjoining room to be served up with the coffee.

Sylvia

Sylvia was twenty, but could pass for sixteen. A gorgeous mop of blonde curly hair and a complexion like peaches and cream were enhanced by a cute turned-up nose and twinkling blue eyes. She was every man's dream of a daughter to spoil, yet there was a hint of wild sexuality in her erotic pouting lips. As a child she'd been a tomboy, and then a high-spirited adolescent. Now, when she should have been grown-up, she was still an extrovert who acted on impulse. The daughter of a British diplomat, she'd spent most of her childhood in Berlin where she'd met her very best friend, Rachel. When she was thirteen her father was posted to Paris and the two girls spent all their school holidays together – an idyllic time. But in late June 1939 her carefree world crumbled. It was a month she would never forget. A phone call had summoned Rachel back to Berlin, where her father had apparently received permission for his family to leave Nazi Germany. Rachel's mother was Jewish, and Sylvia had seen how Jews were treated by the Third Reich: but Rachel was only half Jewish, Sylvia thought, and her father was a prominent doctor. Surely they would be safe.

Two days later she heard their home had been burnt to the ground and that the whole family had perished in the fire.

Sylvia was inconsolable. She hid herself and cried, and ventured out only when Rachel's boyfriend came to visit. It was she who had introduced Rachel to Pierre. She didn't like him much, a feeling she hid rather than hurt Rachel. She would take him horse riding, and they galloped their mounts until the snorting, sweating animals were exhausted and they too were tired.

One day Pierre and Sylvia were washing down the steaming horses after a ride during which they had hardly spoken when Pierre turned to her.

'Do you think the Nazis set fire to the house deliberately?'

'I'm certain of it,' she answered. 'My father says it's inconceivable, but then he's a diplomat.'

'It's too dreadful to contemplate.'

'You haven't been to Berlin,' she snapped. 'You haven't seen their bully boys strutting around deliberately terrifying people.'

'No, I haven't,' he murmured quietly. 'It must be terrible for you. You were friends for so long.'

'You were her boyfriend.'

'Did she tell you we were going to get married?'

'No.'

'We were going to tell everyone this weekend.'

'Oh, how dreadful for you.'

'We were going to consummate it, you know, in bed,' he stammered, 'as I have to report to my regiment in the Maginot Line tomorrow.'

She looked at him. Rachel had never mentioned any of this, but then she had sometimes been secretive. A thought came to Sylvia, so ludicrous, it bordered on the preposterous. She would take Rachel's place. Rachel would want that. She couldn't allow a young man to go to war without a woman's favours. It was unwritten law that a girl would give herself to her boy so that he could march off to war, a man.

'Come to my room tonight,' she whispered. 'I'll try to take Rachel's place for you.'

'You really mean it?'

She nodded. It was like a scene from the movies. She was sacrificing herself for the memory of her best friend. She felt noble, yet so very humble. Ten hours later as she lay in bed listening for his footstep in the corridor, she didn't feel it was such a good idea. She was a virgin, and her experience of boys was confined to hastily grabbed kisses during party games and after dances. Now she was about to give herself to a man she'd never even kissed. Her extravagant behaviour had landed her in a nasty situation, as her mother had forecast only too often. She had opened the curtains and taken the bulb from the bedside lamp so the only light would be from the moon. She didn't want him to see her.

She heard the door open, and heard him whisper as his shadow moved towards her. He stood by the bed, towering over her; as she saw him slip off his robe, she instinctively pulled the bedclothes up under her chin. She heard him fumble with the bedside lamp and curse, before he whipped back the bedclothes and slipped in beside her.

The touch of his naked body was cold to her warm flesh. She felt his cool arm slip around her and his lips crush on to hers. Young men had tried to open her mouth before, but she'd never allowed it. Now, this man had prised open her lips and was licking the inside of her mouth with his tongue. She couldn't stop him; she tried vainly to keep her tongue still, but he winkled it out and sucked it between his lips. She wanted to gag, to draw away from him – she hated this foreplay. She wished he'd plunge his penis into her and be done with it. She felt him bury his face into her neck, kissing her throat, nibbling her ears, caressing her hair. She closed her eyes and tightened her lips: if only he'd get on with it.

He had slipped her nightdress from her shoulders and freed her breasts so he could kiss and caress their soft roundness. She enjoyed having her bubbies fondled, and he was thoughtful and gentle with them, kneading the tender fleshy orbs, kissing the yielding flesh, teasing the dainty nipples. He must have realised her enchantment, for he continued with the titillation until a warm feeling of wellbeing began to rise within her. She relaxed as his lips moved downwards, kissing the warm flesh of her stomach and thighs, his tongue scouring her navel and his hot breath ruffling through her short curly pubic hairs. She tensed as his lips moved towards that soft foliage between her thighs. Her heart fluttered; she had heard whispers of oral sex, but was not yet ready for such intimacies. She clasped his head between her hands and urged him upwards to her breasts. He obeyed without hesitation, and she again became aware of the little thrills which spread from her mammaries to heighten her sexual arousal.

She was hardly aware he had climbed on top of her until she felt the pressure of his knee parting her thighs. Her legs responded immediately. She knew her vulva was already moist with her secreted juices and that she was ready for him. She kicked aside the nightgown and threw wide her legs, prepared to sacrifice her chastity for the memory of her beloved friend. Tears sprang to her eyes as she felt the tip of his hard cock at the entrance of her sweet orifice. The tears were for Rachel and for herself, and for a life that could never be the same – perhaps also for her virginity, which she should have saved to bestow on a man she loved.

41

Pierre's iron rod strained at her hymen, pushing, stretching and thrusting until it ruptured before his invasion and he was deep inside her body. She heard a short sharp screech, followed by a gasp of pain and surprise; she hardly realised it came from herself. She heard herself whimper lamenting her defloration rather than celebrating the pain. He held his swollen prick deep inside her and kissed her tear-stained face until she relaxed. He meant well, but the excitement of being within her, of claiming her virginity had stimulated him too much. A quick spasm warned him that he was nearing ejaculation. She felt him begin to move desperately, pumping, thrusting, driving to impale her to the hilt. He was blatantly gratifying himself at her expense. It hurt, it was depraved. She wanted to scream and punch and scratch him. When his emission flooded into her, he collapsed on to her like a pricked balloon.

She pushed him off; he got up and left. He knew he hadn't been very considerate to her, but then she was a little whore so it didn't matter.

When she switched on the light she saw the blood on the sheet. She made the chambermaid swear not to tell anyone, but the woman told her mother.

Sylvia was sent back to England, to her grandmother who lived in splendid isolation in the middle of Exmoor.

Sylvia's father returned home at the end of the year, but she was left with her grandmother. She had little to do, other than follow the progress of the war and mope. Then, in May 1940, Hitler's forces swept across Europe and Britain was isolated. Sylvia decided she must do something, and against her parents' wishes decided to join the WRNS. It was her father who heard of the hunt for bilingual girls, and her name went forward, thus coming to the notice of Lord C. She jumped at the chance to return to France to avenge Rachel, and as keen as jolly hockey sticks, she travelled to London for the interview. She was forced to stay the night at a hotel, and decided to dine at the Savoy where she might meet friends.

Instead, she met Uncle Paul. He was no relation, but had been a regular family visitor when she lived in Berlin. She'd disliked him when she was a child and had woven make-believe stories around him in which he was a spy or an anarchist with a bomb. She had always believed he was a German, and wondered what he was doing in London. Perhaps he really was a spy.

He insisted she joined him, and afterwards took her to his mews home. She went, believing she might unmask his Nazi activities – what a start for her new career that would be! In her naivety she brimmed over with excitement.

Once they arrived, he left her to make coffee, giving her the opportunity to ferret among his belongings. He was gone for some time, and she had done a lot of rummaging by the time he returned.

'Now, perhaps you'll tell me why you have been searching my home,' he asked coldly. 'Are you a thief?'

'No, no . . . Of course not,' she stammered, wondering how he knew and fighting against her surprise and embarrassment.

'Come with me,' he commanded, leading her from the room into a narrow passage. 'Your activities are on film.'

She saw cameras pointing into the room which she had been wildly searching, and her girlish confidence vanished. She stood wringing her hands like a naughty

43

schoolgirl. She'd been found out, and she'd have to take the consequences. She didn't think any further than that and so was susceptible to anything he suggested.

'What did you imagine you'd find?' he scowled. 'Do you think I'm a spy?'

'When I was a child in Berlin, I thought you were a German.'

'I'm Polish,' he snapped angrily, 'and now I shall phone the police, unless you would rather I gave you a good sound spanking?'

Once she was on the wrong side of the law she knew she'd stand little chance at her interview, and no chance of a commission in the WRNS. She had been spanked before – her school in Berlin had regularly used the strap on unruly girls' bottoms – so the threat held no terrors for her.

'I'd rather be spanked.' She blushed prettily.

He slid open a door in the passageway to reveal a wardrobe containing a rail full of school uniforms.

'Choose one,' he commanded, 'and when you've changed, I'll be waiting in the study.'

Once alone, Sylvia ran her hand through the row of gymslips, all neatly arranged in colours and sizes. She chose maroon, and found a white blouse, knickers and ankle socks pinned inside. It took her back several years, and as she buttoned the gymslip at the shoulders she found herself becoming quite stimulated, perhaps because she had always coveted a maroon uniform.

When she entered the study she was surprised to see her uncle sitting on an upright chair with his sleeves rolled up. He beckoned her, and she walked towards him, smiling confidently. Her tousled golden curls and wide blue eyes presented her as the perfect picture of a well-developed schoolgirl.

'What is going to happen to you?' he demanded.

'I'm going to be spanked, sir.'

She moved to his side, her mature figure bulging out of her gymslip, and obediently spread herself over his knees so that the palms of her hands rested on the floor and her backside was well elevated for spanking. The skirt of her gymslip was raised and she felt the whack of his hand on her knickered bottom.

Sylvia gasped at the smarting pain that invaded her seat, and realised he meant what he said; she was going to get a damn good thrashing. She found herself squawking like a child when the walloping began in earnest, and then, as her posterior began to warm, he jerked down her knickers. She shrieked, endeavouring to cover her bare bottom with her hand, but he roughly twisted her arm behind her back. The ordeal continued until the reddened globes of her scorching rump were ablaze.

'No more, please. Stop. I'm sorry,' she sobbed, lamenting her fate with a sharp intake of breath after every stinging slap, 'Please, I can't take any more . . .'

When the torment concluded, she lay whimpering over his knees, her body limp, her bum glowing crimson – it was as if his treatment had lit a fire in her tail.

'Stand up and stop snivelling, girl,' he ordered. 'And get your clothes off. You've a dozen of the cane to come.'

Her heart sank. She thought she'd paid her debt. She peeled off her gymslip and blouse apprehensively, and stepped out of the knickers around her ankles. She'd never had the cane. She'd heard boys say it stung, but if they could take it so could she.

She watched him flex the cane in his hands, bending it almost double, and swishing it through the air so it whistled menacingly.

'Bend over and touch your toes,' he ordered grimly, 'and count every stroke aloud.'

Sylvia bent over, her fingers touching the floor, her legs straight, her arse raised high in the air, presenting him with a delectable target. From the corner of her eye she saw him raise the cane, felt it snake viciously across her bare buttocks, slicing into the tender flesh. She screamed in surprise and shot upright.

'Each time you get up like that, I shall add another stroke to the total,' he scowled as if the caning aggravated him more than it hurt her, 'and the same if you forget to count aloud.'

She received six more strokes, and each time she bawled out the number as the waspish sting seared across her fundament like charges of electricity. She made no attempt to stop herself screaming, and after every stroke she wailed and wept openly, wiping the tears from her eyes with the back of her hand.

'Now you will stand facing the wall with your hands on your head,' he instructed sternly, 'and you will thank me for punishing you.'

'Thank you for caning me, sir,' she responded tearfully, 'I know I deserved it.'

She stood quietly sobbing, her bum smarting, the twin moons striped with parallel marks. Yet the heat that had been generated in her thighs was signalling an urgent sexual need.

She didn't hear Paul approach, and was surprised to feel his fingers gently massage a cool cream into her ravished haunches. Studiously he covered the whole area of red-hot flesh, first one cheek and then the other, until the sharp stinging dulled to an ache.

She stood upright with her hands on her head, as she had been instructed, not daring to move for fear Paul might prescribe more strokes of the cane. She felt his fingers stray between her smarting cheeks, exploring towards the deep cleft, touching the pubic hairs that hid the entrance to her secret passage. Her whole body trembled as he slid a finger between the lips of her pussy, searching for her clitoris. In spite of, or because of, the smouldering flames in her rump, she was dripping mucous.

'Bend over, Sylvia,' he whispered in her ear.

Without hesitation she grabbed her ankles, but instead of the cane across her elevated rear, his John Thomas burrowed between the wet folds of her vulva and deep into her delicious tunnel of love. He held her by the hips and jerked her back on to his throbbing weapon after every long stroke. The slap of his belly against her tormented globes shot twinges of pain through her whole body and mingled with the sensation of his prick rooted deep in her lair. She howled like a she-wolf as her climax rippled from her in waves of warm ecstasy.

Paul slipped out of her like a cork from a bottle and left her to resume her former stance facing the wall. She didn't hear him leave, and was startled to hear a female voice.

Trying to hide her embarrassment, she turned to see an elderly woman smiling cynically at her.

'My goodness, you've had a proper caning, haven't you dearie,' she droned in a voice that said she'd seen it all before. 'I don't know how he gets you lovely young girls to take the thrashings you do.' She sighed as if the younger generation was a closed book to her. 'I suppose he conned you with them cameras. There's no film in 'em you know.'

The following afternoon she had a successful interview and was told to report to the WRNS division at

Portsmouth for kitting out before her initial training with the other six girls. One of the men on the selection board, Lord Chomsmy, was an acquaintance of her father. She wondered if he recognised her; it had been some years since they'd met at the embassy in Paris.

She walked out of the building at the rear of Whitehall. The door of a Rolls-Royce swung open for her – inside she could see Lord C.

'Hop in, Sylvia, we've a lot to talk about.'

She climbed into the luxurious interior that was the hallmark of such a costly vehicle, feeling tongue-tied and rather embarrassed.

'You wouldn't have passed, but for me,' he smiled at her. 'You were too English for my compatriots' taste. I'd say that puts you under obligation, wouldn't you?'

'Thank you. I'd set my heart on returning to France.'

'And now, young lady, I'd like to look at your bottom.'

She looked at him sharply, surprised and startled by his words.

'Last night,' he continued, 'I dined with a Polish friend who arrived late. He excused himself by saying he had been attending to the bottom of a young acquaintance of mine. I noticed how gingerly you sat at the interview, which suggested the young lady was you. So, then, up with your skirt and allow me to inspect his handiwork.'

Chomsmy patted the seat and wasn't happy until Sylvia knelt, skirt raised, knickers down, so he could survey the bruises on her well-shaped derrière.

'A good job well done,' he beamed, 'and before too long I will see if I can match it, but for now I will be satisfied with a spot of fellatio from those delectable pouting lips of yours.'

By the time Sylvia had adjusted her dress, Lord C.

was lying smugly back against the soft leather seat, his fly already opened to reveal his awakening organ. The idea of a man's prick in her mouth wasn't exactly distasteful to Sylvia, but it wasn't an experience she was eagerly anticipating. She moved her hand towards the rising monster to caress it to its full glory, but he slapped her fingers, and taking her by the nape of the neck pushed her head downwards. She bent right over him, her face in his crotch, her lips brushing his pecker. The male smell of his organ invaded her nostrils as she ran the tip of her lithe tongue over the stiffening shaft. Slowly, she kissed and licked him to full arousal, watching the enormous thing throbbing inches from her nose. Opening her mouth she tried to swallow it whole, but found herself gagging when it pushed against the back of her throat.

Patience, she thought to herself, take it nice and easy. I must be slow and thorough. She circled her pouting lips around the upstanding baton, and sucked him further and further into her mouth until her lips nearly touched his belly. Then, holding him in her mouth, she worked her tongue ceaselessly around his tool.

She eased back her head so that her lips slipped to the top of his pole before plunging it back down into her wide-open throat. The combined movements of her lips and tongue were sufficient to thrill him to the point of delirium, and he could hold back his ejaculation no longer. She felt his spunk flood into her mouth like a gush of warm milk, and she squeezed the ever-decreasing organ until she had drained every drop of its semen. She allowed the spent weapon to slip from her lips, and wondered how she could rid herself of the sperm filling her mouth. She couldn't spit it out, and was toying with the idea of opening the window when he sensed her intent and grabbed her cheeks between her fingers, forcing her head backwards. Like a wayward child taking nasty medicine she was forced to swallow.

The month of initial training passed uneventfully for Sylvia. She enjoyed herself and was one of the stars, for the routine came easily to her with her background of boarding school and physical games. The sergeant lusted after her, saliva on his lips, but he could find no way to seduce her. She left on her seventy-two-hour pass, but as her father had been posted to South America she had nowhere to go but back to her grandmother.

The seccond day was a scorcher and she spent it cycling the narrow lanes of Exmoor attired in a man's shirt, and khaki shorts secured with a leather belt. Rather than return to the house too soon, she visited the local fleapit for the early evening show.

It was half empty and she was surprised when a man took the seat next to her. She was dreamily identifying with Greta Garbo in deep embrace when she became aware of the hand brushing her knee. She remained still, her heart pounding faster than Garbo's in the film, and as she didn't pull away the hand assumed her consent. She felt the light touch become bolder, as the fingers began to explore beneath her shorts. She clamped her legs tightly together, as she wore no underclothes.

She was frozen solid, and couldn't make herself turn her head to look at him, but from the corner of her eye she could see he was in uniform. He would be from the army camp, not far from the village, she thought. He appeared to be satisfied stroking the top of her leg, and she dozed into a state of semi-consciousness, beginning to enjoy the experience. It was then, to her surprise, that he took her hand and guided it into his lap where she was able to feel his erection standing proudly free of his unbuttoned fly.

A second shock wave swept through her, and she tried to jerk her hand away, but he held it with a vice-like grip. She was unable to free herself without attracting attention and making a fuss, so she allowed him to hold her hand and tolerated the rubbing of her cool fingers against his upstanding prong. It was a ludicrous situation; either she pulled her hand away or she wanked him. Slowly her fingers curled around his stiff weapon, and very deliberately she began to toss him off. She moved her fingers tantalisingly slowly, massaging the thick foreskin, digging her fingernails into the knob, perversely enjoying the unsolicited experience. She felt the whole staff swell fit to burst in her hand, and knew he was about to come. She felt him grab her hand, moving it upwards, and before she realised his intent he had ejaculated into her palm.

The sordid incident over, her hand covered in sperm, she felt sick. Why had she gone along with him? She should have changed seats, or slapped his face. Mortified, Sylvia jumped up and ran to the ladies'. She couldn't go back into the cinema. He would see her and sit by her again. She decided to go straight home, but to her horror he was waiting for her outside the toilet. Such was his confidence that he took her arm and marched her out, as if they were husband and wife. Her brain told her to yank her arm away and run for her bicycle, but her legs followed him. He took her to an empty barn just off a farm track.

Sylvia saw he was a lance-corporal, a short, barrel-chested young man with the huge fists and broken nose of a pugilist. As they stepped from the tarmac he

51

produced a thong of leather, and tied her wrists with a running knot. Numb, she allowed him to do it.

Once inside the barn her arms were swept above her head, and the leather that secured her wrists was slipped over a hook driven into a horizontal beam. She hung helplessly, her toes just touching the ground, and wondered how she'd got into such a position. There was no need for it, she knew; she could have left him at any time, as she could have walked away from the man who beat her. She knew she was at the stranger's mercy, and yet she felt an exhilaration, a sexual ebullience as quite suddenly she realised she possessed a streak of masochism. Humiliation stimulated her.

She had no more time for introspection as she felt her shirt wrenched from her shorts and jerked upwards to cover her head. Enveloped by darkness she felt him grab her boobs, squeezing, kneading, pulling the nipples. His hand slid down her warm belly and inside her shorts to the furry pelt hiding her pudenda, his fingers prodded apart the pouting folds and pried into her private lair. She gurgled an incomprehensible protest. He instantly moved behind her and, wrenching down her shorts, slapped the cheeks of her arse with two short sharp swipes. She inhaled sharply, half hoping he would spank her. Instead he knelt behind her and, rudely prising apart the twin moons of her backside, closed his lips over her anus. She whooped in surprise, instinctively jerking her haunches away, but he grabbed her hips and dragged her back towards him, gorging at her tightly guarded rosette. She could feel his tongue endeavouring to pass her sphincter, and writhed in a frenzy of shameful elation. Unable to penetrate with his tongue, he forced a finger into her without further ceremony. She squealed. Her anus was pierced, and worse, she enjoyed it. He unhooked her wrists and dragged her towards a bale of straw. The shirt fell back into place, and she could see again. She was thrown forward across the bale, and held down by a huge hand in the small of her back. She felt his pestle hard at her back passage, and knew he was going to bugger her. She howled in anguish and gritted her teeth as the thick shaft stabbed at her small, tight orifice. She lay quietly panting as his dick pumped backwards and forwards into her rectum, and then she squeaked in surprise a second time as his monster shot out of her arsehole to plunge deep into her quim.

In turn he fucked her two adjacent holes, reaching deep into one before withdrawing and plundering the other. Sylvia bawled, lamenting her fate aloud, but inwardly she was delirious with sexual gratification, unable to distinguish which of her tunnels was host to his invasion. Only when he came did she realise he had shot his load up her bottom hole.

He watched her dress and walked her back to her bicycle. Not until he was gone did she realise he hadn't spoken a word.

Like Madeleine, she arrived at Holsmley Manor to find the colonel sitting in his study.

'You're just in time for tea,' he greeted her. 'Would you care to join me?'

'Thank you,' she replied, impressed by the setting of the magnificent study, and by his distinguished appearance. She was determined to enjoy her time at the manor.

'Strawberries and cream,' he smiled, pointing to the table laid for tea. 'The strawberries are from my own garden, a deliciously sweet crop this year. Go on, help yourself.'

She served him tea and strawberries, and sat eating

from her own plate as he sipped his tea, surveying her over the rim of his cup. She felt she ought to speak, but could think of nothing to say, and Lord C. didn't seem in a conversational mood anyway. He watched her finish her strawberries and cream in silence and then he moved his plate in front of him.

'You enjoy cream with your strawberries?'

'Yes,' she replied, 'they were simply delicious.'

'I have a yen to dip mine in the love juices of a young maiden.' He smiled disconcertingly. 'Would you be willing to pander to an old man's whim?'

She was startled, wondering whether she'd heard him correctly, but he appeared serious enough as he gazed enquiringly into her eyes awaiting her reply.

'You mean you want to . . .'

'Dip my strawberries in your vaginal secretion?' he interrupted, his face a deadpan mask of sincerity. 'Yes, I do.'

'What can I say?' she stammered nervously.

'Say nothing. Just take off your clothes and lie on the table.'

Recklessly she decided to join in the game. She wrinkled her pretty nose and grinned saucily at him. 'You really mean it, don't you?'

'Yes.'

She had nothing to lose but her dignity, and recently, she thought, that had been disappearing fast. Beside he was the governor, the man in charge. She stripped off her light summer dress and french knickers. He pointed to the table in front of him, and she sat on the edge facing him, her knees touching his. With a quiet gentleness he cupped her full unblemished breasts in his hands, stroking the milky-white skin, teasing the pretty pink nipples, kissing the bonny rounded orbs with an eroticism she had never experienced. She looked deep into his eyes and knew she wanted to please this man.

His request no longer seemed strange. She lay back, raised her legs high and gripped the back of her knees so that she presented her luscious pussy to him open-lipped. He took the first strawberry and dipped it into the moist dew of her pouting quim before eating it with relish. Each strawberry in turn was pushed between the folds of her succulent love grotto to be flavoured with her nectar before being devoured. When his meal was completed he leaned forward, sliding his tongue along her wet crack to nibble her clitoris until she was swooning in heavenly ecstasy. She waited with bated breath for him to screw her. He had been worshipping at the altar of her cunt, but now she wanted his prick in her. But he merely smiled enigmatically and signalled her to dress. The colonel's mad tea party was over.

Sylvia enjoyed life at the manor; she respected the colonel, and took to the comtesse immediately. She adored her sophistication, her manners and her old-world courtesy. Yet for the first few days she was unsettled, and decided to talk to Tanya about her worry. Tanya agreed to see her in a small anteroom; she was waiting in one of the two armchairs when Sylvia arrived.

'What's worrying you, Sylvia?' she asked.

'It's a personal problem,' she murmured shyly, 'About sex, really, I suppose.'

'Well, you're in the right place to sort it out. The time you spend here with us will be all about sex.'

'I know, that's why I plucked up courage to talk to you. I really must get my own feelings sorted out, before I can be of any use to you.'

The comtesse offered her a cigarette from a slim gold

case and, taking one herself, lit both with an intricately moulded gold lighter.

'Tell me about it,' she said, exhaling a long stream of blue smoke towards the ceiling.

Sylvia explained her three experiences with sex, and how each had been humiliating. She said nothing of Lord C. She told of how she'd given away her virginity, been beaten and sodomised. She explained how she had been aroused by the events, had even enjoyed them. She had no knowledge of love; she had never given herself to a man she loved or even liked. Her experiences were of deviation, and she was terrified that she now needed sexual humiliation and gratification to satisfy her.

'I can understand your worries,' sympathised the comtesse understandingly. 'You are afraid humiliation is an essential part of your sexual make-up?'

'I didn't like being beaten, but it unleashed an urgent desire for passionate intercourse,' Sylvia explained bluntly. 'I didn't want to be buggered; it hurt, but it took me to the point of ecstasy. Is there a dark side of me that demands humiliation before I can enjoy sex?'

Tanya sat silently, considering the girl's problem. She didn't believe for one moment that she needed humiliation to enjoy sex, but how was she to prove it to her.

'Are you prepared to try a simple experiment?' she enquired.

'Of course . . . anything.'

'Are you totally heterosexual, or have you enjoyed homosexual relationships at home or at school?'

'Girls at school had pashes on each other, and many had things with the female teachers, but I was never that way.'

'Good.' Tanya laughed. 'Now let's see what we can do.'

She got to her feet and signalled Sylvia to do the same. Then, wrapping her arms around her like a lover, she kissed the younger woman full on the lips. The surprise Sylvia felt turned to revulsion when Tanya's tongue slipped into her mouth, French kissing her in a way she had never experienced from a man. She was much stronger than Tanya, and pulled away from her easily, red with embarrassment and anger. The comtesse seemed unconcerned, and sat in the armchair facing her.

'Lift up your skirt,' she commanded coldly. 'Right up. Hold it there.'

Reluctantly Sylvia did as she was bid, feeling somehow that whatever Tanya did would be for her good.

'Open your legs wide . . . wider.'

Sylvia felt the comtesse unfasten her cami-knicks at the crotch and tuck the thin silk up under her raised skirt so that she stood open-legged and naked from the waist down. Pondering what humiliation was to follow, she watched Tanya pour a liberal measure of oil into the palm of her hand and then felt it being rubbed between her thighs into her comely nest of pubic hair. The smooth oil soon soaked her short curly thatch, covering the soft pouting folds of her quim with a thin film. She watched Tanya thoroughly massage the oil into her own hand. Suddenly she felt oily fingers exploring her private aperture. The fingers and thumb were bunched and slipped easily past her greased labia into the recesses of her dry, unwilling channel.

In spite of the oil soaking her fist, Tanya could feel Sylvia resisting her progress by contracting her vaginal muscles. Slowly, she rotated her fist pressing it little by little, upwards into Sylvia's unwilling tube. She sharply slapped the inside of Sylvia's thighs to make her part her legs even wider and to allow Tanya's knuckles to pass the gaping entrance into the spongy pliancy of her vaginal cavity.

Sylvia shuddered at the intrusion within her, gasped at the assault, lamented the humiliation being heaped upon her. She stood impaled on another woman's fist; a hand was shoved right up her, filling her yielding snatch to capacity. Only when Tanya began to move her fingers inside her, stretching the elasticity of her pliable tunnel-walls to breaking point, did she complain.

'Stop it,' she squealed. 'Enough. For chrissake, take your hand out of me!'

Tanya allowed her fist to slip from the girl's gaping quim and wiped herself fastidiously on a towel. Sylvia heaved a sigh of relief as her vagina was rid of the invading hand, but was aware of a soreness, for the fist had not been welcome.

'Did you find that humiliating?'

'Yes.'

'Did you enjoy it?'

'No.'

'Did it give you any sexual gratification?'

'No.'

'Then we can safely say humiliation isn't automatically a sexual experience for you. Does that make you feel any better?'

'I suppose so,' Sylvia said reluctantly.

'Now, we must prove you can achieve sexual arousal without humiliation playing any part. Do you agree?'

'Yes.'

'I think I can persuade the colonel to help us. He doesn't turn you off sexually. I mean you've already had experience with him, haven't you?'

'What is it you want me to do?' she asked dubiously.

'Go to his bed tonight,' the comtesse explained, 'and

take your pleasure of him. I shall instruct him to be passive, so there can be no humiliation. You will be able to satisfy yourself that you can enjoy sex without it.'

She went to his room at midnight. It was a warm, sultry night, and she found the colonel stretched naked on the bed waiting for her. She looked down at him. He was a big man; his once-muscular body was running to fat, but he was still in good nick for a man of fifty. It suddenly struck her that he was as old as her father. It made him more approachable – not that she'd ever had any desire to sleep with her father, but she'd loved to cuddle him when she was a small child. All of a sudden she wanted to cuddle this man; she needed to feel warm and safe. She dropped her flimsy negligée, and fell at his side, pushing her soft femininity against him. He seemed to know what she wanted, because he turned on his side and wrapped her in his strong arms. She cuddled close, nuzzling his chest, reaching her arms around his back and shoulders. He made no move to disturb her, allowing her to cuddle up to him like a loving girl child as she traced patterns on his back with her teasing fingers.

An hour passed before she rolled him over on to his back, spread herself across his chest, and began kissing him. She brushed his lips like the touch of a butterfly and caressed his face, neck and shoulders, sometimes licking his skin with the tip of her dainty tongue. Her gentleness aroused him; she could feel his penis gradually awakening, and slipped her hand down to caress it with the tips of her fingers. It was as hard as a rock. She pulled at his shoulders, signalling him to turn on his stomach, and burrowed her way beneath him. He knelt above her, kissing her soft red lips, her snow-white breasts, her pert pink nipples. She wrapped her arms around his neck and her legs across the small of his back, swinging below him like a baby monkey. The blunt tip of his pego was between her open thighs; she could feel it prodding against her cleft as she clung athletically below him. An avid urge to take him inside her rippled through her body. She implored him to breach her, to violate her.

'Ravish me,' she whispered urgently. 'I want your cock in me . . . please . . . as far as it will go. Please fuck me.'

She manoeuvred her body until his knob was touching the glutinous folds of her agitated pussy, and wriggling desperately she managed to guide it to the spongy entrance of her anxious fanny. Taking a deep breath she worked her thighs in such a manner that his quivering tool slid blissfully into her haven. She screwed him, taking her own sweet time by moving herself beneath him, enfolding his John Thomas in the resilience of her heavenly playground until she felt herself coming in delightful little ripples which trickled down her cleft and lubricated her nut-brown bumhole. He was still hard inside her, and she struggled to exchange their positions until she was mounting him. She endeavoured to accomplish this acrobatic feat while holding him tightly inside her. She succeeded, and laughing aloud she sat above him, his prick completely swallowed in her love box. Sitting high above him, she moved her body up to the tip of his throbbing shaft before sliding down on to him like a fireman down a pole. The mucous dripping from her swollen vulva had spread to soak her curly bush, her lower stomach and her open thighs; each time she slapped down to root herself on his rampant penis their bodies squelched as if they were wrestling in mud.

Knowing she was about to orgasm for a second time, Sylvia twisted herself around to face his feet, reaching down to grab his ankles so he could view his prong clenched by the circular muscles of her stretched vagina.

The wide expanse of her curved arse entranced him. She certainly possessed the most beautiful bottom. He felt his storm gathering, and began urgently driving his swollen weapon into her, feeling her answer his every breathtaking thrust. He was on the point of orgasm when he roughly pierced her tight bumhole with his index finger. She squealed in surprise and released her flood; simultaneously his semen shot far up into her uterus.

He lifted her to lie in his arms, and they slept.

The following morning the comtesse visited her room.

'Did you find enjoyment?' she asked without preamble.

'I certainly did,' Sylvia smiled, like a cat with a saucer of cream.

'So you no longer have a problem?'

'I think I might have.'

'For heaven's sake, Sylvia, what?'

'I think I might become a nymphomaniac,' she grinned.

Ingrid

Ingrid sat waiting apprehensively. Yesterday, on her sixteenth birthday, she had lost her maidenhead. Today she was to be birched.

Born in a small fishing village on the west coast of Denmark, she had been bundled off into domestic service when she left school. Her first job had been in a big house in Copenhagen. She'd liked it and the family had been kind to her, but when they had moved to a smaller house, she'd had to go. She had been in her present position for six months, and she wasn't particularly happy. It was a big house in the country, not far from Elsinore, but the mistress was strict and distant. A Scottish lady who had married a wealthy Dane, she ruled the servants with a rod of iron.

Ingrid had made the mistake of falling for the second-footman, a gangling youth in the mould of her favourite movie star, Gary Cooper. The lad wasn't backwards in his relations with girls, and Ingrid was soon enjoying stolen kisses in quiet corners of the house. Her little romance gave her the feeling of wellbeing, keeping her mind off the drudgery of her life, although when he grew bolder and squeezed one of her breasts, she became uneasy. She allowed it to continue, however, and soon he was slipping his hand inside her bodice to fondle the plump softness of her bubbies. He would tiptoe up to her quietly when she was working, and wind his arms around her as he kissed the back of her neck. She adored those illicit moments; when his hand cupped a naked breast and his fingers caressed the eager nipple, she was quite breathless with happiness. It was only when he attempted to grope beneath her skirt that she became angry, brushing his hand away. Her mother had warned her to keep her legs together in the company of men.

Then, on her sixteenth birthday, the staff had given her a little celebration. It happened that the family were out that day, so the butler purloined wine from the cellar and the cook supplied tasty morsels of food. Ingrid had enjoyed the party immensely and drank too much wine, so when her true love led her upstairs she did not have the wit to protest. He sneaked her into the mistress's bedroom and made love to her between the linen sheets of the big bed.

It was an unseemly fumbling affair between a drunken girl unable to protest and an eager, lustful youth. He ripped her clothes from her body, and she struggled against him until he consoled her by gently kissing her succulent young titties, taking each whole tender globe into his mouth and sucking deliciously. His need to have her, however, overcame his gentleness: prising her legs apart he crudely shoved his fingers into her tight lair, causing her to scream in pain. She fought against him, but he held her down and forced his pulsating rod deep into her body. She had never been touched there, certainly never fucked, and the crude invasion of her virgin vagina caused her excruciating pain. She screamed aloud. He shot his bolt over her belly almost immediately, although she had no knowledge of it. When she opened her eyes it was to see her mistress towering above her. She had never seen anybody so angry.

Both she and the second-footman were to be birched. He was to get fifty strokes, she thirty. The alternative was immediate dismissal without pay or references. He went. It was simple for him, Ingrid thought, he could change jobs easily enough. She would have to go home to face her mother's wrath and her father's disappointment. She would rather suffer the birch. She wondered whether it would hurt. She knew she was to be punished in front of the whole family, which was humiliation enough.

The door opened, and the mistress's personal maid, Greta, approached her.

'You are a silly girl. The mistress is absolutely furious. I've never seen her so angry.'

Greta was a woman in her mid-thirties, quite attractive, but very conscious of her post. It was the first time she'd spoken directly to Ingrid, except to give her orders. Ingrid didn't reply. What could she say?

'She's going to birch you herself,' she announced. 'She's sure to lay it on really hard.'

Ingrid thought she detected a smirk, and she guessed that Greta would enjoy seeing her suffer.

'You are to undress to your petticoat. When you're ready I'll escort you.'

Ingrid found herself shivering as she undressed. She was on the verge of tears. It surely wasn't right to birch sixteen-year-old girls; there must be a law against it. She shook her long blonde tresses free as she pulled her dress over her head. She was a big girl, tall and mature for her age, with deep blue eyes and a pouting sensuous mouth. Her breasts were already full, and her thighs ripely curved. In a few years she would develop into a statuesque Scandinavian beauty, of the type so admired by men the world over.

'Remove your underwear,' commanded Greta.

Hesitantly, now certain she was to be birched on her bare behind, she stepped out of her drawers. Thinking about it made her blush. She watched Greta leave, to return in a few minutes and lead her into the great hall. At the far end a semi-circle of chairs surrounded a tall wooden box with a padded velvet top. She was led to the box and made to stretch over it.

'Stretch yourself right over the box, Ingrid,' Greta snapped. 'Now stick your bottom further out. That's better. Let me get your petticoat out of the way.'

She spoke as if she were arranging covers on a sofa, Ingrid thought cynically as she felt her derrière bared for all to see. She could imagine the picture she presented, her toes just touching the floor, her bare arse stuck high into the air, and her head hanging down between her arms with her golden hair cascading to the floor. She felt like a medieval slave girl prepared for flogging. She heard the audience arrive in silence and take their seats quietly, as if it were some religious occasion. The mistress stood beside her swinging the birch menacingly and, although it looked formidable, it wasn't the heavy rod she had dreaded. It consisted of half a dozen cane-like switches tied together. Ingrid heaved a sigh of relief.

'You will receive thirty strokes,' the mistress growled, 'and if you struggle from your position, I shall double the number.'

Ingrid heard the ominous swish of the birch. Instantly a vicious sting invaded her rump. She squealed aloud, a high-pitched scream involuntarily forced from her throat by the searing whip of the birch rods across the tender flesh of her trembling buttocks.

A second later she bawled at the second stinging stroke.

'Silence, girl,' called the mistress, 'or you'll get more.'

As her maid predicted, the mistress thrashed her severely. Each stroke was full and measured as she raised the birch high above her head before bringing it down as hard as she could to further torment the smarting cheeks of Ingrid's young buttocks. She paused after each ten, though whether it was to give her sobbing victim respite or to rest her arm was debatable. Throughout it all Ingrid forced herself to be still; her stomach was firmly wedged to the padded top, but her legs kicked frantically at each stroke, and her head shot upwards as she squealed. The thrashing felt like a thousand wasps abusing her smarting hindquarters. By the end of the ordeal her face was wet and her eyes blinded by tears. Her arse burned as if it were on fire. She was totally exhausted.

Greta led her to her own bedroom, the cruel command of her mistress ringing in her ears: 'You will be back at your duties in one hour.'

She allowed Greta to help her out of her petticoat and on to the bed. The cotton sheets were cool to her naked body. She closed her eyes, the blistered cheeks of her ravished bum burning like a furnace.

'Is it bleeding?' she asked.

'No. The flesh is red and bruised, but the skin's not broken. Does it hurt much?'

'It stings like hell.'

'Should I put some cream on, to soothe it?'

'Do you think it will?'

'I think so.'

She winced and moaned in agony when Greta's fingers touched her, but the cool cream eased the blazing pain.

'Is that better?'

'A little.'

Greta continued caringly to massage the cream into the tingling flesh of Ingrid's outraged keister. In spite of the sore ache, Ingrid drifted into a shallow sleep. She awoke to the realisation that Greta's fingers had strayed between her thighs, and she was being caressed in her most secret parts. Her first reaction was to call for the woman to stop, but she was tired and the feeling was pleasurable. She allowed her thighs to be gently parted, and felt the probing fingers at the lips of her vulva, massaging the tenderness beyond. A ripple of pleasure turned to a shudder of delight when the tips of the exploring fingers touched her sensitive young clitoris. She found herself more aroused than she had ever been, and began to pant like an animal as those active fingers slid inside her pussy. She closed her thighs on the trespassing hand, and realised she was soaking wet. Sticky juices were seeping from her body.

She was about to cry stop when Greta urged her up on to her hands and knees and slid beneath her. She felt the woman's head between her open legs and her thighs being pulled downwards until her gaping twat was touching Greta's impatient gob. Hot lips sucked avidly at her, a flickering tongue probed inside her wet quim, and hands kneaded her lush titties, which hung beneath her like two delicious peaches. A tinge of disgust ran through her when she became conscious of what was happening: another woman was making love to her. She wanted to scream, to wrench herself free, but the fire in her backside had spread to her loins and she found herself grinding her crotch down on to Greta's face and her whole body shuddered as she orgasmed into Greta's eagerly awaiting mouth.

Ashamed, she struggled from the bed, quickly dressed and fled to her duties.

Some weeks later a new butler arrived, an Englishman in his late fifties who appeared to take a liking to the disgraced Ingrid. When, out of the blue, he proposed marriage, she accepted. As his wife she would regain respect among the other servants and cease to be the butt of all their jokes. They married a month later, and on the first night of their two days' honeymoon in Copenhagen, she discovered he was a homosexual. Her sex life consisted of masturbating him or sucking him off while he looked at photos of young men. He couldn't bear to touch her as a woman, although he was kind to her in every other way. He was well travelled, and an educated man, so she learned much from him, including his native English language. She was determined to leave him, but before she did she would learn everything he had to teach her.

In the end, however, it was he who deserted her. On 3 September 1939, when Britain declared war, he packed his bags and left, saying he would send for her when he was settled. He never did.

At Christmas, Ingrid went home on holiday and stayed. When the Nazis invaded in the spring her whole family fled to England in their fishing boat. Within sight of land they were attacked by a Dornier, and sunk; she was the only survivor. After a fruitless search for her husband, it was suggested to her by the Free Danish government that she take a domestic job in London; she had wanted to join the women's services, but couldn't be accepted until her nationality was established.

The young couple who employed her were titled. He worked in Whitehall, but she had never done a stroke in her life. Ingrid had been there for less than a week, when the husband came home with exciting news.

'Darling, I heard today they are looking for young women who can speak a European lingo.'

'So?' replied his bored wife.

'So, you can speak Frog like a native.'

'What do they want them for?'

'Security work of some kind, something to do with Churchill's new espionage units.'

'Surely you don't expect me to get involved in anything so sordid. You'll have me driving an ambulance next.'

'You'll have to find something soon, darling. National service for women is very much on the cards.'

'If it comes, Mummy will get me into some sort of voluntary work.'

Ingrid was standing in the hallway and overheard the conversation. She realised it was just what she wanted – a chance to get back at the Nazis who had killed her whole family. She must have the address to ask for an interview. She saw the master approaching. He was a tall, thin man in his late thirties, dressed in the regulation City gentleman's black suit.

'Sir,' she whispered.

'Yes, Ingrid?' He paused in front of her.

'I must have that address, sir,' she pleaded, 'so I can try for an interview.'

'It's classified information, I'm afraid.'

'Please . . .' she wheedled.

He saw she was desperate, and decided to use the situation to his own advantage.

'What do I get in return?'

'What do you want?'

He grabbed her hand and led her to the nearby toilet. He locked the door.

'You know what oral sex is?'

'Yes, sir.'

'Well, get on with it.'

She dropped to her knees, her fingers busily unbuttoning his fly. He sat on the seat as she eased his prong free of his trousers. It was already half erect. She knelt between his legs, bending her head forward so that she could take his steadily rising cock into her mouth. Her soft lips closed over it, and she could feel it swelling in her mouth. She sucked sweet and long, like a young girl with her favourite-flavoured lollipop. Within seconds the pole was rock hard, and quivering at the back of her throat. Her mouth was so full she could hardly breathe. She eased back her head and her luscious lips slipped up the shaft until she had only the tip left in her mouth. She caressed the rampant weapon with the tip of her tongue before plunging her head forward and taking as much into her mouth as was humanly possible.

He looked down at her. She had swallowed a great mouthful of his throbbing cock, more than any other girl had managed. She moved her lips so expertly, sending feelings of delirium through his loins. She didn't look up at him; she concentrated on bringing him to a quick climax. He could hold himself back no longer; he knew he was on the edge of orgasm. He grabbed her long hair, and jerked back her head to watch his prick slip from her mouth. Then, quite deliberately, he shot his spunk all over her face. His great sigh of relief drowned her small squeak of disgust. She had closed her eyes, but could feel his gum spatter on her lashes and her cheeks. Then his fingers were on her face, crudely rubbing his sperm into her, spreading it all over her cheeks, nose and forehead; he massaged her skin as if his spunk were a cream to

70

enhance her beauty. He got to his feet, and left her standing in the toilet.

A few minutes later she heard him return. A card slipped under the door. It had a name and phone number on it. She picked it up and went to the bathroom to scrub her face.

At Whitehall she was one of the last to go into the interview room, and even Lord C. had become a trifle tired of seeing pretty girls. When Ingrid entered, however, he came to life. He thought he'd never seen such a glorious arse. He promised himself he would see more of it – and not only see it, but give it one.

When Ingrid arrived at initial training camp it wasn't surprising that the sergeant thought very much the same as Lord C. The seat of her ATS skirt stretched so tightly across her superb fundament that it outlined the delectable twin moons, the like of which he'd never seen under a uniform skirt. At twenty years of age, Ingrid had developed into the full beauty she had promised to be. She was truly voluptuous, an earthy beauty who exuded sexual promise. The sergeant watched her wherever she went, plotting devious ways to get her knickers down.

His opportunity came quite unexpectedly. Ingrid asked for an interview, and in his office handed him a letter from her solicitors in London. They had information concerning her husband, and requested she visited their offices in Holborn.

'Do you know what this means?' he asked.

'No, not really.'

'You have enlisted under a false name, and given false details of your married state.'

'Am I in much trouble?'

'My God, you certainly are,' he exaggerated melo-dramatically. 'You'll be dismissed from the service, and can kiss this job goodbye.'

'Oh, no! I so much want to be a spy against the Nazis.'

'I shall have to inform the colonel.'

'Must you?'

He was silent for a moment, as if seriously consider-ing her case. 'Well, we'll see,' he smiled. 'There may be a way around it.'

'Thank you.'

'And you'll need leave to go to London?'

'Yes, please.'

'That will be difficult, too.'

'I'm sorry to be so much trouble. You will help me, won't you?'

'I'll try.'

He waited several hours, growing more and more horny, before he went to seek her out. He found her in the gymnasium working out with the other girls. The instructor worked them on the ropes and wall bars before finishing with a fast ball game. Taking a seat, the sergeant watched the girls; he leched over their long bare legs and the short skirts that barely covered their plump posteriors. He loved to see their bouncing titties as they ran and jumped; the sight was enough to make him want to masturbate on the spot. He loved to imagine the same scene with them all being put through their paces, naked.

The ball game was fast and furious. When it had finished the sergeant called Ingrid and led her to the equipment room next to the gym. She was breathing heavily; her face was hot and flushed, and the sweat ran from her body after such strenuous exercise. She looked so ravishing, he could have eaten her.

'I think I can straighten things out for you. No one need know.'

'Oh, thank you, sergeant,' she cried gratefully.

'And arrange leave for you to go to London.'

'I could kiss you,' she purred.

'It will have to be more than that.'

'Pardon?'

'I shall need a proper reward, for all the trouble you've caused, madam.'

She looked at him, and hung her head prettily. 'You want to fuck me?'

He nodded. Her heart missed a beat. He had no way of knowing that she was every bit as randy as him. She had never had so much regular exercise in her life, and not only was she fit, she was happy. She was almost bursting out of her skin, and her desire was for a man. She had fantasised about all the instructors, especially the sergeant, so it would be no hardship to be screwed by him. She needed a man, not only because she was randy, but to make certain she was a hundred per cent heterosexual after her experience with Greta. She saw the gleam of pure lust in his eyes as she quickly pulled her thin blouse over her head and undid her bra. Her exquisite boobs hung naked, deliciously round, plump and tender, like ripe fruit to be handled delicately. He reached forward and gently squeezed a pink nipple. She shivered as it hardened to his touch, and unfastened her flimsy gym skirt, allowing it to flutter to the floor. He watched breathlessly as her fingers slipped into the waistband of her knickers, pushing them down her long legs to her ankles.

Her young body shone with sweat: she was truly magnificent. He had imagined she would be attractive naked, but in reality she was superb. Each erotic curve, from her shoulders to her thighs, was exquisitely defined. Her belly, as flat as a board, emphasised the globular spheres of her comely bosom, while from between her closed thighs peeped a hint of pure golden pubic fur. He undressed as she removed her shoes and tossed her knickers aside.

'Let's have you running on the spot,' he snapped.

She was puzzled, but didn't question him. Her military training was already paying off. He couldn't keep his eyes off her bouncing melons, and by the time he had climbed out of his uniform, her body was once again glistening with perspiration. He led her by the hand to a pile of mats, and knelt over her. She was still out of breath, her chest and stomach moving rhythmically. He placed his lips between her breasts, where the sweat ran freely, and sucked the salty liquid into his mouth. Inch by inch, his tongue moved over her body, sucking her perspiration from her and savouring it as if it were holy water. He licked her breasts, stomach and neck before parting her thighs to taste the feminine fluid between her legs. He nibbled at the soft downy floss, but deliberately skirted the inviting lips of her pouting labia. He would return there at his leisure. He turned her over to survey the splendour of her bottom, the twin mounds so exquisitely rounded to produce a derrière of bewitching beauty. He wanted to slap those smooth pliant cheeks, to watch them wobble like jelly, but he refrained. All in good time. He moved his lips over the silky white skin, so supple and sensuous to the touch; he kissed and nibbled the soft flesh, while gradually moving towards the hidden valley between. She felt him part her nates and she shivered a little. Soon her most secret orifice would be revealed. She was aware of a wetness, and discerned he had squirted spittle from his mouth on to her anus, which he began gently massaging with his fingers. She tried to move, but felt his lips close tightly over her rear entrance, his tongue circle the tight little hole. What was his intent? Was she to be taken up the arse?

His tongue, however, was but visiting, and she felt herself flipped over like a fish on a slab and his mouth closing on to her willing twat. She swooned as he gorged upon her love-box, and parting the fleshy outer lips with his fingers, he nibbled hungrily at the inner sanctum with tongue and teeth. She writhed in an ecstasy she had never before known as his lips teased her so-sensitive clitoris and his tongue probed into her welcoming crack. The juices from her vaginal walls flowed freely into his mouth and he drank thirstily of her. The insides of her thighs were drenched with her mucus, which he licked greedily from her.

When she was hot with want for him, he raised her body and presented his rampant cock at her gaping orifice. She whimpered, at the zenith of her passion, as his monster slipped so very slowly into her yielding passage. She strained to part her legs even further. There must be no barrier to stop him. She must have every inch of his pulsating sex inside her, even if it reached her stomach walls. She felt the thick rod reaching deep within her until their bodies met and he could go no further.

They lay still for a moment, at peace, content to hold each other. It was the calm before the storm. He slowly began to move his John Thomas out of her honeypot, sending her into a frenzy of sensuality. She struggled and writhed beneath him, clawing at his back and biting his shoulders. She wound her legs around his thighs and squeezed, as if she were a boa constrictor trying to crush its prey. He rode the storm, spitefully thrusting his tool in and out of her gaping twat like the piston of a steam engine. Her nails dug into his flesh causing enough pain for him to retaliate. He slapped the curve of her buttocks with the palm of his hand, once, twice, until she squealed. He gripped her thighs, and squeezed; she felt his hot ejaculation spurt deep inside her body. She responded with her own climax, whimpering as it trickled from her. He collapsed on to her, covering her sweaty body with his.

Five minutes later he dressed, bending to kiss her nipples before he left.

'Tomorrow I shall spank your butt.'

'Why?'

'Your punishment for telling lies.'

'Then what was this in aid of?'

'Your reward for behaving yourself!'

'You bastard,' she grinned.

Ingrid was left in no doubt she was heterosexual, and the following morning she marched into the sergeant's office after first parade. He was sitting behind his desk.

'And what can I do for you, Miss Ingrid?'

'I've been told to report to you for a good spanking, sergeant,' she replied, standing strictly to attention.

'Oh, yes.' He smiled. 'And was there anything else?'

'What do you have in mind?'

'A bit of lechery, perhaps?'

'Whatever you say, sergeant.'

He walked around the desk and perched on the edge facing her.

'All right, Miss Ingrid, let's get on with it. We'll have that skirt raised and those knickers down.'

She did as she was bid, and stood before him with her skirt hoisted above her waist and her knickers lowered sufficiently to bare her behind.

'Turn around, miss.'

He drank in the provocative beauty of her delectable

derrière, which positively invited spanking. He took her by the shoulders and moved her sideways to within easy reach.

'Bend forward from the waist,' he ordered. 'Now bend your knees, and stick your butt out.'

She stood, leaning forward so that her upper body was at right angles to her legs, holding her skirt high. Her bent knees served to push her arse right out, to present a perfect target. He jerked her knickers down past her knees, and raised the palm of his hand. She drew in her breath with a cry when it landed, but remained in position. He spanked her soundly, each slap landing with a resounding crack across the fleshiest parts of her quivering fundament. The noise of his palm against her bare flesh echoed through the building, so all his staff would know she had been spanked. She gasped at every smack, whimpering and moving her legs to lessen the effect. Her treatment continued until her buttocks were glowing a healthy pink.

By then the sergeant had become unbelievably horny for her. He moved around to face her and began to strip below the waist. In spite of her sore backside, she was as randy as he. She followed his lead, and soon they faced each other, ready for action. She saw he had an enormous hard-on, while she was conscious of a wetness between her thighs. She flung her arms around his neck, and felt his hands cup the smarting cheeks of her bum. Instinctively she jerked herself upwards, her legs circling his waist, her feet crossed in the small of his back. He stood supporting her with his hands under her buttocks while she hung around his neck like a huge human necklace. She eagerly manoeuvred her thighs until she could feel the tip of his prong under her moist pussy, and groaning, she slowly impaled herself on him. The position was too uncomfortable

77

to last long, and his arms ached supporting her frantic movements as she slid blissfully up and down his rampant pole. She gasped as she climaxed and he could feel her glutinous juices trickling down his balls. It hastened his own orgasm, and he discharged into her on a downward stroke of her thighs, causing her to howl with delight. She returned her feet to the floor, and smiled up at him. He kissed her forehead.

'You'd better change out of uniform, ready to catch your train to London.'

The solicitors told her that her husband had been traced, but he had been killed in a road accident. His will didn't mention her, and he had left what little money he had to a young man. She said she didn't want to contest the will, and caught the next train back to camp.

When she changed trains on to the local line, she found she had to wait. To pass the time she had a couple of gins in the station bar.

When the train arrived, she climbed into an empty compartment. At the first stop a schoolboy, a lad of about sixteen, dressed in grey flannels and school blazer, joined her. A handsome youngster, he reminded her of her youngest brother. When the train stopped between stations, she asked him whether he knew the reason.

'We have to wait for the up express,' he replied. 'Sometimes it's quite a while.'

She looked out of the window at the green peaceful English countryside and wondered how long it would be before she saw Denmark again. The boy cleared his throat.

'Excuse me, you're not British, are you?'

'I'm from Denmark.'

'My friend spent his holiday there last year. He says all Danish girls are frigid.'

'Does he?' she smiled.

She closed her eyes to sleep. The gin was making her drowsy. She dreamed she was being kissed, and woke with a start. The boy was sitting beside her, his lips brushing hers. She pushed him away angrily.

'What are you doing?'

'Don't be angry. I wanted to tell my friend I'd kissed a Danish girl.'

'You can't do things like that,' she scowled.

'I'm sorry.'

He continued to sit beside her, and she knew he was blatantly looking down her blouse at the provocative swelling of her boobs and the deep valley between them. She wore no bra.

'Can I see your breasts?'

'What?' she cried unbelievingly.

'My girlfriend showed me hers. Only I bet yours are much bigger.'

He smiled innocently at her, as if it was the most ordinary request in the world, and she found her fingers undoing the buttons of her blouse. She wondered whether it was the gin or his likeness to her dead brother that was making her do it; but she had no real idea why. Slowly she pulled the material away to expose her marble white globes in all their naked glory.

He gasped at their beauty, and after an eternity of looking, bent forward to kiss them. She was floating in another world, irresponsible, uncaring, just allowing things to happen. She was aware of his eager lips on her nipples, and knew they were responding to his kiss. He attempted to cup an orb in his hand, but he was sweaty and she pushed him away. He returned to sit opposite her, where he remained silent for several minutes, content to gaze at her uncovered boobies. She watched him under half-closed lashes, knowing that whatever he asked she would comply. Why, she didn't know.

'Can I see between your legs?'

She felt a little thrill of apprehension shoot through her. Perhaps she was an exhibitionist at heart.

'Turn your head,' she murmured shyly.

She was as nervous and as silly as a schoolgirl. She whipped off her knickers and popped them in her handbag. Then, having eased the hem of her dress above her stocking tops, she sat on the very edge of the seat with her legs wide apart. She watched him open his eyes, and knew he could see her pouting slit, nestling in its surround of curly short golden hair. She pulled her dress higher to be certain her snatch wasn't in shadow, and waited for him to lean forward to touch her. When he did so, it was roughly with the impatience of youth. She winced, and pulled away as he shoved his middle finger into her without ceremony.

'No,' she cried, grabbing his hand, 'gently – like this.'

She took his fingers and guided them along the swollen lips of her vulva, and then led them inside her willing quim towards her anxiously waiting clitoris. Slowly, she took her hand away and leaned back, closing her eyes. She didn't see him whip his trousers down and reach forward to grab her behind the knees. She was perfectly relaxed, wondering why he had stopped fingering her, when her legs were suddenly jerked upwards over her head. She squawked with surprise as her knees touched her shoulders and her feet pointed straight up towards the carriage roof. The utter confusion she felt when she realised what a ridiculous figure she must cut was completely forgotten when she felt his stiff young cock pushing at the lips

80

of her pussy, threatening to penetrate right inside her. She squealed for him to stop.

'Oh, my god, what are you doing? Let go of me, you horrible boy!'

He had her legs pinned to her shoulders and was leaning forward over her, perfectly placed to thrust his young weapon into her unprotected hole.

'What you're doing is rape,' she screamed. 'Let go of my legs. Let me put them down.'

His answer was to plunge inside her, his anxious tool slipping easily into her moist passage until it reached the hilt. She ceased struggling as he thrust backward and forward inside her without care or finesse. She felt him spend himself, gasping as he came inside a woman for the very first time. He yanked up his trousers, and holding them together with one hand, he pulled open the door and jumped out on to the grassy embankment. Silly boy, she thought, he was probably scared by her talk of rape. As if she would have reported him. After all, she'd been a willing party until then, and if he'd been a bit more sophisticated she'd have continued to be. She adjusted her clothing and smiled as she wondered what sort of roué he'd be in ten years time.

Two weeks later she arrived at Holmsley Manor. It was bigger than she'd expected. She was invited to join Lord C. for tea in the library after she had changed out of uniform. She took her time preparing herself and entered the library adorned in a pretty cotton summer dress worn over her bare legs. She thought Lord C. looked very aristocratic, much more so than any of the gentlemen she'd been employed by.

'Ingrid, isn't it?' he welcomed her.

'Yes, sir.'

'You'll join an old man for tea?'

'Thank you, sir.'

'They're serving hot buttered toast,' he smiled, 'but with your consent, I would prefer it to be buttered bum and toast.'

'Pardon?' she murmured.

She thought she couldn't have heard him properly, or perhaps it was an English joke she didn't understand.

'I shall butter your bum and lick it off to eat with my toast,' he explained simply. 'That way it gives plain boring old toast a certain zing.'

'I'm sure it must, but I don't really fancy . . .'

'You wouldn't deny a poor old man a whim?'

She realised he was the guv'nor, and to refuse could count against her. It was only harmless fun anyway.

'I'm sorry. What would you like me to do?'

'Slip off your knickers, and lift your dress, my dear, so that I may admire your comely seat.'

She did as she was commanded, standing before him with her dress raised well above her waist, her magnificently proportioned rump gloriously naked for his admiration. He drank in the beauty of those milk white twin moons, so perfectly contoured, so delicately curved. He kept her standing for more than ten minutes, certain he had never seen an equal. It was almost too delectable to be spanked. First, he would have some fun with her, and then, in military parlance, he would fuck her arse off.

The maid brought the toast and butter, and he beckoned Ingrid nearer. The extra large pat of butter had been heated, so that it would spread easily. Using a broad flat knife, Chomsmy spread it evenly over the whole expanse of her fleshy posterior. Then, conscientiously, he licked every millimetre of her twin moons.

When all traces of the butter had disappeared, he stood and scooped his index finger into what remained of the pat of butter.

'And now for dessert,' he grinned. 'I'll have you bending forward and parting your knees, young lady.'

She did as she was bid.

'Grip your knees, and stretch out that lovely arse.'

The sight of her curved bottom stretched out before him sent a shudder of anticipation down his spine; his tool was already stiffening.

'Bend your knees,' he urged.

She obeyed, and the cleft almost disappeared as that small wrinkled bottom-hole was boldly displayed. His index finger smeared the butter around the tight little orifice, and he trembled. His tool was swollen and ready for action. Without warning, he jabbed it against her greased anus; grabbing her hips, he pushed. For an instant her sphincter held against his invasion, but then the ring of muscle that guarded her rear entrance parted, and he slid smoothly up into her anal passage.

He gasped for breath; he had impaled her to the hilt. He felt exhilaration. She had the most beautiful arse in the world, and he was fucking it.

She groaned as he began to move inside her, and then, as if deciding she liked this new experience, she bent her knees even further and drove backwards, meeting his every thrust deep inside her rectum. He came quickly, such was his elation at capturing her virgin bum-hole; pulling free his bursting weapon, he shot his load all over her fleshy butt.

'Rub it well in,' he muttered, 'it will mix with the butter. You'll have the fairest arse in Christendom.'

Ingrid settled into life at the manor, and although she wasn't the best pupil on the espionage course, she enjoyed the comtesse's talks on sex and seduction.

Jeanne

Jeanne opened the front door of her basement apartment in the Republique district of Paris. A young man stood smiling at her. She pulled her loose robe closer around her, but was unable to hide the promise of the fabulous body beneath.

'Yes,' she said.

'Can I come in, mam'selle?'

'Why?'

She thought she'd never seen such a wonderful smile. It lit up his smooth boyish features, making him as handsome as any film star.

'You're so beautiful, mam'selle. I would like to fuck you.'

'Would you now,' she giggled.

He pushed past her into the apartment, and she closed the door behind him. She stood with her back to it, looking up at him. She couldn't imagine a more sexy man. He slipped the robe from her shoulders, and it fluttered to the floor. She stood naked. She was small, barely more than five feet tall, but her breasts were full and succulent. Her black hair was long and delicately waved, while her hazel eyes lit up a pretty girlish face enhanced by two smiling dimples.

She took his hands and guided them to her two delicious orbs, which had made him gasp in admiration. He kneaded the soft malleable flesh between his fingers, fondling the small erect nipples until they swelled to the size of plum stones. She covered his large hands with hers, and held him as if she was afraid he'd fly away. While he massaged her two full moons, he closed his lips over hers, and his tongue played games in her mouth that sent shivers down her spine.

He released her swollen breasts, and pushed her gently to the floor. The carpet was rough beneath her back, but she didn't notice it for his mouth was closed over her rounded melons: sucking one, and then the other. She could feel a wetness between her legs, and knew her juices were flowing from her anxious rosebud, which was already aching for his touch. She closed her eyes with delight and he was suddenly naked, kneeling over her and threatening her quivering bubbies with his rampant member. She took the throbbing weapon between her fingers, and guided it into the valley between her creamy plump mammaries. He was a willing captive. She squeezed her pliant mounds against his imprisoned staff, urging him to fuck them. He moved his cock inside the sweet softness of his prison, causing a delicious friction that stimulated him to climax. He ejaculated under her chin, and his semen splattered over her throat. He knelt watching her as she smiled up at him, while she massaged it into her breasts; and then, daintily she sucked each of her fingertips. He picked her up, and carried her into the small kitchen.

'Now, you can cook my dinner, woman,' he growled.

'I didn't get that fuck I was promised at the door,' she replied.

'Do you let every stranger who knocks at your door, fuck you?'

'Yes.'

He slapped her bottom playfully. They had been living together for six months, and it seemed like six days. She adored him. They both studied at the Sorbonne, and she had become infatuated with him soon after she enrolled. He, however, was politically left wing and a member of the Communist Party, while her parents were rich provincial folk. She had quarrelled with her father, and he had disowned her when she went to live with her lover.

Tonight he was going to a political rally. She usually accompanied him, but there was a very real possibility of violence, and he didn't want her exposed to it. The rally was organised by fascists, and the communists intended to stop it. She worried about his safety, as she ironed furiously to calm her nerves. She didn't hear him come up behind her. He encircled her with his arms, his hands cupping her ample boobs.

'I can't go without saying au revoir to my two sweethearts,' he whispered, tenderly squeezing her breasts.

'Be careful, please.'

She was wearing shorts and bra. He undid her bra, and cupped her breasts again, pinching her dainty nipples.

'What about our unfinished business?'

'There's not time, is there?'

'There's always time,' he grinned.

She felt his fingers unbutton her shorts, and they fell with a flop to the floor.

'Does pussy want to come out to play?' he whispered.

'Feel!'

His fingertips moved tantalisingly down her thigh, and along the plump overhang of her buttocks to the deep crevice beneath her nether cheeks. He explored

86

her damp pudenda nestling in its soft cushion of pubic fleece. She opened her legs and he slipped two fingers into her, massaging her swollen vulva and fondling her pulsing clitoris.

'Pussy wants you,' she moaned. 'Hurry, hurry. She's waiting.'

She bent forward so that her hands rested on her knees and her long black hair cascaded around her face. He presented his cue at the entrance of her waiting quim, and cupped her gorgeous swinging bubbies in his hands. Her love-box was already dripping with nectar, as he sank into her spongy passage like a stone into water. She gasped, and worked her thighs to aid him, pushing back onto his shaft to meet his every breathless stroke. As they copulated, he kneaded her tender orbs. There was so much moisture trickling down the inside of her thighs, she wondered whether she had peed herself in the frenzy of intercourse. And then, he added his juices to hers, lovingly ejaculating his sperm deep into her sticky tube.

She never saw him again: he was killed that night. She mourned bitterly, refusing to return to her family. The only person she would see was Pierre's friend, Reggie. Reggie was an Englishman, a budding novelist and a fellow left-wing sympathiser. He was in Paris to write his 'great novel' and scratched a living writing short stories. He had spent much time with Jeanne and Pierre, and was head over heels in love with Jeanne. After the loss he comforted her, and kept silent about his love until she was out of her dark abyss. After the second month she promised to marry him, and although she moved into his apartment they weren't yet lovers. Patiently he coaxed her back to her family.

The wedding, in her home village, was a splendid affair, and as they left the church she realised how much she loved him. She couldn't wait to tell him. After the formal speeches, she whisked him into the garden, to the little summer house she'd loved as a child. It seemed strange for a bride in her wedding dress to tell her husband, for the very first time, she loved him. He moved towards her to take her arm and kiss her, but she fell to her knees, her anxious fingers fumbling at his fly. Overcome by her sudden display of passion, he tried to lift her to her feet.

'No, darling,' she muttered, 'let me do it. I must show I love you in my own way.'

He rested his hand lightly upon her lovely head, allowing her to fish in his trousers for his slumbering prong. It wouldn't take much rousing, as he had felt a twinge of lust the moment she dropped to her knees. She eased it free and, lifting her bridal veil, took the whole quivering shaft into her warm wet mouth. He could have yelled with pleasure as her soft red tongue zealously licked his throbbing pego. She sucked divinely; one moment teasing with the tip of her tongue, and the next moment swallowing his whole shaft deep into her throat. His hands moved behind her head, encouraging her to hasten the sensuous movements of her mouth for his storm was gathering. She recognised the signs as his thighs trembled, and gulped his prick deep into her throat ready for his emission. He crushed her face into his crotch, and spattered his spunk over the back of her mouth. When he had stopped shivering she slipped his limp cock from her mouth, sucking the tip to make certain she had every drop of his precious sperm before smiling up at him and swallowing.

It was the beginning of a sex life to equal her life with Pierre, but soon after their honeymoon war broke out. Reggie decided he must return to England to enlist, and she sailed with him. He'd had a book accepted, and they used the money to enable her to live in digs near him. They had an unforgettable Christmas together. Soon afterwards he was posted to France. They decided that she should work while he was abroad, and she got a post in a private school that had been evacuated from London. It was a co-ed secondary school for boarding and day pupils, and when it was evacuated most of the day pupils accompanied it. Many of the staff had joined the services, and the standard of teaching and discipline was low. She was engaged as French tutor and assistant house-mistress.

During her second week she received a message to report to the headmaster's study immediately, and found part of her duties was to be present when girls received discipline. Corporal punishment was the school rule, and boys and girls alike received it upon their bare posteriors. The only concession to gender was that the girls were punished with a slipper, instead of the cane. The headmaster, a big man who had stayed on after retirement because of the war, insisted he had the sole right to punish the pupils, but a woman had to be present when the girls were beaten.

Arriving at his study, she knocked and entered. The two girls to be disciplined had been made to stand on upright chairs in the middle of the room. The youngest was about fifteen, a dark-haired young beauty who was well developed for her age. The other was older and taller, a blonde with slim shoulders and no bust, but ample thighs and buttocks. The girls had obviously been sent from the sports field in disgrace for they still wore their hockey kit: short pleated navy skirt, blouse and long socks to the knee. They must have been on opposing sides for one wore a white blouse and socks, while the other wore light blue. Jeanne realised that her presence was a necessary evil for him. She was certain he was the type of man who would have thrashed the girls harder, and even sexually assaulted them if she hadn't been present.

The headmaster picked up a battered slipper, and stood glaring at the two girls.

'No girl, ever, has been dismissed from hockey and sent up to me,' he thundered, 'and in front of visitors. I'm going to give you such a slippering you'll remember it all your lives.'

'Yes, sir,' they murmured.

'Come down off that chair, and prepare yourself.'

The younger girl climbed down from the chair, and he sat on it. She must have been on the receiving end of a spanking before, as she appeared to know exactly what to do. She took her place by his side, and reaching under her games skirt she nervously eased her knickers down to her knees.

'Come on girl, get on with it,' he snapped impatiently, 'I've got more important things to do than slap your bottom.'

She hastily whipped her skirts up around her waist, and stretched herself over his knees.

'Legs straight, both hands on the floor please.'

She was draped helplessly over his lap, her toes and her palms on the floor, and her cute bare bottom raised prettily for spanking. And spank her, he certainly did. Each time the slipper whacked down across her plump young nates, the hearty slap echoed like a gunshot. The girl was soon in tears.

'Stop,' she howled. 'I'm sorry. I promise I'll be good.'

The headmaster paid little attention to her squeaking, and only paused to push her hand away when she tried to rub her inflamed rear. No one counted, but she must have suffered a dozen full-blooded thwacks on her blazing seat. When the headmaster finally threw down the slipper, the girl's bum was as red as a turkey cock.

'Stand by the wall,' he ordered, 'and watch what you'll get when you're older.'

He signalled the other girl to get down from the chair.

'I've had you before, haven't I?'

'Yes, sir.'

'This time I'm going to cure your bad temper once and for all,' he barked, holding a tawse for her to see. 'I'm going to use this tawse on your backside, and you can be thankful it's not the cane.'

Jeanne had never heard of a tawse, a broad leather strap with the business end divided so that it possessed two parallel tails.

The headmaster nudged the girl towards the desk, cleared a space, and signalled her to bend over it. She began to obey.

'Lift your skirt, girl. You don't imagine I'm going to whip you over that?'

She lifted her pleated skirt, and without being told, eased her knickers down her thighs to bare her behind.

'Right down, to your ankles,' he ordered, 'then let's have them off.'

She bent across the desk, her stomach and breasts pressed into the wooden surface, her feet wide apart and her cute bottom raised for his attention.

'Sit in front of her, and hold her wrists please.'

Jeanne did as she was requested, and found herself looking into the girl's pretty face and along her back to the curve of her bare posterior. She couldn't see the tawse land on the tender flesh, but she could imagine the white skin turning from pink to red as the two leather tails landed in unison across those unprotected buttocks.

The girl closed her eyes, and screwed up the muscles of her face every time the strap landed. She yelped and squawked at each stinging blow, and after only a few whacks she kicked her legs wildly to try to break free from Jeanne's grasp.

'You cow,' she spat at Jeanne, 'you fucking bitch.'

'What was that?' the headmaster barked.

'Nothing really,' Jeanne replied calmly, 'just name calling.'

'She doesn't learn, does she?' he grunted, producing a long thin cane. 'Perhaps a few strokes of this will convince her.'

Four times the cane hissed menacingly through the air, to whip across her fundament. She squealed at every stroke, dissolving into wild sobs and wriggling her lower body to ease the pain.

'Pull up your knickers and go,' he said, 'and show the other girls what they can expect if they're sent to me.'

Jeanne watched the two pretty girls shuffle out of the room clutching their soft derrières, and knew they'd be the centre of attention in the dormitory, that night.

'Thank you, Jeanne,' she heard the headmaster say. 'No doubt we shall be meeting again under the same circumstances.'

She hoped not.

That night she felt as lonely and homesick as any of the pupils. She missed Reggie terribly, and for the first time was conscious of being in a strange country. Taking a post in an English boarding school hadn't been a good idea. It was so different from anything in her native France, and she toyed with the idea of going home to her parents.

She walked to the senior students' room, which was

reserved for the older girls and boys. Several were reading, but most were listening to Tommy Dorsey on the radio. She was surprised to see a young man in naval uniform, and he was introduced as an old pupil who was on embarkation leave. He spoke to her in fluent French, and she discovered his family had lived in Tunis when he was a boy. They talked together, and the others gradually drifted away. She glanced at her watch. It was ten-thirty, time for lights out.

'I must go,' he said. 'It's a lovely moonlit night. Won't you walk to the gate with me?'

She agreed, and once they were outside on the gravel drive she took his arm in sisterly manner.

'Where are you staying?' she asked.

'Nowhere. I'll catch the last train.'

'That went half an hour ago,' she laughed.

'Then I'll catch the first one tomorrow morning.'

'Where will you sleep?'

'On the station, in the hedge . . . does it matter?'

'I suppose not, you're young.'

'And lonely,' he sighed.

'Surely not. Sailors have a girl in every port.'

'I don't. I came down to say good-bye to my girl friend here, but she didn't want to know.'

'Know what?'

'When a boy goes off to war,' he stuttered shyly, 'a girl usually, you know . . .'

'Sleeps with him?'

'Well, perhaps not,' he sighed angrily, 'but gives him a kiss or something.'

'You came all this way to kiss a girl?'

'Something like that. All my mates have girls to send them away happy.'

Suddenly she felt as sad and lonely as him. She wanted a sympathetic cuddle too.

'Come on, we'll go to my room. You can give me a kiss,' she smiled, 'would you like that?'

'Would I!'

She led him to her room, not knowing or caring why she did it. She was lonely and frightened in a strange country, and the boy was young and innocent. Just at that moment they needed each other. She had only one thought in her head, and she didn't try to hide it. She helped him out of his tight jersey, and unfastened his bell-bottoms.

'I can't let you go to war a virgin, can I,' she laughed. 'You're still a virgin aren't you?'

'Yes,' he blushed.

'And you'd like to alter all that?'

'Yes, please.'

'And so you shall,' she smiled at him. 'Just like all the best stories you shall have a woman before you sail off in your battleship. Why, it's almost a woman's duty isn't it?'

She felt a touch of bitterness at the way life had treated her. Her lover was dead; her husband was away fighting a war; and she was locked in a dreadful school that she hated. At least she could give the boy pleasure, and lose herself in illicit sex for a few moments. He lay on the bed watching her. She unbuttoned her dress, and pulled it over her head.

'Undo my bra,' she teased.

She felt his fingers fumble at the catch, and finally unhook her. She turned to face him, allowing the bra to fall to the floor. She heard him draw in a breath of astonishment when he saw her naked breasts. They were beauties, she knew that. Pierre and Reggie had both adored their globular beauty, and every man she met looked at them in a way which simply said, I could suck those.

94

She knelt above him, allowing her two delectable peaches to hang down to touch his lips. He kissed their softness, as she swung them like ripe fruit in the wind to brush against his face. When she had teased him sufficiently, she lowered her shoulders to allow those two deliciously tender orbs to rest either side of his nose. He reached up and took them in his hands, squeezing and fondling them, teasing the dainty pink nipples with his fingertips. He wound his arm around her back, and pulled her down to him, so that he could squash her scrumptious boobs into his open mouth. He gorged on their bulbous softness, only allowing them out of his mouth to suck a quivering nipple.

She felt excitement rising within her, and knew her honey-pot would be soaked in mucus. She turned her body around to face his feet and, straddling his head, lowered her open thighs so her slightly parted labia brushed his nose. He held her hips, pulling her down so that her glutinous quim was over his open mouth. Hungrily, he worked his tongue into her hot vulva, sucking and licking until his mouth was full of her heavenly nectar. He swallowed, and began again to probe her enchanted cave, pausing only to tease her dainty clitoris between his lips.

She knew she was about to orgasm. Her body shuddered, and she cried out as she clasped his stiff young pecker between her lips. She ran her sweet tongue up the whole shaft several times, and knew by the way he trembled with passion that he wasn't far from climax. Swiftly, she turned her body and knelt over his thighs, lowering her rapacious twat down onto his eager tool. She could feel it throbbing within her, and fell forward so her supple gourds squashed against his chest. She could sense the storm gathering in his young body. She pressed her lips onto his, and moved her sweet arse in long rhythmic thrusts which sucked his whole shaft into her secret passage. He screamed like a child when she squeezed his ejaculation from his swollen member.

Jeanne lay quietly on top of him until she felt his limp cock slipping from her.

'Now, my young matelot,' she smiled, 'you can go to sea a man.'

It was the first screw she'd had since Reggie was posted to France, and she felt like a fat cat.

On the day of the invasion of France, Jeanne received a telegram telling her Reggie had been killed the week before. She knew she must leave the school and move on to more important things. The headmaster was sympathetic, and gave her the name of a friend at the War Office. She waited several days to collect her thoughts before she went to see him. He gave her another name, and she was shuttled from one department to another until the name of Lord Chomsmy cropped up. It was just what she wanted, a chance to revenge Reggie and Pierre, and maybe see her family again. A week later she passed the interview with flying colours.

There was no doubt she was the most incompetent girl at the initial training camp, but because she always tried so hard the sergeant was tolerant of her. He admired her trim figure and magnificent breasts, but didn't lust after her. She was the only girl he treated as a daughter, and although the others noticed they didn't comment. They realised she had enough trouble on her plate trying to become a soldier.

It was her little-girl-lost look that led to her next sexual encounter. She was on her first map-reading exercise, and had become hopelessly lost in the woods.

At her wits' end, she screamed desperately for help. She felt relieved when she saw a big corporal walking towards her. She knew him by sight, as one of the many instructors.

'Well, what have we here?' he chuckled. 'A little lost boy soldier.'

She had to admit she did look a bit like a boy. Her small figure was swamped in khaki denims; her long hair was tucked under her steel helmet; and her face and hands were as grubby as any schoolboy's.

'I'm a girl,' she giggled.

'You're playing at boy's games. I shall have to treat you as a boy.'

'All right, what ever you say,' she said, 'but get me out of here.'

'Didn't they tell you that little boys playing soldiers in the woods should beware of nasty old corporals?'

'That's enough, you're being silly,' she said nervously. 'Just show me the way back to camp.'

'Let's have those trousers down, little boy,' he sneered.

It was pointless struggling. He grabbed her, and she felt her trousers and drawers dragged down to her ankles. She was made to kneel on her hands and knees, feeling so very vulnerable with her bare arse stuck in the air. She sensed his weapon was out, and threatening her from behind.

She felt the end of his iron knob probing her small brown hole, and realised she was about to be buggered. She'd only had it up there once before, when during a night of unbridled passion Pierre had taken her in every orifice. It was one thing submitting to a lover, but another having a stranger's cock breach her anus. She screamed in protest, forcing him to hesitate.

'Don't you like playing little boy's games?'

'No, you brute,' she sobbed, 'God no. I hate you.'

'OK. We'll play girl's games.'

As he spoke he forced his tool into her reluctant quim. She heard him laugh, as if pleased by his own wit and versatility, but the excitement brought about his ejaculation, which shot out between her thighs and covered her dainty bush with his sperm.

Later, she told the sergeant about the incident. He advised her to say nothing, but the next time she saw the corporal he looked as if he'd been in a train crash.

She was glad to arrive at Holmsley Manor, the final part of her training. Jeanne liked Lord C. and considered him to be a real English gentleman. She was pleased when he invited her to take tea with him. They ate cucumber sandwiches, and he told her the history of the manor until the maid arrived with a bowl of cherries and two peaches.

'I think fruit adds the final touch to teatime,' he smiled, 'but presentation is all, don't you think?'

She was unsure of his meaning, so she kept quiet.

'If you allowed me to decorate your lovely body with these cherries, I'm certain it would add to their taste. What do you say? Are you prepared to humour an old man?'

She thought he must be playing some obscure game, unless it was some kind of test of her reaction.

'Please,' she replied, 'do as you wish. I'm sure you don't mean to harm me.'

'Thank you my dear. Now, if you'll remove all your clothing, I'll get the cherries.'

She stripped naked, and turned to see he had clipped six clothes pegs to a line. From each peg hung a string of cherries.

'If you stand with your feet apart and your hands behind your back, we'll begin our little feast.'

She did as he instructed, and saw him unclip two pegs from the line to transport two strings of cherries across the room. He clipped a peg to each of her ear lobes, and draped the strings of cherries over her shoulders to skirt her breasts like long dangling earrings. Before he fetched the second pair he teased her dainty nipples with his fingertips until they pulsed with excitement. She gasped in astonishment, as he clipped the pegs onto her nipples so that two strings of cherries hung from her delightful orbs. Finally, he knelt and pinched the fleshy outer skin of her labia, before attaching the last two pegs to the lips of her quim.

'And when we have eaten the cherries,' he smiled, 'two peaches soaked in female nectar to finish.'

As he spoke he nudged aside the pegs clipped to her labia, and pushed the two peaches deep inside her slit. She felt like seven kinds of fool, standing there decorated with hanging cherries and with two peaches up her twat. If it was a test to embarrass her, he had succeeded. However, it didn't finish until they'd eaten all the cherries, and gorged on the tangy peaches. He kept a straight face throughout, and when the fruit was eaten, he patted her sweet bottom and told her to get ready for dinner.

Jeanne was the only girl who didn't dislike Nigel. She thought he was silly, but like most French girls had been brought up to believe the British upper classes behaved that way. She gathered from the other girls that he had a monster willy. When she was summoned to room 14, the chamber used for sex lessons, she went armed with a bottle of olive oil. Before Nigel had time to speak, she had his shirt off and was rubbing oil over his chest.

'What am I,' he grumbled, 'a sardine to be tinned?'

'It is a trick taught to me by a working girl in Paris.'

'Oh, I see,' he groaned, 'Froggie nonsense.'

'Froggie nonsense, no,' she grinned, massaging the oil into his upper body. 'You will like it.'

'Anything for a quiet life.'

'Good, now off with your trousers.'

'Ah,' he brightened up, 'you want to see my little willy?'

'That's not what I hear.'

'What do you hear?'

'That it is one 'ell of a whopper.'

She helped him to complete his undressing, and blinked in amazement when she saw the size of his cock. She fell upon him with the oil bottle, massaging it into his stomach and buttocks and pubic hair. She stripped off her own robe, and set to work again with the oil. She got him to rub it into her body, and could see he was enjoying himself. He massaged every crack and cranny of her curvacious female body, soaking her titties and her bush, and smearing it between her thighs and down her shapely legs. When they were both covered, she pushed him onto his back and poured the remainder of the bottle over the tip of his shaft.

She gently massaged his whole organ with her oily fingers, fondling the helmet with her fingertips to lubricate it completely. Then, facing his feet, she mounted astride him, and inserting the end of his monster penis between the oily lips of her vulva, she lowered herself down onto it. His greased stallion bore into her tunnel with unexpected ease. The walls of her vagina seemed to stretch at his approach, and she swallowed up his charger without hurt. She smiled when she thought she had taken him completely into her. She was mistaken, he still had several inches left out in the cold.

Abruptly, he flipped her over onto her back and jerked her legs apart. Once again his monster sank into her oily hole. She accepted it even further into her body than before, but it still wasn't the end. He swung her legs upwards so she was bent double, her knees behind her ears, and her quim stretched to its absolute limits. Little by little, he infiltrated the last inch into her overflowing tunnel.

Aided by the oil, their bodies slipped and slid as they fought to relieve themselves of their pent up emotions.

Nigel had never enjoyed a shag so much, and made a point of telling his uncle. Jeanne, who had believed her pussy to be too small, was now convinced she had been born with the biggest cunt in France.

Christine

Christine smiled nastily and served: the ball shot over the net like a rifle bullet, giving her opponent no chance.

'Game, set and match,' chanted the umpire.

The two girls walked back to the dressing rooms to the applause of the spectators. Christine had been a leading player for a couple of years; her opponent was a younger girl who showed all the promise of a world-class player. It had been a real needle match. There was no love lost between them, and a show of bad temper before the match had led to the side bet.

'OK, you crummy little bastard,' Christine snapped, 'now I've beaten your pants off, you can eat my meat.'

The younger girl looked like thunder as tears of frustration and hate welled up into her eyes. Christine chose not to notice, and stepped out of her panties. She perched on the edge of a bench, her legs wide open, and the youngster had to kneel to get her head between Christine's open thighs. The tears, so near the surface, began to trickle down the girl's face. Christine smiled. She was no lesbian, but it certainly wasn't the first time a girl had sucked her off.

Tennis and sex were the most important things in her life. She was an Australian, brought to France by her mother, who thought it would further her daughter's tennis career. When she had shown exceptional promise at school, her ambitious mother had begun to outline her daughter's career. She would win all three major world titles by the age of twenty-one. Christine's birthday was the next day, and she hadn't reached a quarter-final yet. Maybe it would have been different if her mother had taken her to the USA to be coached, but instead her mother had chosen France for the social life.

Christine watched the girl's dark curly head creep upwards between her thighs, and could feel the warm breath ruffling the soft fleece surrounding her expectant twat. She felt the girl's lips fasten on her vulva, and grasping the back of her head shoved the girl's face into her crotch so she was forced to eat the glutinous mucus that had begun to run from her vagina. It would teach the big-headed little cow a lesson.

Christine possessed a magnificent athlete's body. She was a well-built girl, standing five-eleven in her stockinged feet, and her long shapely legs went on for ever. Her breasts were full and rounded, while her attractive open face was topped by a head of curly blonde hair. She was like a blonde amazon when she strode onto court, but her face always wore a smile and her eyes constantly twinkled with a zest for life. She hadn't a care in the world, and thought of nothing beyond her own pleasures.

The girl's tongue slavered at her crack, probing the gummy slit while searching for the sensitive clitoris. Christine urged her on.

'Come on girl,' she snapped. 'Get your tongue moving. Suck me dry.'

As she spoke, she orgasmed. Her slippery gum trickled down the girl's throat. She knew the little brat wasn't a lesbian, and the thought that she must be hating it heightened Christine's enjoyment. She watched the girl shoot upright, and rush to the wash basin to spit out a mouthful of love juice.

'I'll beat you next time,' she spluttered, 'and you can suck me off. See how you like that.'

'You probably will,' smiled Christine, 'but there won't be any side bets.'

She dressed and left the club, dodging her mother who was full of bile because of Christine's father's surprise visit. She thought about her father. How dare he arrive out of the blue and criticise them both. He'd worn uniform. He had been recalled when war broke out, and been posted to Europe in early 1940. She remembered his stories of the First World War, when he'd served in field intelligence. She was never quite certain whether her mother had left him in order to bring her to France, but there had been one hell of a row. He had arrived from London yesterday, with tales of Hitler's forces being strong enough to capture western Europe. It scared her mother into arranging a passage back to Melbourne. Well, she wasn't going with her. Everybody knew the Maginot line was impregnable.

Afterwards he'd turned to her saying she'd never done a day's work in her life and that all she lived for was pleasure. He said she was greedy and spoilt, and should join the women's services or something equally ridiculous.

The next evening was her twenty-first birthday ball; she determined to live it up, and bugger daddy. She drank much more than she could take, and by midnight she had little control over herself. Two young American tennis players had been watching her, and reckoned she was ripe for plucking. They both fancied her, but she'd never allowed them near enough for a tumble. After dancing with her, one of them led her to a small room with a piano.

'Hey, where are you taking me?'

'I hear you're a wow on the piano.'

'Who told you that. I'm not so hot?'

'I hear you're mustard.'

'On the piano?' she tittered.

'No, over it.'

'What do you mean?' She glanced at him stupidly. 'You can get lost.'

'Go on. How about a quick poke?'

'Piss off.'

'Daddy wouldn't like it,' he sneered.

The mention of her father did the trick. If it would spite him, she'd let them all poke her.

'Come on then,' she growled aggressively, 'and bring your buddy.'

She walked unsteadily to the piano, deliberately lifted the full skirts of her evening dress so the folds ruched around her waist, and knelt on the piano stool. Her long shapely legs were encased in silk stockings, her forearms rested on the keyboard, and her arse stuck out provocatively. The knickers she wore hardly covered her behind, and her twin moons were clearly visible.

The first guy stepped forward, and eased her knickers down her thighs, manoeuvring them under her knees and down her legs. While he was thus engaged, the second guy was busy running his fingers along the thick fleshy lips of her quim. As he fondled her love-grotto, so she arched her back to thrust her butt out even further.

Both men had their trousers around their ankles, and the first one stepped forward to present his iron-hard ramrod at the entrance to her orifice. One long thrust of his hips was enough for his rod to slip into her tunnel to the hilt. She moaned, sensually delighted, and was surprised when he immediately withdrew. Her surprise was short lived for when he stepped aside, the second man took his place. They took turns to root into her, each standing aside to allow the other his turn to invade her hot wet tunnel. She had never been taken in such fashion, and the idea of two pricks plunging into her alternately excited her. She groaned and whimpered as she orgasmed, but still the two men continued to slurp in and out of her willing slit.

When they came, it was like Siamese twins. A rush of cream from one drenched her pudenda; it was followed immediately by a flood from the other. She was full to the brim with spunk. She stood up thinking what a whore she was to allow it, never mind enjoy it.

Three hours and a bottle of champagne later, the same two yanks approached her again. The party had broken up, and most of the guests had gone home. The talkative one spoke to her.

'Lovely party. How about continuing it at our place?'

'I think I've had enough to drink,' she giggled, 'don't you?'

'We weren't thinking about drinking.'

'You want to screw me again?'

'We thought you might like a foursome on your birthday.'

'I'm sorry, I haven't got a girlfriend who will jump into bed with you.'

'We've got someone.'

'Is she anyone I know?'

'It isn't a she.'

'Oh,' she exclaimed wide-eyed, 'three men. I've never had three at once.'

'Now's your chance.'

106

'OK,' she breathed after the shortest of pauses, 'you're on.'

This would really shock father – and mother too – but it was her twenty-first birthday and she could do what she liked with the rest of her life. She would stay in France and wait for the silly war to finish, when she would be able to play serious tennis again.

The third man who joined the two Yanks was a Mexican tennis player. She knew him quite well, and didn't like him much, but what the hell.

Once they'd got her into the back of their Mercedes they began to undress her. Within minutes she was naked.

The streets were deserted, but when a solitary car came up behind them, they hoisted her into the back window. She knew her bare bum was illuminated by the lights of the following car, but she didn't care a jot. When they screeched to a halt; the Mexican slung her over his shoulder, while the Yanks followed with her clothes. She squealed with carefree abandon. She cared not a toss for the world. Today was her birthday, and she was going to take three cocks at once, and gobble them up inside her. So much for male superiority.

The men waited for her in the bedroom, all three of them sitting on the bed – three upright pricks saluted her. She ran laughing towards them, and they took her without preliminaries.

She mounted the first Yank, whose weapon urgently sought among her soft curly bush for the entrance of her tender quim. She reached between her thighs, and guided his eager tool into the moist passage which led to her heaven. The pego slid into her as a hot spoon into butter. He gasped with pleasure as she took him to the hilt.

107

Almost immediately a second prick was presented to her mouth. The second Yank was holding his stiff rod in his hand, and waving it under her pretty nose like a magic wand. She opened her mouth, which was soon full of prick. She gasped as the monster knocked against her tonsils before she had time to close her lips over the shaft. She sucked greedily, working her tongue over the whole member as if it was an ice cream.

The feeling of fullness inside her pussy delighted her, a feeling that was about to be doubled – she could sense the third organ probing her most secret hole. It was the Mexican's anxious tool that demanded entrance to her forbidden rear entrance. She arched her back, so the cheeks of her arse would part to display her puckered bumhole. The prong inside her love-box was burrowed to the hilt, and she felt another nudging at her sphincter. That ring of muscle which guarded her backdoor suddenly gave way, and the invading weapon was able to breach her last defence.

'Happy birthday,' laughed the Mexican.

'Please, take one out,' she gurgled, but the words became garbled as the third prick was shoved back into her mouth. Well, she had asked for it, now she had to relax and try to enjoy it.

She sucked at the prong in her mouth as if she was biting on a bullet. The two prongs filling her loins pumped alternately, until the one up her bum began to move faster. She knew the first explosion was near, but was surprised when the prick in her mouth discharged a flood of sperm into her throat. She spluttered and was forced to swallow when the second explosion shot spunk into her bowels. She realised she was on the point of her own orgasm, and climaxed in unison with the third man.

* * *

108

A fortnight later she was invited to a tournament in Belgium, but she arrived late and was forced to sleep in a dormitory for young workers. That night the Nazi invasion began. The dormitory was hit by a stray bomb, but she knew nothing of it; she awoke badly shaken in hospital. She was uninjured, but detained overnight because of concussion.

It was in that hospital that her life changed. She was conscious, and needlessly worrying the nurses, when she overheard a conversation. All the young workers had been killed; she was the only survivor.

'Fate isn't kind,' a voice said. 'All those honest, hard-working young people lose their lives, and that spoilt parasite is spared.'

'It's the way of God,' came the reply, 'but it's difficult to understand why the only one of no use to man nor beast should be the one to live.'

It shook her rigid. She had never realised that was how she appeared to others. On top of what her father had said it made her seriously consider her life. She would show them all that she wasn't bloody worthless. She'd help fight the war against the Nazi bastards who had bombed them.

She travelled to London, and found her father. He doubted that she would ever change, but promised he'd keep an eye open for anything that might suit her. A couple of weeks later, however, he told her about Lord C. and said he'd arrange an interview. She found she had all the attributes necessary to join Lord C.'s circus, and passed the interview with flying colours.

At the initial training camp she fitted in well, her fitness and physical abilities helping her enormously. She found it much easier than most of the other girls, and perhaps because of that she drifted back into her old ways. She broke several rules, and on the second week was caught staying out all night. The sergeant called her to task.

'I don't think you're the right woman for the job.'

'Why not? Rules are made to be broken.'

'Some are, some aren't,' he smiled wryly, 'and here they aren't.'

'What's so special about this place?'

'We have a month to knock you into shape and to make you realise it's a tough job you've got ahead of you. You've got to learn discipline to stay alive.'

'I suppose you're right.'

'You know I am. As a tennis player, you know very well that you couldn't win a Mickey Mouse tournament without it.'

'I'm sorry. I'll buckle down to it.'

'It's too late.'

'Oh come on,' she cried. 'I need this job. It's something I've promised myself.'

'It's my job to report you to the colonel.'

'Can't I persuade you otherwise?' she murmured coyly.

'You could try.'

'What if I offered you my arse?'

'To do with what I like?'

'Within reason,' she smiled.

'An idea springs to mind.'

'Go on?'

'The RSM has a silly fantasy. I owe him a favour.'

'What would he want me to do?'

'Whenever he drills a squad of servicewomen he has an overwhelming desire to march one off the parade ground, and shag her silly.'

'That could be arranged,' she laughed.

'And what about me?' he enquired, leaning back in

his upright chair behind the big desk. 'Don't I deserve a small reward?'

'What did you have in mind?'

'I've got a bloody great beat on, just sitting here talking to you. There's plenty of room under the desk, and I bet you suck like a dream.'

She dropped to her knees, and crawled under the desk towards him. She could see how the material stretched across his crotch, and knew he wasn't fibbing. There was a rock-hard cock in those trousers.

Christine undid his fly buttons with nimble fingers, and his prong shot out as if it were on elastic. She slid her fingers under his testicles, easing them free of his trousers with her cupped hands. Ignoring the great prick sticking up in the air like an anti-aircraft gun, she nosed between his balls, licking them one by one. She could feel the anxious prick quivering against her forehead. She took it between her fingers and thumb, and swallowed it into her warm wet mouth. She could feel the helmet swell to bursting point as she rolled it between her moist lips. He would come quickly, and she would have done her penance.

Suddenly she heard a knock at the door, followed by the sound of footsteps in the room.

'Sorry, sarge.'

It was a soldier's voice, a young voice. It was probably the young soldier who worked in the outer office.

'I'm not alone, soldier.'

'So I see, sarge.'

'What can you see?'

'A female bottom under the desk, sarge.'

She could imagine the smile all over the young bastard's face.

'On the desk you will see a ruler, female bottoms for the use of,' growled the sergeant. 'Give it a couple of slaps will you?'

Christine's mouth was so full of cock that she could only gurgle. He grabbed her head so she could say no more. She hated having her backside smacked. It was the one thing she'd never allowed a guy to do to her. Now, some nasty young soldier was going to whack her bum with a ruler, while she was on her hands and knees under a desk. It was degrading.

She felt the wooden ruler thwack across her butt, and squeaked in indignation. The second blow was harder, and although her thick uniform skirt took the sting out of it, she was furious. To show her displeasure she dug her teeth into the sergeant's shaft, and then quickly commenced sucking again in case he ordered the soldier to wallop her again.

'Will that be all, sarge?'

'That's it. Sorry to disappoint you soldier.'

The interruption had served to ruin all chance of a quick ejaculation. He was in control again, and she found she had to work hard to bring him to the boil. She rolled the stiff pole around her mouth, pushing it deep into her throat, and fondling the root with her fingers. She slid her tongue up and down the pulsing shaft, before plunging it back into her gob again like a huge stick of celery. Slowly she dragged an orgasm from him. She felt his prong swell and tremble, before it gushed into her throat leaving her with a mouthful of sperm.

Two days later the RSM took them for a drill parade. The other girls were surprised, because he usually had little to do with the servicewomen. He was a big guardsman, some six foot six, with a florid face and bristling moustache. He barked commands at them in a rough manner. After a few minutes of intensive drill, he stamped towards Christine.

'What's your name, servicewoman?'

'Christine, sir.'

'I'd like a few words with you, Miss Christine. Fall out, and follow me.'

He marched her across the big tarmac parade ground towards a row of Nissen huts. At the end of the row was a piece of hidden wasteground surrounded by a brick wall. He called her to halt, facing the brick wall.

'You're a useless cunt on parade, Miss Christine,' he snapped. 'What you need is fucking. Get your knickers down.'

It had begun to drizzle, but that didn't deter him. She fumbled beneath her skirt, and eased her drawers down to her knees. Her skirt fell back into place.

'Lean forward, hands against the wall.'

She obeyed. The palms of her hands were on the rough bricks, and her body curved forward. He stood silently watching her for a moment as if drinking in the reality of his fantasy. Then he knelt down and helped her out of her knickers.

'Spread your legs, woman,' he ordered curtly, 'and bend right over.'

She hitched her skirt above her knees, and stood with her feet wide apart. She put her weight on her hands again, leaning forward against the wall so her backside was stuck well out. She felt him grab the hem of her skirt, and drag it up over her thighs until her bare buttocks stood out for all the world to see. He didn't attempt to take off his trousers, but jerked free his throbbing ramrod and jammed it between the cheeks of her arse.

'Say you deserve to be fucked,' he growled in her ear.

113

'I deserve to be fucked,' she parroted, 'I'm a naughty girl. Stuff your big hard cock up me. I've been so bad. Teach me a lesson.'

Her words galvanised him into action. He had pushed his cock between her legs, and it rested against her belly. He massaged it into her soft curly bush, and she groaned when she felt her vagina responding to his urgings. Grabbing her hips with his enormous hands, he presented his zealous prong at her orifice. With one long thrust he breached her. She felt herself fill as his cock sank deep into her. His body weight bearing down upon her was too much, and she nearly collapsed.

'Grab your ankles,' he growled.

She belt double and gripped her ankles. She was soaking wet from the persistent drizzle. Her legs were wide apart, and her body bent like an inverted U. In such a position her butt was high in the air, presenting her wide open snatch for his delectation. He made no attempt to please her, as his prong moved into her passage like a steam piston. Her body rocked, and she would have toppled over but for his grip on her hips.

When he came the bastard wasn't even prepared to give her his sperm. He withdrew, and shot it over her backside. She wailed, but he was gone. Her lower body was dripping, and raindrops trickled down her legs.

It was because of the incident with the RSM that she took the chance of putting one over on the gym instructor. He was demonstrating basic unarmed combat, and she had a fair working knowledge of judo. When her turn came on the mat, she completely surprised him with a throw that landed him on his back. The girls drew in their breath, and some giggled. He said nothing, and she went to the back of the line for the next demonstration.

When her turn arrived, everyone was expectant; would she make the instructor look a fool again? She was quite confident as she countered his move, and positioned herself to throw him again. Instead she found herself pinned to the mat by her shoulders with her legs in the air. She was unable to resist as he pulled her knickers off, and tossed them into a corner. The other girls laughed and clapped, and she felt a bloody idiot as she joined the end of the line to continue the lesson knickerless.

Not a word was spoken, and she had the wit not to complain. She'd tried it on, and failed.

Afterwards, he told her to stay behind. The other girls trooped away, looking at her meaningfully. She thought she was for the high jump again, and wondered what it would take to buy the ape off. Instead she was pleasantly surprised.

'I like your style, young lady.'

'Thank you.'

'Sorry about the knickers, but I couldn't lose too much face in front of the other girls.'

'I understand.' She smiled. 'Does your gentle sophisticated manner work with all the girls?'

'Touché,' he grinned.

She had forgotten her damaged pride, and was beginning to like him. He was powerful, and handsome in a rugged way with a tough stocky body. His huge shoulders and barrel chest make him look like a small tank. When she looked at him closely, she was surprised she had even attempted to throw him.

'We've got the gym to ourselves,' he said. 'Fancy a work-out?'

'What sort of work-out?'

'Any kind you like,' he grinned, 'but let's put it this way, I'm as randy as hell.'

So was she. At that moment there was nothing she'd enjoy more than a tumble with the tough little corporal. She stood up and whipped off her blouse and short games skirt. Turning round, she saw he was naked too.

They chased around the gym, laughing insanely like two young children. When he did a series of cartwheels she followed, and he caught her legs in mid-air, so she was standing on her hands. He held her legs wide apart and, dipping his face between her thighs, kissed her luscious quim. He ran his tongue along the fleshy outer lips, and pulled at her pubic hair with his lips. She squealed in girlish delight as his tongue poked into her upside-down cunt, licking the inner lips, and searching for her pert clitoris. Only when she was so juicy that he could suck her freely flowing mucus into his mouth did he move his head away.

She squeaked to be let down, but instead he took a rubber dildo from a nearby shelf, and sank the phallic object between her open legs and into her gummy slit. It penetrated her moist passage until it had completely disappeared into her. Attached to the end were thin straps, which he fastened around her waist to stop the dildo slipping out of her.

He released her, and pointed to the parallel bars. She followed him on every piece of apparatus – the bars, the ropes and the rings – as they went through an orgy of exercises. The sweat ran from her, her muscles ached, and the rubber dildo inside her caused continual friction against her vaginal walls. She felt like a bitch on heat.

The corporal swung up onto the wall bars, hanging by his hands with his back to the bars. She saw his stiff prick pointing at her like a signpost.

'Climb onto that,' he said.

She undid the straps around her waist, and removed

the rubber dildo from her itching twat with a sound like a suction pump. It had been bloody uncomfortable, but it had served its purpose: she could have screwed the cookhouse tomcat. She climbed the wall bars, moving her body over him until she hung like a monkey with her open thighs on the level of his face. She was as horny as hell.

She lowered her thighs towards his penis, found the tip with her cunt lips and sank onto the shaft. He was sucked into her greedy hole as if he'd been pulled under by quicksand. He was swallowed in one long lusting thrust of her thighs, and held immobile by the vaginal walls of her prison of love. The physical exertion took its toll, and hard as he struggled to delay his climax he failed. His whole body shuddered as he creamed into her. She pushed hard against him, her body pinning him painfully against the wall bars. She whimpered with pleasure when she received his hot long spurt.

She buckled down and enjoyed the remainder of her initial training, but was glad when it was over and she could go to Holmsley Manor to get down to the real business.

The trains weren't running to time, and she was late arriving. She expected to be told off, but nothing was said. Instead Lord C. welcomed her civilly, and invited her to take tea with him. She was delighted to partake of such an old established English custom, and changed into a thin summer dress for the occasion. Tea was served in the impressive library. After they had finished the cucumber sandwiches, Lord C. smiled at her in a particularly knowing way.

'As you've been a good little girl I thought you would like a lollipop,' he said benignly, handing her a red lollipop on a stick.

'Thank you,' she said, nonplussed.

'Suck it my dear,' he smiled.

She dutifully popped it into her mouth, and sucked at the sticky sweetness. She wondered if the old boy was off his rocker, or whether it was some sort of initiative test.

'Now, if you slip your panties off, you can put your lollipop where the big girls put them.'

She was surprised, but did as she was told. She lifted her bottom off the chair, raised her dress and slipped her panties down her thighs.

'Pop it into your grown-up pussy,' he instructed.

She eased her backside forward onto the edge of the chair, and raising her dress to her waist, she slid the sticky wet lollipop between her quim lips until nothing but the wooden stick was visible.

'You're too big to suck lollipops. We'll have to find something more grown up for you.'

He rang the bell, and a tall, slim young man entered.

'Nigel,' said Lord C., 'the lady has outgrown lollipops. Have you something a big girl could suck?'

'Yes, colonel,' he replied. Jerking open his fly he produced the biggest cock she'd ever seen in her life.

She'd started to play the colonel's silly game, so she would have to continue. The young man approached and stood in front of her. His great limp cock hung inches from her nose. She could hardly ignore it, so, wrapping her hand around the root, she swung the heavy tip into her mouth. No sooner was it engulfed in her wet mouth than it began to swell. She smiled dutifully, trying to take in more and more of it. She sucked valiantly at the huge lollipop, working her lithe tongue around the helmet. She had temporarily forgotten the real lollipop stuck up her twat until she felt Lord C. twist it suggestively inside her. A stab of

118

annoyance made her close her legs, but he still held the stick and manipulated it inside her unwilling pussy.

The monster in her mouth was as hard as a rock and beginning to tremble. Soon it would explode down her throat. She had grave misgivings at having to swallow a gallon of hot sperm.

'And when little girls become big girls, where do they put their grown-up lollipops?' asked the colonel.

In answer, she was swung upwards by two sets of hands to be suspended above the great phallus. She wrapped her legs around the young man's waist, her arms tightly around his neck, and prepared to be impaled. She felt Lord C.'s fingers pull the lollipop from her, and part her vulva for the victorious entrance of the champion. When she had accepted as much as she could manage, she moved her butt outwards, then plunged down again, impaling herself to her limit.

She was too heavy for Nigel to support standing, and Lord C. helped him to sit before stepping back to admire the way Christine had taken the initiative. She found it a long, arduous job, but after a time it began to excite her. Her loins were on fire, and she orgasmed and orgasmed again, whinnying like a young mare. Finally, when he shot his load into her; she whooped in sheer wonderment.

A week later she was worried. At first everything had been fine. She was enjoying the course, and all the different aspects of her training. Her carefree way of life and open approach to sex made everything come easily to her. It was when she faced the fact that she would have to come to terms with sado-masochism that she began to worry. She'd kidded her way through a couple of talks by the comtesse about its place in sex and seduction, but she knew she wasn't ready for anything practical. The other girls seemed willing to participate if needs be, and that added to her worry. She didn't like being the odd one out: the only one with a problem. She screwed up her courage, and went to see Tanya.

'I can't bear the idea of allowing a man to beat me,' she explained.

'Were you spanked as a child?' Tanya enquired.

'Never.'

'And since then, during lovemaking perhaps,' she asked, 'hasn't a man put you across his knee and smacked your bottom?'

'In fun, when making love, I've allowed men to slap me,' she replied, 'but never very hard or very often.'

'Then we must start at the beginning.'

'You mean I have to be spanked?'

Tanya smiled. For such an uninhibited girl, she was showing a great deal of reluctance.

'I don't think there's much point in spanking you, Christine,' she said, grinning. 'Besides, you're too big to put over my knee. We'll leave that to the men.'

'I thought you might introduce me into the shallow end, so to speak?'

'I will, Christine, I will,' Tanya replied soothingly. She produced two instruments of corporal punishment. 'We'll start with these.'

Christine drew in her breath. Tanya had tossed a leather strap and a wooden paddle onto the low table between them.

'Today we'll begin by giving you a taste of the strap. Tomorrow you can sample the paddle.'

The comtesse stood up, and swung the leather strap. The business end was about a foot long, and made of light pliable leather – nothing like the heavy thonged one Lord C. liked to play across her arse. She

120

instructed Christine to raise her skirt and lower her knickers, and indicated that she must stretch over the arm of the sofa with her fundament raised well in the air.

Christine whinnied with surprise at the first stroke. The leather strap had caressed the soft flesh of her luscious twin moons, and all she'd felt was a pleasant tingling sting. Tanya followed with several more tittilating whacks, which warmed the skin without hurting. Christine wriggled her buttocks. She didn't dislike it. Tanya brought the strap down sharply with a stinging crack, and Christine yelled in horror. A red stripe appeared across her plump white posterior where the strap had made its mark. She started to get up, but Tanya pushed her head back into the cushions.

'No,' she whispered, 'we've hardly begun.'

She swung the little strap in earnest, and each thwack across Christine's bare backside brought a squeal of protest and indignation.

After a couple of dozen vigorous strokes, Tanya threw down the strap and signalled Christine to get up. She stood rubbing her tingling backside with both hands, an expression of horror on her face.

'That wasn't too bad, was it?' asked Tanya.

'Bad enough,' she grimaced, 'it's not something I'd do from choice. Is my arse very red?'

'Good heavens, no, girl; you've hardly been touched,' laughed Tanya, 'it's a delicate salmon pink. Tomorrow I'll redden it up for you.'

The following day Tanya was as good as her word. She ordered Christine to remove her dress and panties, and bend over the table. She explained she was to be paddled, and showed her the flat wooden paddle so popular in America for the disciplining of female bottoms. She added she intended to use the paddle as it was meant to be used, and there would be no pandering to Christine's shyness or fear. She was true to her word. The wooden paddle whacked down across the plump fleshy cheeks of Christine's seat. Each one echoed like a thunderclap, and each one was followed by a scream and a curse.

The paddle turned her squirming bum a deep red. She beat her legs in the air to ease the sting in her tail.

'And before you ask, it is bright red today,' Tanya smiled. 'Tomorrow it will be one big bruise, but you've passed with flying colours.'

Meik

Meik graduated from Amsterdam University in the summer of 1939, but was unable to get the job she wanted. She was an excellent linguist, speaking fluent English and German, but her degree wasn't good enough to allow her to follow her father into the diplomatic service.

She had been born in the Dutch colony of Java. Although her mother looked a pure European, she was actually half Javanese, and the blood had come out in her daughter. Meik's skin was an attractive light brown, almost olive, and her features were definitely Asian. Her dark almond-shaped eyes, high cheek bones and shining black hair made her look exotic. Her slim, sylph-like figure was pure oriental; but her full breasts and curved buttocks owed much to her European blood. Whatever her breeding, she was a real beauty.

In spite of her birthplace, Meik was very proud to be Dutch. She was fiercely patriotic, and it was the zealous passion, bordering on fanaticism, with which she approached her work that grated on her colleagues. She accepted a post with Dutch security, but when the British SIS asked for a liaison officer the organisation was glad to send her. She moved to the Rotterdam office, where the British also found her to be enthusiastic. When she asked to be allowed to follow up some tom-fool lead, they agreed just to keep her quiet.

The British had received a dodgy tip-off that a Nazi spy ring was operating from a bawdy nightclub near the waterfront. She ignored all warnings, and got herself a job as the cigarette girl there.

Arriving for work, her initial shock was her costume. It consisted of a very short flared skirt and a low-cut self-supporting bodice. All underwear was taboo, so all she had under her flimsy skirt was a suspender belt to support her long black stockings. The tray of cigarettes that she carried around her neck stopped her bending forward too often, but when she did her bubbies popped out for the punter's titillation. In addition, the punters paid by pushing the cash into her corsage.

From outside the place looked a tumbledown old building, but inside it had been tarted up to appear like a sophisticated luxury club. The lights were dimmed and softly coloured to give a cosmopolitan effect.

By ten o'clock the club was bursting at the seams. It was the time for the first floor show. Two leggy young ladies danced onto the floor and went into a strip routine. Meik was too busy to watch, pushing her way between the tables when the customers beckoned. She had guessed her behind would be black and blue from slaps and pinches. All the men seemed to know she was nude beneath her dainty skirt, and took full advantage of it. The method of tipping, however, horrified and embarrassed her.

'Open your money box honey,' a customer drawled, 'I got something for you.'

He held up a rolled up note, and she gasped in surprise as his hand fumbled up her short skirt.

'Come on, open up honey if you want the goodies?'

It suddenly clicked: the accepted way of tipping her was to push money up her cunt. She felt sick with humiliation as she was continually mauled in her most secret and sensitive place. Only her iron will and her determination to succeed kept her from tears.

After their striptease the two girls minced through the appreciative audience, provocatively jiggling their boobs and waggling their bums. They were soon covered in small denomination notes, which were stuck to their naked bodies by the spit of the cheering punters. Larger denominations found their way up into the girl's grateful money-boxes.

A second-class torch singer followed, plastered with make up and very obviously over the hill. The audience tolerated her, as they knew the best part was her finale. Naked below the waist, she strode towards the audience, where coins had magically appeared on the edges of tables to be picked up by the elastic lips of her groping twat.

The houselights were dimmed, and the star of the show was announced. A woman walked out into the spotlight. She was dusky, beautifully curved, and dressed as a traditional belly dancer. The music began, and the woman slowly twisted and spun. Her belly and thighs moved sensuously, as her voluptuous body jerked to the rhythm. The sparkling jewel set in her navel seemed to hypnotise the audience. The punters began cheering long before the act finished, and coins began showering onto the floor.

The tempo changed, and slowly and tantalisingly the woman began to strip. She was no strip artist, but the audience cheered and stamped their appreciation. Soon she stood dazzlingly stark naked. The audience quietened when she began to dance. It was the same belly dance, but this time the beat of the music was wilder. She danced sinuously, with animal movements. Passion oozed from her every pore. Her eyes shone like stars, and her pupils dilated. She was drunk with the ecstasy of the music, and the exhibitionism of her dancing. She covered the whole floor, jerking, twisting and spinning. Her lithe body contorted into wild patterns. It was more than just a belly dance: it was primitive and obscene. The punters sat mesmerised. They drank in her swinging breasts and gyrating belly, her naked thighs and buttocks. She moved faster and faster as the tempo gathered to a crescendo. She jumped high with her hair flying and her thighs akimbo.

The music stopped.

The sweat glistened on her skin as she crouched panting on the floor. Slowly the music started again, and she postured to it. She exaggerated each movement as she slowly circled the floor, her legs wide apart to display her quim to as many eyes as longed to see it. Her movements became grotesque as she bent double, but all eyes were focused on the spot between her thighs, the music and the dancing were forgotten. A ripple of excitement came from the audience as she took a beer bottle from a table. It broke into a roar of encouragement when she placed the neck against the lips of her slit. The punters showed their appreciation as she shoved the bottle up. It was no longer stimulating, it was obscene, but all eyes watched with a terrible fascination as the whole bottle slowly disappeared into her gaping twat.

It was three o'clock before Meik had the opportunity to slip into the private rooms at the back of the club. If she could find any evidence of Nazi involvement, it would all have been worthwhile and the supercilious British would have to eat their words. Most of the punters were drunk, and they had lost interest in the little bare-bottomed cigarette girl. She slipped through the door marked private, where she came upon the manager's office. If there was any evidence, it would be there. She was so nervous her fingers shook, but soon she was so engrossed in her search, she didn't hear the footsteps in the passage.

The door swung open, she was caught.

'What the hell . . .?'

The manager moved swiftly towards her, pinning her arms behind her back. There was no point struggling; he was a big man and there was no hope of escape. A woman was with him.

'She must be a police undercover agent,' he grunted. 'We can't take chances – she'll have to go in the river.'

The full consequences of her foolhardy escapade came home to her. She could end up dead.

'No,' she squealed, 'I'm not the police.'

'Who the hell are you then?'

'I can't say.'

'You'll have your pretty face carved up if you don't.'

'I work for,' she hesitated, 'British Intelligence.'

'A likely tale. What the hell would they want with us?'

'They believe you have Nazi connections.'

They both laughed.

'Those stupid English will believe anything,' the woman grinned, 'but if she's telling the truth we'd be better off freeing her. Her disappearance might bring the cops sniffing around.'

'Maybe you're right. Find out where she comes from in the morning.'

She was unceremoniously bound and gagged. A length of rope secured her wrists behind her back, another tied her ankles. She was thrown onto a sofa, where she stayed until the following afternoon. By that time she was cramped and hungry; she had been forced to pee on the floor. When the door finally opened, two big pug-ugly men barged into the room.

'You're a lucky girlie,' grunted the first one. 'We've been sent to take you home, but not before you get a taste of what happens to nosy young ladies.'

The two musclemen grinned nastily. The first picked her up like a child, and slung her face down across the wooden tabletop. He moved behind her, and she felt her ankles being freed. The second man took up a position by her head, holding down her shoulders with his ham-like fists. Only when her flimsy skirt was ripped off and her legs forced apart did she realise she was about to be raped. She screamed into her gag, but only a strangled sound came out. She heard them laugh. She struggled violently, attempting to free her body in blind panic and rage, but was rewarded with a stinging blow across her buttocks. She screamed again in surprise and pain.

Quite suddenly, she accepted the inevitable, and was still. Immediately, she felt the cheeks of her arse parted by two rough hands, and a man's iron-hard rod was thrust against her defenceless quim. She fought to keep it out, tightening her vaginal muscles, but it was hopeless. The marauding weapon forced its way into her aperture. The second man chose that moment to rip off her gag, and stuff his rampant prick into her mouth. Meik spluttered and choked, surprised and horrified at the second attack on her body. She didn't know which was the worse, the pain of the baton burrowing into her wretched fanny or the humiliation of the prick filling her mouth. She tried to pull back her head, but an enormous hand grabbed her by the hair. She knew that if she continued to struggle her vagina could be permanently damaged, and she could easily choke on the object in her mouth. She lay still, endeavouring to relax and praying it would end quickly. It did. She felt sick when both men ejaculated almost simultaneously. To have one rapist's sperm flooding her womb revolted her, but to be forced to swallow the other's spunk nearly choked her.

'Now we're taking you back where you belong, baby,' growled the first heavy, 'but the boss says to warm you up a bit. Make 'em see we ain't gonna tolerate no snoopers.'

She was gagged again. Producing another length of rope, the men wound it around her from shoulders to waist. Her breasts were encircled around the base so they puffed out. They tied her ankles again and wound the rope upwards around her legs to her hips. She was trussed up with rope coiled around her body until only her head, feet and backside were visible. They placed her face downwards on a big carpet, and sat on chairs either side of her. She found it impossible to see what was happening until the first man held a wooden desk ruler under her nose.

'We're gonna beat your bum bright red, to show your pals we aren't to be messed with.'

He was as good as his word. They thrashed her naked haunches, paying little heed to the squeals behind the gag. They plied their rulers alternately across her smarting nates, trouncing her butt for what seemed eternity. When the ordeal was over, her scorching keister was a fiery scarlet.

The worst embarrassment was yet to come, as she was rolled in the carpet and delivered to her place of work. Everybody was there when the carpet was unrolled. When she emerged they seemed concerned at her terrible predicament, until they saw her bruised and reddened posterior sticking out from the ropes. No one could hide a smile.

Two months later Meik was in England. She had escaped the Nazi invasion. In spite of her experience she had continued to work for British SIS, and when the organisation left the Netherlands it took her along. In London she offered her services as an agent to the Free Dutch government. It was unable to use her, and British SIS turned her down, unjustly blaming her for leaving several boxes of classified material behind.

Sitting on a bench in Hyde Park, she felt miserable: nobody wanted her. She didn't even notice a handsome young army officer sit by her side.

'Excuse me, I don't mean to be rude, but are you from Malaya?'

She looked up. He was a strikingly handsome young man wearing officer's service dress with the single crown of a major.

'I'm Dutch. I was born in Java.'

'I'm sorry.'

'You're sorry I'm Dutch?'

'No, I mean . . . because the Nazis have invaded your country.'

'Yes, it's devastating.'

'Were you there, or do you live in Britain?'

'I escaped a week ago, and desperately want to go back.'

'Surely you don't mean as a spy?'

'That's exactly what I mean.'

'As it happens,' he said slowly, 'I'm in intelligence.'

'Could you help me?' she asked eagerly.

'It's possible.'

He told her he'd been working as an agent in Belgium, and had escaped through the German lines two days ago. He was on a forty-eight-hour pass before going back to France, where he would stay in Paris if the country fell.

He rang a secret Whitehall number, and got her an interview for the next day. She promised to spend the rest of the day with him, as he knew no one in London. They walked and talked together. Later they lunched at the Savoy, during which time she fell under the spell of his easy, suave charm. He suggested they take a room, and she agreed.

In the room, he ran a bath for her. When she was naked he crept up behind her and, swinging her up into his arms, dropped her gently in the water. She hadn't been bathed since she was a very small girl but she enjoyed it. He gently soaped her, massaging her body with his hands, meticulously rinsing her skin. His fingers touched her all over, washing her mature body as if she were a child. He made her feel comfortable, innocent, cared-for, and never once was his touch carnal.

He helped her from the bath, and wrapping her in a big towel he dried her body, showing the pure kind of love a man usually reserves for his daughter. She relaxed, allowing herself to be spoilt, and she felt so warm and safe. Not a word had passed between them, and when he carried her into the bedroom she expected to make love on the bed. Instead he put her down on the thick carpet, and knelt over her. With a tenderness she'd not known since she left her mother's arms he kissed her forehead, the tip of her nose, her eyes, the curve of her chin – gentle kisses like the caress of a butterfly. He nibbled the lobes of her ears, and buried his face in her neck. The tenderness he showed her made her blood tingle. She stroked the back of his head, and guided him to her breasts. He worshipped

131

each plump, rounded orb with his lips, kissing each nipple in reverence.

Meik knew she was being romanced, the kind of romance from a women's novel. There was no lust, no desperate want. And then, as if he'd read her thoughts, she felt her legs raised, and he was sliding inside her. It was such a slick and practised movement, she was hardly aware she was being seduced until she felt him hard inside her. Even then, his only thought was to please her. He worked his practised tool inside her willing vagina with infinite skill, bringing her to one rippling orgasm after another. She clung to him, dazed, but strangely unsatisfied. Even when he climaxed, there was no unbridled passion. She was quietly relaxed, but uncertain what to make of him.

Their afternoon of love-making had made her miss the bank, and the large wad of cash she had to open an account was still in her handbag.

That night they dined and danced at the Troc. In bed he was a different man. The quiet gentle lover was gone, and in his place was a lustful roué. He took her sitting on an upright chair, facing the mirror. She straddled hs thighs, her back to him, watching herself in the mirror. In bed he mounted her, forcing her legs upwards until her knees were behind her ears. Doubled up, with her legs wide open above her head, she wished he'd revert to his former guise. Yet, as his pounder plunged deep into her eager tunnel she urged him on by digging her nails into his back. He answered her by throwing finesse to the winds, and shagging her as if she was a bitch on heat. She moaned as his pestle pummelled into her willing fanny, and soon her gum trickled down her thighs onto his testicles.

She remembered nothing after his orgasm flooded her. The booze and the lovemaking had exhausted her.

Awaking next morning, she felt bruised but content. He wasn't beside her, nor was he in the bathroom. Her suspicion grew. Looking in her handbag, she saw that her money had gone. The only thing he'd left her was the hotel bill. Even the interview was a fraud.

That, on top of everything else, made her feel the bottom had fallen out of her world. Then came Dunkirk and the fall of France, and like many others she thought it only a matter of time before the Nazis were in England. Churchill, however, would have none of it, and Whitehall was buzzing with rumours.

The SIS told her of Lord C. – a perfect way to get rid of her – and within days she was accepted.

She entered into initial training with all her usual verve, and in no time was a star pupil. The sergeant drooled over her oriental beauty, but could devise no way of getting inside her knickers. Meik was in her element, and she enjoyed every minute.

The only fly in the ointment was her weapons instructor, who made it bloody obvious that he fancied her something rotten. On the pistol range he would stand behind her, ostensibly to correct her stance, but whenever the opportunity arose he would squeeze her titties. On the rifle range it was worse; he would lie beside her when she was in a firing position, and his hand would stray between her legs to fumble her.

Everything came to a head in the grenade pit during her first attempt to throw live grenades. When her turn arrived she stumbled into the throwing pit to find him there. Whether it was his presence, or the fear of Mills bombs, she had never been so nervous. She took the pin out, but on the command 'throw' she froze. Her body trembled, her arm was frozen solid, and her fingers wouldn't release the bomb. The instructor had seen it before, but when coaxing failed he had to prise her fingers open. She dropped the grenade, which he casually tossed over the parapit.

'You could have killed us both,' he exaggerated.

'I'm sorry. Oh God, I'm sorry.'

'So you should be.'

'You saved my life.'

'Then, I deserve a reward, don't I?'

'What do you want?' she replied without thought.

He took her shoulders, and pushed her down onto her knees, her face inches from his crotch. She knew what he wanted before he said it.

'Suck me off,' he grunted.

She had no alternative but to obey. If she screamed, the whole sad story would come out and she'd be deemed a failure.

Meik struggled to unfasten the metal buttons of his denims, and dug her hand inside to free his penis. She didn't notice they had moved off the duckboards, and that she was kneeling in a muddy puddle. She yanked his cock out, and stuffed it in her mouth. It was already hard as a rock, and she intended there would be no refinements. She gulped it as far down her throat as she could to satisfy his initial lust. Then, closing her lips over the shaft, she began to suck and massage him simultaneously. She was counting on drastic action to accelerate his orgasm, but he towered above her thrusting his hips forward for more. She inserted a hand inside his trousers exploring between his open legs, caressing his hanging testicles, but to no avail.

She recalled a tip overheard in a washroom some-where. She manoeuvred her hand behind his balls and locating his arsehole, dug her index finger into his anus. He grunted in surprise, and climaxed before he realised what had happened. She felt her mouth fill with hot sperm, and jerked her head away to spit it on the ground before he could stop her. He grabbed her chin, forcing her to take his cock again, but there was no spunk left in him.

Soon afterwards she passed out of training with flying colours. Her commission was granted in the Dutch navy, and she headed for Holmsley Manor, full of confidence.

Lord C. was waiting for her in the library when she arrived, but Meik had arrived too late to play his little teatime game. Lord C., however had devised another little surprise for her. He had a penchant for oriental girls; he adored their smooth satin skin, which he liked to believe had a flavour of the mysterious East.

After she had changed, Meik walked confidently into the library. She saw Lord C. as a big old shaggy bear, and he held no fear for her. She wore a pretty silk dress, which reached just below the knees, and she looked cool and appealing.

'I'm sorry you're too late for tea. Perhaps you'd care for a sherry before we commence our evening's ablutions?'

'No thanks. It's a bit early.'

He caught her staring, puzzled at the presence of a big shaving mug of foam on a nearby table.

'You're thinking it's a strange time for me to shave?'

'I was wondering.'

'The answer is simple. It's you I wish to shave.'

'Pardon?'

'Humour an old man.'

She smiled. The old boy had gone a bit daft, unless it was some sort of joke.

'As you wish, but you won't need a razor. There's no beard on my chin.'

'But between your legs?'

'You mean you want to . . .?'

'With your permission.'

She couldn't hide her shock and surprise at the strange request, but she knew she had to agree.

'All right,' she agreed, 'you can shave me.'

'On the sideboard you'll find a pair of scissors. Use them to trim your muff, before I lather you.'

She found the scissors and sat on an upright chair facing him. He watched her remove her knickers, and arrange the skirt of her dress so that it circled her waist. Then, curving her back and parting her thighs, she began snipping away at her pubic hairs. She had a thick matted bush of black hair like the short shiny coat of a mole, but Lord C. loved to see oriental women with their quims smooth and naked.

Soon Meik had trimmed her fleecy bush so short that her delectable young slit looked as if it were hiding in shadow. She leaned back, and he began to lather the shaving soap between her legs, using the brush and his fingers to cover her from arsehole to navel. Next, he picked up a safety razor. It was an intricate task, and he was no barber. It took him longer than he expected, as he had to be careful not to nick her delicate skin or the fleshiness of her labia. When he had rinsed and dried her she looked as smooth as she had been before puberty. Only the rolled flesh of her vulva lips broke the smooth contours of her belly and thighs. He knelt before her, as if to inspect his handiwork, and his lips closed over her sweet dell. She closed her eyes, elated by the cunnilingus he was suddenly bestowing upon her shaven love-grotto.

She felt him kiss the naked skin surrounding her hairless jewel, nibble at the inrolled flesh of her labia, and gently bite her excited clitoris. His efforts to please filled her with rapture. She came in floods, and he drank deep of her nectar.

Bewitched by his delight of her body, she swooned. He helped her to her feet, and slowly unfastened the buttons of her dress. She held up her arms, and he pulled it over her head to leave her standing ravishingly naked. He cupped her light brown bubbies, kissing each in turn and fondling the pert nipples. He kissed her on the lips, feeling her lithe tongue slip inside his mouth. Then, taking her by the hips, he lifted her onto a table. As she rolled backwards, she raised her legs high, grasping her ankles and holding them well apart. Her bum was perched on the very edge of the table, and her gorgeously nude vulva looked so vulnerable between her open legs.

'Now, I'm going to fuck you,' he murmured.

'Please, I want to be fucked.'

She was still moist from oral sex, and his rampant knob slid easily into her willing pocket.

'Talk to me,' he said. 'Tell me about it.'

She had never done such a thing before, she would have been too embarrassed to mouth the words. Yet now they came tumbling from her.

'I do want it, sir. Please stab me with it.'

He was in to the hilt, his belly pushing between her thighs and his balls slapping against her bottom.

'Screw me now. Harder . . . quicker . . .'

He worked his truncheon like a piston, and each time he withdrew he peered between her legs to look at his cock imprisoned by her smooth hairless quim. It delighted him.

'Fill me up. Make my pussy tingle.'

'You're a hot little whore,' he mused in her ear.

'I'm a slut. Go on, fuck me. Make me come.'

'Tell me you want it?'

'I want it. Don't stop,' she shrieked, 'I'm coming.'

He felt her body shiver and tremble. It was as if a great wave was washing over her, as he dragged an orgasm from her. And then, her delirious excitement spread to him, and he found himself on the point of climaxing. He gripped her thighs.

'Christ, I'm coming.'

'Do it,' she bawled. 'Now . . . quickly.'

As his semen streamed into her, so her vagina gripped his penis as if she were trying to milk him of every last drop. His cock slipped from her, and she sat up aching in every muscle. She couldn't wait to get to her room to inspect her newly shaven quim in a mirror.

It wasn't that she didn't enjoy Holmsley Manor; it wasn't that she didn't enjoy the sex; but the espionage was devious underhand work and Meik was in essence an open, straightforward person. She hated deception, especially in sex. In time, however, she learned to live with it.

Jacqui

Jacqui was the one girl Lord C. didn't choose – he was outvoted by the interviewing panel. She certainly had all the right qualifications and background, but she was a bit too world-wise, a bit too sure of herself for his liking. At twenty-eight she was several years older than the other girls, and he didn't see her as a good influence.

She was French Canadian, with that special shade of red hair which turned heads. Her auburn mane was eye-catching and perfectly toned to her delicate white complexion. She had green eyes which were set rather deeply in an oval face, and her whole personality seemed to be reflected through them. She was an outgoing character, and like most redheads she was quick tempered. Over the years, she had learned to be her own woman, to use her sex to get what she wanted. In fact, sex meant little to her other than a weapon to exploit all men and some women. She had all the attributes which Lord C. sought, yet he doubted her. He would be proved wrong.

Jacqui was born in Quebec, where she attended convent school. Her father, whom she adored, was a journalist who spent much of his time abroad. When she was fourteen, her father was posted to Germany. Her mother joined him, but Jacqui was left to finish her schooling in Canada.

At seventeen she left convent school, and joined her family in Berlin. It was there she was introduced to sex, and realised the part it would play in her life. She fell under the spell of a dedicated National Socialist, a young man who followed Adolf Hitler and his Nazis. He was tall, blond, and incredibly handsome in his brown uniform. She was captivated by his apparent charm, courtesy, and impeccable manners.

He invited her to spend a day on his parents' farm. After lunch led her to the barn, where he chased her playfully into the rafters, and smothered her in kisses. In the well below them was freshly cut hay. He suggested they dived into it as if it were a swimming pool. She agreed, and when she saw him stripping off his shirt and shorts, she followed suit.

He stood like a naked Adonis before her. She had never seen a man unclothed before, and although she adored his slim, muscular body, it rang no bells for her. She undressed, but for her drawers, and felt no shame or embarrassment. He grabbed her by the waist, and playfully ripped off her knickers. She struggled a bit, but it was no big deal. She felt excitement, but it was not sexual. He dived into the hay, and was swallowed up by it. Screaming girlishly, Jacqui followed him.

The smell of the freshly harvested hay intoxicated her. She felt him grab her wrists and kiss her passionately, his tongue searching inside her mouth as if for hidden gold. She was quite aware she was about to lose her virginity, and was curious. Sex was a strange paradox to her. In the convent it had been held to be wicked and sinful. Later, when she discovered the act of copulation, she was amused. She thought it ludicrous, both the act and the nuns' fear of it.

He had fumbled under her blouse before, but now

when he kissed her naked breasts, sucking the nipples into his mouth, she found it not unpleasant. He kissed her belly, running his fingers over its smoothness, and she picked up handfuls of hay and scattered it over his head and back. Only when his lips ventured into her bush of pubic hair did she feel a twinge of embarrassment. She urged him upwards. He turned onto his side, brushing the hay from his hair, and she could see his penis sticking out like a barber's pole. She wanted to laugh, but instead she threw her legs open to receive him. It wasn't a success; he stabbed into her entrance, but her maidenhead remained a barrier. He was nonplussed, unsure of what to do. He didn't want to injure her. She guided him back to her tight aperture, and holding him in place bade him plough into her. It pained her when her hymen surrendered, and her blood was spilt. Once inside her tunnel, he pumped his organ vigorously until she felt his seed flood her aching channel.

She decided sex was as painful as it was ridiculous. There was no pleasure in it. She decided she would use it as a weapon, or a bribe, to get her way in this world which belonged to men.

Her idea was reinforced the following week when she accompanied him to a political gathering. After the meeting, a noisy affair, they were invited to the private party of Mad Otto. She noticed the older men and women drifted away, leaving the young and the beautiful to attend the party. It was held in a large room at the back of a hotel, which was complete with a small stage and dance floor. The band played American swing and the beer flowed. Most members of the company were merry before the festivities began, and they all seemed to know the ropes. When the MC ordered everybody on the floor, they obeyed. She saw

141

her partner smiling at her knowingly, and realised there was something afoot. The music stopped, and the MC ordered the men to remove an item of clothing from their partner. She realised it was going to be that sort of night. The game continued; each time the music stopped, so the women lost more clothing. The dance floor was soon filled with grinning men and naked women. Then, without warning, the lights went out and the MC shouted that the women must undress their partners before they came on again. She found herself struggling with the strange buttons and belts of his uniform.

The evening became progressively rowdier. The MC went from table to table demanding their participation in games of wild unfettered sex. Women made to kneel blindfolded were expected to guess the owner of the prick in their mouths. Blindfolded men tried to guess the identity of the girls whose quims they were licking. At intervals games were played on the dance floor. A favourite was a bastardised musical chairs, where men stood with their cocks out, and the women had to grab one in their mouths when the music stopped. Other games ended with the winning couples copulating in public, or in private. She avoided being among them until she was chosen to masturbate on stage, using a huge dildo, to the tune of the British national anthem. She refused. She rushed blindly into the street, pursued by a pack of rowdy drunks.

Luckily, she ran straight into the arms of a policeman, and she arrived home draped in a police overcoat. After that incident, her parents decided she must leave Berlin, and work for a living. She chose journalism, and went to New York. After a couple of years as a junior dogsbody, she became an assistant working on a gossip column.

Her first big interview was with a politician's wife, who was a well-known socialite and a lesser known lesbian. Jacqui could sense from the woman's smouldering looks that she was attracted to her. As she needed a sensational interview, she decided to take the bull by the horns.

'Would you be more comfortable if we continued this interview in your bedroom?' she smiled coquettishly.

'My dear,' replied the woman in surprise, 'I had no idea you were . . .'

'You were doing your best to find out.'

'Perhaps I was,' she grinned, 'how naughty of me.'

She led Jacqui to the bedroom where, holding her arms firmly at her sides, she kissed Jacqui on the lips.

'May I undress you?' she purred.

'If I get the interview I need, you can do what you like to me.'

'Agreed.'

Jacqui allowed herself to be undressed. The woman was slow and loving, with none of the haste invariably shown by men. Slim feminine fingers caressed her body, smoothing the silk of her lingerie before touching the flesh beneath. When her final garment had been discarded, she watched her stockings being rolled down her long legs, and felt red lips kissing her skin in the wake of the cobwebbed silk. It was the prelude to a thousand kisses rained on her breasts, belly and thighs. Her pink nipples were reddened under the constant onslaught of eager lips, and her belly was wet as if it had been licked by a cat. She felt the woman's head between her legs, and her own face within inches of a black matted minge. A skilful tongue ran along her labia, probing inside to seek and tease her inner lips and clitoris. Was it her imagination, or did a female

143

tongue move quicker, more skilfully? Her orgasm certainly lasted longer.

It was strange and rather exciting, but the woman was no more than an inanimate object to stimulate her. She knew she would be expected to suck the gaping maw above her. She parted the labia with her fingers, and pushed her mouth deep into the woman's gummy twat. It smelled of exotic perfume and bodily fluid, and was slippery to her lips. She had to admit she preferred the taste of a man's cock, and the feel of a man's skin. The woman stood up, and she saw her produce a huge double-headed dildo. She watched as one end, as big as any prick she'd ever seen, disappeared slowly up the woman's twat. She watched her fasten the strap around her waist, and approach the bed. She looked like a she-male, for the second head of the dildo stuck out of her bush like a man's prick. She felt the big rubber dick press against her moist fanny as the woman spread over her like a lover. She discovered her vagina wouldn't accept it like a real prick, and she had to relax her muscles so it could slide into her tunnel without hurting. It felt cold, hard and impersonal, sunk into her warm quim. What was worse, the woman could burrow into her with that artificial prong until she was physically exhausted. There would be no climax to end it. She prayed it wouldn't be too long.

Her boss knew exactly what had happened, and realised the potential of his new assistant. A month later she was sent to extract a story from a well-known young lecher. His eyes rarely looked higher than her silk-clad legs as she sat cross-legged before him. She suggested, with a smile, he might find his memory refreshed if she continued to interview in the nude. She got her story.

By 1939 she was a successful and experienced journalist. That year her mother died, and she left her job to look after her father in Paris. She took a junior post with a Parisienne newspaper until the spring of the following year, when her father insisted she return to Canada. He stayed on to cover the Nazi invasion of France, and the last she heard of him was in the Ardennes.

In Canada, she received an official communiqué stating he was missing. Determined to find the truth, she sailed for England. She found he had been attached to the 23/55 Hussars, and through the regiment found the survivors who had returned from Dunkirk. In a convalescent hospital she located the soldier who had seen her father die. Dressed in hospital blue, sitting in a wheelchair with both hands heavily bandaged, the man looked sadly at her.

'I'm sorry, miss,' he murmured. 'He was a wonderful chap. We all liked to listen to him. He told us more about the war than all the bloody politicians.'

'Thank you,' she whispered.

'He went quick. Direct hit it was. He wouldn't 'ave known anything about it. Lucky really.'

'I must leave, now I know for certain. Is there anything I can do for you?'

'Not really, miss.'

She leaned forward to display most of her firmly rounded bosom to his gaze. She saw a desperate longing in his eyes, and realised his sexual deprivation. She could see he had a hard on, but his bandaged hands wouldn't allow him to relieve himself.

'You can't do anything for yourself, can you?'

'No, miss.'

'Do any of the nurses lend you a sympathetic hand?'

'Pardon, miss?'

'Give you sexual relief?'

'No, miss. Afraid not.'

She threw her light raincoat over his lap, and slid her hand under it towards his crotch. His tool was as stiff as a ramrod. She swiftly pulled aside his pyjama trousers, and her fingers closed around his anxiously throbbing cock. He closed his eyes as her long cool fingers gently and expertly massaged his tormented shaft. He smothered a groan of pent-up frustration, and came into her hand. A young nurse passed as he climaxed, and guessed what the lovely redhead was doing for the wounded man. Jacqui smiled up at her; perhaps the nurse would carry on the good work.

Leaving the hospital, she went straight to the Canadian embassy to discover how she might best join the war against the Nazis. She wanted revenge for her father. It was like a nagging pain. Someone whispered Lord C.'s name; a few days later she was called for interview.

Jacqui found initial training difficult. She was happy to learn about weapons, but drill, PT and other military training seemed pointless. She noticed the sergeant leching after all the girls, and saw an opportunity for an easier life. At the end of the first week she stayed in bed, when all the other girls tumbled out for morning parade, asking Ingrid to explain she was ill. As she expected the sergeant soon came marching into the Nissen hut. She had made sure she looked wan and delicately female, her red hair spilled out over her pillow.

'If you're sick, Miss Jacqui,' he barked, 'you see the MO. You don't laze about in bed.'

'I'm really not too bad, sergeant,' she replied quietly, 'I'm not a case for the doctor. I'm just tired.'

'Tired, or just bloody lazy?'

'I do find it a trifle exhausting,' she smiled up at him, 'I wouldn't mind so much, but there's really no point in most of the rushing about, is there?'

'And you want permission to lie in bed?'

'Well, not exactly.' She propped herself up on her elbow so that the bedclothes slipped aside to reveal the curvacous depths of her delectable orbs, 'I was thinking of light duties?'

'Were you indeed.'

'I could be very co-operative in other ways. It's all the running about outside I dislike.'

'You prefer indoor games?'

'If you like.'

He moved to the bed, standing close to her head. With a slow deliberation she began to unbutton his fly. She watched him as she did so, and smiled to herself. It wasn't difficult for a girl to get her own way. Her hand slipped inside his trousers, enabling her to wrap her long fingers around his semi-rampant tool to free it from his uniform. With an expertise born of practice, she manipulated the helmet of his throbbing prong with her cool fingertips until the whole shaft was quivering with excitement. She kissed the tip so very tantalisingly, flirting with her tongue before taking the whole pestle into her soft wet mouth. She sucked so sweetly, he was aroused beyond reason.

'Get out of bed,' he snapped.

When she was slow to obey he grabbed her under her armpits, and lifted and twisted her until she found herself with her feet on the floor and back to him. She was dressed in her pyjames, the jacket of which was wide open. He grabbed her breasts from behind, trapping her nipples between two fingers, and squeezed until the hardened points shivered with bliss. She

147

jerked her head back to rest on his shoulder, and he buried his face in her neck. She felt the cord of her pyjamas being untied, and watched her trousers flutter to the floor. She bent well forward resting her palms on the bed, and pushed out her rump ready for copulation. Her sweet slit invited him to enter. He sank into her in one thrust, his balls slapped against her buttocks.

She had complete control over herself. No sooner had the sergeant recovered from his surprise at his easy entry, than she gripped his pego with her vaginal muscles, and held him like a vice. When he moved inside her, so she tightened or slackened her muscles at will. It was she who was controlling the fuck, and it excited him. He didn't try to dominate her. He was happy for his tool to be milked like the teat of a cow. When his gathering flood neared, he desperately wanted to gouge into her. He held back, however, and was rewarded when she brought him to an earth-shattering climax.

'Now that was heaven, Miss Jacqui,' he cried. 'Do I get afters?'

'Why not, if you're still hungry?'

'I'll be in the Bell and Crown, eight o'clock,' he said, turning to leave.

'What about me? What should I do now?'

'Get yourself dressed, and get on parade.'

'You bastard,' she shouted, but he was gone.

She couldn't come to terms with the sergeant's behaviour. He had shagged her, and then told her to get back to work. He'd treated her as if she was a skiving little shopgirl. She'd never been defeated by a man; her body and sexual expertise had always got her what she wanted. Who was that ignorant pig of a sergeant to use

148

her, and then deny her wishes? She was angry. He must be taught a lesson. She'd see him tonight, and humiliate him in some way. She was never short of ideas. She knew he'd be conceited enough to be there, expecting her to come. Probably believing she couldn't wait for another length of his precious John Thomas.

Sure enough, when she arrived at the Bell and Crown, he was playing darts in the saloon bar. They sat drinking Scotch, and talking. She found herself fascinated by his life in the regular army. At closing time he led her to a room at the back of the inn, which the landlord was pleased to let to members of the military and their 'wives'. It was an olde worlde room, complete with beams and a sloping floor. The bed was big and comfortable, covered with a thick feather mattress that almost enveloped them when they sat on it.

'I guess you were kidding this morning,' she said, 'but now, I expect your promise that I'm on light duties before we go any further.'

'No can do,' he replied flatly.

'Then, I'm off,' she said swinging her feet off the bed. 'No promise, no fun.'

'You must please yourself, but let me put it like this. You'll get little enough training for the job you'll be sent to do. You'll need every bit and more to survive, and my job is helping to see you don't get your pretty arse blown off.'

She was silent. For the first time she saw it wasn't a game. He was right, she was preparing to go to war. Suddenly, she felt grateful to him.

'I'm sorry,' she murmured. 'I take your point.'

'OK,' he grinned, 'then let's make love.'

She went down a draughty corridor to the bathroom

but found only cold water. A second later he burst in, stark naked. They ran back to the bedroom hand-in-hand like honeymooners. Once inside, he grabbed her and twisted her upside down with a quick flip. He stood her on her hands, back to him with her legs hanging over his shoulders.

'Stop it, you idiot,' she squealed. 'I shall be sick.'

He couldn't answer because his mouth was full of cunt. He stood gorging on her delectable pussy, pushing his tongue into that spongy dell.

'Come on, be fair,' she pleaded, 'I feel like a fish hung out to dry.'

He made her walk on her hands to the bed, and flipped her over so she landed on her back. She gurgled with delight as she was buried in the thick mattress. She had never been with a man who treated sex so lightheartedly, and she enjoyed it. He began tickling her feet, and then her ribs, and she laughed so much she was gasping for breath. She remembered her father tickling her as a child, but that was a long time ago. No one had done it since.

The sergeant straddled her lovely body, sucking her gorgeous melons with wide-open mouth as if he were trying to eat them. She felt his rod anxiously feeling for her orifice. She eased her thighs apart and he infiltrated her Elysian grotto, the fount of so much pleasure. Once he was rooted deep within her she closed her thighs. He was trapped. He turned her over, and she was above him. They were glued belly to belly, thigh to thigh, their legs closed, her toes resting on his instep.

'Squeeze,' he whispered, 'with that heavenly cunt of yours.'

'Like this,' she giggled, tightening her muscles until he felt his whole shaft gripped by the elasticity of her vagina.

'My God, I've never come across the like of it,' he moaned. 'You haven't got a third hand in there, have you?'

'It's a God-given gift,' she laughed.

'Better than being double-jointed!'

She continued to exercise her tunnel walls on his willing prong while he remained passive inside her. He gently moved his hands over her slender back, and the superb roundness of her creamy buttocks. His fingers stroked her hair, and moved down her spine before exploring the crevice between those delightful twin moons. Their bodies were still, and she milked him until her vulva ached and he exploded inside her.

He rolled her over, his penis still inside her, and knelt above her. Tenderly, he kneaded her soft bubbies, the pliant mounds like putty in his hands. He leaned forward and kissed her mouth, breasts, and the curve of her shoulders. Her dazzling red hair was tangled about his neck and face, and he attempted to gently loosen the auburn tresses. He was becoming hard and randy again. He parted her knees to spread her legs at right angles to her body.

In such a position her love-box was completely exposed, and her dainty pudenda slightly parted. She again welcomed his John Thomas as he sunk deep inside her tube, but this time he meant to screw her with an animal violence. He straddled her and rode her, driving in and out of her glutinous twat, the sweat squelching between their writhing bodies. She grasped his arms, her nails digging into his flesh, and then she screamed.

'Christ,' she shrieked, 'I'm coming!'

Her screams stimulated him to ever more frantic action. It was as if he was trying to get inside her, balls and all. He missed the point of her sudden surprised shriek. He wasn't to know she had never orgasmed with a man before. She had been poked a hundred times, but only ever come by her own hand. She groaned and clung to him, bringing him to a shuddering climax.

For the remainder of her initial training, Jacqui settled down and got on with it. At times it was difficult, but she kept her mouth shut. She was glad enough of her leave when it came, and took up an invitation to stay with an old school friend who lived in Oxford.

Marge, who had married an Englishman, was looking after his father while her husband was away fighting the war. Unfortunately the old chap was senile, and she wasn't able to leave him for long.

The first day of her leave Jacqui volunteered to stay in the house, so Marge could go to London. She rose at nine-thirty, and didn't bother to dress. She pottered about in the kitchen in a short silk robe, and took the old boy up a cup of tea. He stared at her with a blank expression, but said nothing. She put the tray on his bedside table, and leaned over him to tidy the bedclothes. The poor old man was nothing but skin and bones.

Then, the unexpected happened. She became aware of a bony hand under her robe, moving between her legs and feeling for her minge. She froze in horrified astonishment. The old fellow was touching her up. She sprang from the bed, slapping his hand.

'Susan,' he muttered, 'Susan, why did you slap me?'

She knew Susan was the name of his late wife. His mind was completely addled. She was ashamed of herself. Why had she slapped him? She was pathetic, treating a sick old man like that.

'Sorry,' she said. 'I'm not Susan. Sorry, I shouldn't have hit you.'

She went to the bathroom and was towelling herself dry when she saw him at the door. He stood motionless staring at her. His pyjamas hung on him like a scarecrow, and she could see through the gap at the front that the old boy had an erection. She deliberately let the towel drop, so the poor old chap could see her naked body. Why she did it, she had no idea. Was it to make up for slapping him, or because she knew it must have been years since he'd seen a woman naked?

She put on a flowery summer dress, and decided to help by doing some housework. She washed the dishes and did a bit of dusting, and the old fellow followed her like a little dog. She fastened his pyjama jacket and pulled the trousers together, and sat him down while she began to vacuum. She couldn't decide whether she was sorry for him, or annoyed by his pathetic leching after her. She forgot about him as she wove around the furniture, and the noise of the vacuum cleaner drowned his approach.

As she bent over to rearrange a cushion on the armchair, she felt a hand on her buttocks. She switched off the machine and was about to reproach him, when she changed her mind. She remained bending forward, her hands resting on the seat of the armchair. She had butterflies in her stomach wondering what the old man would do. She dropped onto her elbows to raise her bottom even more provocatively. Her full skirt was being raised, and she held her breath as he eased her knickers down to her knees. It was a weird sensation, and she wanted to stop the madness she had started. She knew she couldn't; she had gone too far. The old fellow was probably worked up to a pitch he hadn't known for years, and to stop him might cause a heart attack. How could she explain it to Marge?

She felt the end of his knob rubbing against her soft furry bush, and reaching between her legs she guided it towards her slit. She parted her legs, relaxed, and felt him push his gnarled old pego into her moist snatch. Soon she was completely impaled. She moved her backside to the rhythm of his feeble thrusts, and wondered how many years had passed since he last screwed a woman. She felt quite noble. For all his age he certainly had stamina, but unable to move her position, she became tired. She wagged her behind faster trying to help him to climax, and suddenly it struck her – the old chap might have difficulty doing just that. She began to wonder if she should call it a day when, out of the blue, he stuck a horny old finger up her arsehole. She squealed, and shot upright in surprise.

'You dirty old sod,' she shouted.

The muscles of her quim had automatically tightened, and gripped his shaft like a claw. She heard him moan as she pulled away, and felt his watery semen splash between the cheeks of her bum. She wondered what the hell Marge would say if she discovered she'd seduced her father-in-law.

She went out for an hour during the afternoon, and when she returned saw Marge was back from London. The house was quiet; she didn't call out for fear of disturbing the old man, but noticed his bedroom door was open. She glanced in. Marge was bending over the side of the bed, and the old chap was rooted up her. She knew Marge had seen her.

'You must be horrified,' she said later. 'I'm so ashamed. You won't tell anyone, will you?'

'No, I won't tell anyone, but why do you do it?'

154

'It's the only way I can control him. You'd never guess how highly sexed the old devil is.'

'I would.' She smiled. 'He screwed me this morning.'

When she arrived at Holmsley Manor, she was a trifle apprehensive. She knew Lord C. hadn't been impressed by her at the interview, and had looked positively thunderous when she'd addressed all her answers to the other panel members. She'd also been silly to ignore him when he visited them at initial training camp. Now, apparently, he was their colonel and commanding officer. She hoped he didn't bear a grudge, but unfortunately for her Lord C. was already planning her comeuppance.

She was shown into the library and asked to sit down.

'Miss Jacqui, our worldly-wise Canadian redhead,' grinned the colonel cynically. 'You will have something to prove to me if you expect to pass your training here.'

'I'll try my best, sir.'

She had decided to be conciliatory and passive. There was no point aggravating him further. After all, he was the boss with powers to pass or fail her.

'When the girls arrive I usually play a little game with them to embarrass them – to make them realise their training in eroticism has begun. I don't believe you would be easily embarrassed, would you?'

'No, sir.'

'Tell me why not?'

'Sex is purely physical to me, sir, as natural as eating and drinking. I don't connect it with love or romance.'

'Don't you derive any pleasure from it?'

'Yes, of course I do,' she grinned, 'but physical pleasure like eating and drinking.'

'So, there's not much we can teach you about it, and

155

you have no reservation about using your body like a harlot's?'

'You can't shock me like that,' she smiled, 'I believe I'm the ideal woman for your wants, and yet you don't see it, do you?'

'I do. Oh, I do,' he replied. 'But you're a bit too self-sufficient, a bit too cocky.'

'I need taking down a peg or two?' She laughed at him outright.

'Perhaps we'll have to see if you're as cold blooded as you boast.'

'Oh, I am. I am.'

He took a beautiful long-stemmed glass from the sideboard, and showed it to her with a little bow.

'Then, piss in this, and I will drink a toast to you.'

He spoke casually, as if it was quite usual for him to drink a toast of female urine. She realised she was being tested and, other than an initial surprise, she showed no embarrassment. She stood, and hitched up the skirt of her naval uniform. He held the glass at arm's length between her open legs, and watched her pull aside the crotch of her french knickers. She was trembling with embarrassment, and all her internal muscles seemed to have frozen. She bent her knees, pulled open the outer lips of her twat, and tried to pass water. It wouldn't come. She bore down on her bladder, and a few drops tinkled into the glass. She could see him smiling. He thought he had defeated her. She relaxed, breathed deeply, and concentrated her mind on other things. Suddenly, warm urine gushed from her to fill the glass.

Lord C. sat back, raised the glass to her, and drained it without blinking an eyelid.

He was a cool one, she thought, unless he enjoyed drinking girl's pee.

'Now it's my turn,' he said, unbuttoning his fly.

She stood motionless, shocked. It was one thing to pee in a glass, and watch a man drink it. Now, she was expected to drink his urine. She couldn't. She knew she couldn't. He would have won.

'Kneel down and open your mouth. We won't need a glass,' he laughed. 'You can drink straight from the fountain.'

She forced herself to kneel, and saw his penis aimed at her face. She had to go through with it. She opened her mouth and immediately a stream of piss flooded it. She choked, spluttered, and moved her head. The stream continued, soaking her face and trickling down her chin onto her jacket. She tried to swallow, but couldn't. She squished the evil-tasting piddle out of her mouth.

'Stop squirting it out like a basking whale,' he snapped. 'Swallow it.'

She couldn't. She couldn't open her throat to swallow. It was too much to ask. She squirted it out of her mouth again, and knew she had been defeated. She wanted to cry.

He rested his hands on her shoulders, and kissed her damp forehead. His sympathy was too much to bear. She burst into tears.

'I've decided to cane you,' he announced solemnly.

'Oh no, you can't do that.'

'You mean, you're going to leave us?'

'No, I didn't mean that,' she replied bitterly.

'Then you're going to be caned, aren't you?'

'I suppose so.'

'And you deserve it, don't you?'

'If you say so.'

'No, it's you who must say so.'

'All right, I deserve to be punished.'

157

'You'll have to be more submissive than that, if you want to stay here.'

'I'm sorry,' she muttered after a long pause, 'I was a very silly girl, and I deserve to be caned.'

'It will be my pleasure, but first, go and clean up for dinner, and I'll introduce you to my nephew.'

She sat next to Nigel at dinner, and his continual blathering drove her up the wall. She could have done without him, but understood from the other girls he was one of the staff who controlled their destinies. After coffee and liqueurs, several of the girls excused themselves. She, however, found herself propelled towards room 14, which Nigel insisted she should see. When she saw the mirrored walls and king-sized bed, she knew why she was there. She was about to object, to tell him she was too tired, when she thought better of it. He was such a silly weak character, he probably only had a quick squirt in him. Better let him have a leg over, and there would be nothing she could be blamed for.

He fumbled with the strap of her evening gown and, frightened he might tear it, she pushed him away and undressed herself. She found no embarrassment in nakedness, and her spirits rose when she heard him whistle in admiration. She knew she had a magnificent body, but it did no harm to be reminded. He insisted on blindfolding her before leading her to sit on a padded bench. She wondered if he was shy; the thought made her smile. She heard him undressing. Suddenly she was pushed backwards, and her wrists locked to a bar behind her head. She was frightened. She hated being restrained. She was about to object when her legs were swung up and over her head.

'Don't,' she shouted. 'Let me go free. This is bloody ridiculous.'

In answer her ankles were locked over her head onto the same bar as her wrists. She knew she was completely helpless, her feet behind her head, her legs wide open, and her soft bush displayed like a welcome mat around her fully exposed snatch. She felt an oil being poured around her hole to prepare her for the entry of the warrior. She wondered why she was blindfolded – perhaps his dick was so small he was ashamed of it.

Slowly, as his prick invaded her tunnel, she understood why she had been oiled. Nigel's weapon was larger than most men's.

Again and again his monster penetrated her resilient tube, and each time he filled her to capacity. Unable to move her arms or legs, she was completely at his mercy. She felt like a trussed turkey being stuffed for the feast. The young man might look like a wimp, and talk like an idiot, but he had a cock long enough to knock a girl's hat off.

She relaxed, anticipating the next stroke, opening her thighs in readiness to receive that truncheon once again, when she suddenly shrieked. He had stuffed his cock up her arse.

Stimulated, he withdrew from her anus to plunge his charger back into her snatch. Unable to restrain himself, he exploded into her.

Nigel took off her blindfold and untied her. Dressing, he moved over to the door.

'I hear you're in for a good caning?' he sniggered.

'Yes,' she replied.

'Across your pretty bottom?'

'I expect so.'

'Are you looking forward to it?'

'No, I'm not.'

'Then stand facing the wall and wait for the colonel,'

he snapped. The door banged shut behind him as he left.

She must have stood facing the blank wall for nearly twenty minutes. She wondered why she was being so submissive. Normally, she would tell them all to go to hell, but she knew she was in their power. If she played up, she'd be out on her ear, or get a double dose of the cane. She didn't fancy being thrashed, but a few strokes of a cane wouldn't kill her.

She heard Lord C. enter.

'Turn and face me, young lady.'

She turned, unashamedly naked, but trembling in anticipation of her punishment.

'Put your hands on your head.'

She obeyed, knowing she presented a picture of a naughty girl awaiting a good whipping.

'You know what's going to happen to you?' he asked.

'You're going to cane me, sir.'

'Have you ever been caned before?'

'No, sir.'

'Do you agree to the punishment?'

She knew he was humiliating her. He knew that talking about it would pain her as much as the sting of the cane.

'Yes, sir. I'm sorry, sir. I agree to your punishment,' she muttered. 'I deserve to have my bottom caned, and I'll be a good girl in future.'

The words stuck in her craw, but they did the trick. She saw a smile of satisfaction wrinkle the corners of his mouth.

'As you have apologised so nicely, I'll be lenient. You'll receive six strokes.'

'Thank you, sir.'

'Feet apart, bend over and touch your toes.'

She assumed the position he wanted. Her long legs

were straight, her spine curved downwards like a bow, and her arse was stuck high in the air. It was because her feet were wide apart that the cheeks of her beautifully rounded buttocks were stretched apart to display her pretty pussy. The position was as humiliating as the words she'd been forced to utter.

She felt the cane bite into her tender seat, and shot upright, squealing like a little pig. He waited for her to touch her toes again. The second stroke made her whimper, and at the third she burst into a flood of tears. He swung the cane impatiently at his side, waiting for her snivelling to stop. When she was quiet, he whipped the last three strokes across her tormented bum. She yelped as each struck the fleshy cheeks of her perfectly presented posterior. She wailed and blubbered as if she had sat on a hornet's nest. A continuous scorching sting blazed across her inflamed nates, and by looking between her legs into the mirror she could see her reddened buttocks. There were six plainly marked parallel welts across the white skin where the lash of the cane had lacerated her unblemished derrière. She sniffed, and wiped her eyes with the back of her hand.

'I suggest we start our relationship anew, Miss Jacqui, and forget what has passed.'

'Yes, sir.'

'Then stop snivelling, girl, and go to your room.'

She didn't wait to dress. She scuttled down the corridor towards a cold bath, which she hoped would cool her burning rump. She had been whipped and humiliated, and could do nothing about it. If today was anything to go by, it was going to be a tough war.

PART TWO

London

Lord C. sat in the small lecture room with the comtesse at his side, studying the seven girls who sat in front of him. To all intents and purposes their training was finished, and they'd all done well. It had started as a bit of a lark, but now he truly believed the girls could play an important part in the war. Unfortunately, the experiment had hit a snag before it could get off the ground. He had called a meeting to explain it to his girls. He looked around at them. By chance, the three blondes were sitting on his left: the athletic, hedonistic Christine, from Australia; Ingrid, the naïve Scandinavian beauty; and Sylvia, the thoughtful English rose. On his right sat the three brunettes: the worldly-wise Madeleine from Belgium; Jeanne, the intellectual French girl; and the zealous Meik, their oriental beauty. The auburn-haired Jacqui from Canada sat between them looking cool and sophisticated. Add to these the elegant Tanya, and he was absolutely certain he had eight females capable of seducing the world, never mind the Third Reich.

'Ladies,' he began, 'I'm afraid we have a large problem. A problem we must solve ourselves if we are to continue as a unit. Central Intelligence has refused to recognise us, which means we will receive no help from its vast organisation. As we cannot survive without access to Central Intelligence's contacts, communications, transport and so on, I'm afraid we're a dead duck.'

The girls fidgeted in their chairs; their mood of utter despair hung over the room like a damp cloak.

'Is there nothing we can do?' asked Jeanne quietly.

'There is a possibility, a slim chance.'

'Then let's hear it,' interjected Christine.

'You are prepared to swap sex for secrets, that's what you're trained for. You are prepared to seduce and compromise our country's enemies, but are you willing to do the same to your own security services?'

'You mean compromise the bigwigs in intelligence, and blackmail them into recognising us?' asked Sylvia.

'Blackmail is a bit strong, Sylvia,' he smiled. 'You'll land us all in the Tower.'

'There's no need for blackmail,' explained Jacqui. 'If we can become the mistresses of a couple of these mutton-headed prigs, then we would be in the position to infiltrate their service. If we do that, they will have to admit we are capable of doing it to the Nazis.'

'And, if they don't,' grinned Madeleine, 'we'll show the evidence to Winston Churchill.'

'Yes,' they chorused.

'I thought you'd all agree,' said Lord C. 'I have already looked into it. There are three possible targets, and all hold senior positions. I've hired private detectives to ferret out their general background, and the comtesse has thought out a plan of action which she will outline to you.'

'Our first task,' said Tanya, 'is to ascertain the type of female who turns the target on. To do this, we will all covertly show ourselves to the target, and his reactions will be watched. It should be simple to see whose breasts he ogles, whose backside his eyes follow.

Whoever is the lucky girl will lead the operation against that target. She will get him to pick her up, and she will winkle out his hang-ups and fantasies, so we can play on them to land him like the big wet fish he probably is.'

The first target was Sir Reginald Huett-Bly of K2 division, SIS. A widower of five years, he continued to live in his family house in Surrey. He was alone, as both his sons were in the forces, and his last live-in servant had recently left to earn a decent wage in a munitions factory. He worked in Baker Street, and regularly caught the 19:10 train home to his local station.

Tanya decided he should view the girls on Mary-lebone station while he drank his usual pink gin before boarding the train.

It wasn't difficult for the girls to display themselves as he sat in the bar. He admired them all as any red-blooded male would, but when Sylvia walked by he couldn't keep his eyes off her. Tanya signalled to Sylvia, who began to put the plan into action.

She grabbed Jeanne and Madeleine, and stood talking and giggling to them within sight of him; his eyes never left the trio. When he boarded his train he watched them saying goodbye, before Sylvia climbed into his compartment. She took off her coat, so he could admire her figure, and leaned out of the window to wave farewell as the train moved out of the station. She smiled briefly at him before settling down with a book.

She knew she mustn't appear flirtatious or forward, because that would scare a man of his age and background. She knew the station where he would alight, and when she got to her feet he politely took her case from the rack for her.

During the journey she had visited the toilet to loosen the heel of her shoe, and as she stepped onto the platform it gave way. She sprawled forward onto the concrete, and he dashed forward to help her.

'Are you hurt?'

'No, I don't think so,' she gasped. 'I think the heel of my shoe broke.'

He found the heel, and handed it to her.

'Is anybody meeting you?'

'No.'

'Are you able to walk?'

'I think so,' she replied hesitantly, grabbing his arm to steady herself.

'Perhaps we could share a taxi. Where are you going?'

She gave him an address, and he hailed a cab.

When the taxi pulled up outside a house, however, she looked as if she was on the verge of tears. She pulled a letter from her handbag and showed it to him. It was headed 'The Shaw Secretarial College', but the taxi driver told her there had never been such a place at that address. She had been conned. Sobbing, she told how she'd paid for a week's course, so she could join her friends who worked in London.

Sir Reginald told the taxi to drive to his address.

'You must come home with me, until you decide what to do.'

'May I?' she murmured, dabbing her eyes. 'You're very kind.'

She thought that once she was inside his home it would be plain sailing. He made no mention of her staying the night, however, and didn't attempt to make a pass at her.

'When you've had a cup of tea, we'll see about getting you back to London,' he said.

It was the last thing she wanted.

'I shall have to ask my friends to put me up at their flat.'

It wasn't going to be as straightforward as she'd expected. Somehow she had to weave a suggestion of sexual activity into the conversation.

'They're both typists who work for the same firm,' she said, 'but they don't like it much, and are thinking of leaving.'

'Oh, why?' he asked casually. 'I thought secretarial work was secure employment for young women.'

'Their boss is too strict; whenever they make a mistake he spanks them,' she said glibly, hoping it would lead somewhere.

'They don't have to tolerate that.'

'Not now, perhaps, but before the war jobs were hard to come by,' she said. 'Anyway if they leave I shall apply for one of the jobs.'

'So you don't mind having your bottom smacked?' he grinned.

'My dad used to spank me,' she replied. 'I didn't mind that.'

'I would have thought it was a bit undignified to be put across a stranger's knee?'

'Perhaps you're right,' she smiled, 'but I'm not really old enough to worry about my dignity.'

'You're a strange girl,' he laughed. 'Now, I'd better ring the station to find the times of the trains.'

It looked ominously like she was going to get the brush-off. She had to be more direct. It was the only chance.

'Now the bombing's begun, I'm a bit frightened of returning to London tonight. Let me stay here. You can spank me if you like, and then I'll know whether it hurts my dignity.'

'I don't know . . .'

'Come on,' she urged, 'don't be an old stick-in-the-mud. I thought all men enjoyed slapping girl's bottoms?'

He thought she was a strange young woman. He'd never met anyone like her. So natural, naïve and trusting.

'All right,' he smiled, 'you can stay, but there's no need for the other thing.'

'Thank you,' she smiled, touching his hand. 'You're a nice man. We'll talk about it later.'

Sylvia, however, had no intention of talking about it. She was determined that he would spank her, and that it would be a prelude to other things.

She rustled up a spartan meal from his near-empty larder, and he produced a good bottle of wine. After the meal, she insisted he enjoyed several brandies and a fat cigar. While he listened to Bach sonatas on the radio, she slipped into his bedroom and found a pair of his pyjamas. She re-entered the room, walking coyly towards his armchair clad in nothing but his pyjama top. When he saw her, he nearly spilt the brandy. She was a picture: impishly appealing, dainty and wistful like a shy, coquettish young virgin.

Sir Reginald drew in a deep breath, and wanted to prick himself to make sure he wasn't dreaming. What had begun as an ordinary mundane day was turning into one of unbelievable bliss. She stood facing him, swamped in his pyjama jacket, a jacket so big it nearly reached her knees. It hung on her like an old sack, but none the less it made her look bewitching and desirable.

'I've come to have my bottom smacked,' she murmured coyly.

He'd dreamed of such moments. Her golden hair

170

tumbled loosely to her shoulders, and several unruly locks had fallen forward to partly cover her face in a beguiling peek-a-boo manner. The rumpled jacket, open to her navel, just covered her nipples, but revealed the erotic valley between the swellings of her delectable bubbies. She held one hand behind her back, as if she was hiding something from him. She smiled saucily, and brought the hand forward to reveal she was holding a hairbrush. She presented it to him.

'That will sting like billy-oh,' she whispered.

He took the hairbrush in a kind of trance. Truth was certainly stranger than fiction. It didn't occur to him to look for anything sinister behind it. They were in the privacy of his house, and they had met by chance. There was no way it could be blackmail, and what else was there?

Sylvia spread herself across his knees, and the pyjama jacket rode up to the sensuous curves of her sweet derrière. He quickly jerked the material upwards until it lay across her shoulder blades. She had the most adorable rump, it was so round, plump and shapely. Those unblemished twin moons simply invited spanking.

He thwacked her rump with sharp, stinging slaps of the hairbrush. The strokes were hard enough to smart, and to make the fleshy cheeks wobble like jelly, but not to discolour or bruise too much.

'My poor bottom,' she wailed.

She kicked her legs, and squirmed on his knees. Her behind was beginning to smoulder with a deep heat. The hairbrush walloped her arse again and again. It stung, but she knew she was halfway to her objective. She gripped his ankles and caressed his legs, digging her fingernails into his flesh each time he whacked her. Before it was over she was sobbing openly. Large tears trickled down her face; when she stood up he kissed them away, while stroking the cheeks of her sore bum with the palms of his hands. She took her inflamed butt to the shower, and allowed cold water to splash onto it until the surface heat had abated. As she gently patted her rear dry, she heard him running the bath. She saw it as a further opportunity, as she had an uneasy feeling he would want to tuck her up in her own bed after spanking her like a naughty schoolgirl; he was that sort of man.

She knew, however, she had to get into his bed, from where she could manipulate him. She walked from the shower towards the bath, and allowed the towel to drop from her body. He paused open-mouthed, his body frozen in the act of soaping his shoulders. She posed before him, and he was intoxicated by her wanton nakedness. All was still, it was as if they were in a time-lock.

'Here, let me wash your back,' she smiled.

She took the soap from his hand, and, deliberately leaning over him so her boobs pressed into his face, she began soaping the curve of his back. She felt his hands, slippery with soap, begin to caress her thighs. He ran his fingers down her spine, and stroked her tender rump. It throbbed to his touch, but she didn't flinch. She scrubbed at his back with her soapy hands, and when she was finished she pushed him back into the water.

Kneeling by the bath, she dipped her hand beneath the surface to fish for his John Thomas. He watched her pull it clear of the water, and quickly raised his hips, afraid she might pull it out by the roots. Her energetic hand massage had him as hard as iron within seconds, and she had leaned over the bath to swallow his cock in her mouth before he could say Jack Robinson.

He marvelled at her. He had never met such an uninhibited girl. He never really believed they existed outside fiction. He propped his fists under his backside to keep his rampant tool above water, although he believed she'd be up to pushing her face beneath the surface just to gobble the whole length of his staff. As it was, her hair cascaded into the water, and her chin was wet from dipping below the surface. She sucked like an angel, and her deliciously soft lips urged his quivering member to such Elysian heights that he couldn't remember being so horny for many years.

As soon as she felt his excited prick begin to tremble under her lithe tongue, she allowed it to slip from her mouth. She saw a brief look of utter disappointment and frustration cross his face, but it vanished when she stepped into the bath. By placing a slender foot each side of his belly and holding onto the sides of the bath, she was able to crouch so that her pudenda was above his upright cock. She put a hand between her thighs, running her fingers the length of her open vagina, endeavouring to ensure she was ready to receive him. Grasping his quivering prong between her thumb and forefinger, she placed it at her entrance and sank impatiently down onto it. She heard him groan with delight, and sensed she was thrilling him with her sexual capers.

He moved his fists from beneath his body, so that their genitalia sank, and therefore their copulation must continue under the water. She raised her thighs, sliding slowly up the shaft of his agitated pole until her cunt lips were holding the tip of his knob just above the surface of the water. Then, like a diver plunging into the waters of a murky river, she drove down onto him until she hit bottom. Her arse had disappeared below the surface, and they cavorted beneath the water. She fell forward onto his chest with an enormous splash that sent the water cascading onto the floor, and pushed her tongue into his mouth with such force that he nearly choked. He wound his legs around her back, clasping her firmly to him beneath the water, while she pumped her vagina up and down his penis. He felt a great knot gathering in his loins, and an excitement such as he hadn't experienced in thirty years. She sensed his thrill within her, and bit deep into his shoulder. He let forth a shout of pain and pleasure, as his sperm shot out into her receptive tube.

She helped him out of the bath, and into bed. He was panting as if he'd had a heart attack. In bed she cuddled around him, and knew she'd succeeded in her task. Next morning he left her sleeping, and went to work. All day he dreamed about her. In the evening when he arrived home it was to a nicely prepared meal, but what he really desired was her lusty young body. She had snared him hook, line and sinker. She would ply him with alcohol and sex, and his tongue would loosen. In the few days she had at her disposal, she prayed she'd find a way to worm her way into his place of work.

Meanwhile the girls were stalking the second target. Tanya had discovered from the man's talkative ex-wife that he enjoyed being sexually dominated. She suggested Jacqui might be the girl for the job. Jacqui had never played the dominant role in her life, but she agreed. Christine was to work with her.

Jacqui was told that the man in question could be found at the Star and Garter in the Strand every lunchtime. She arrived to find the lounge bar packed with office workers and military personnel. Several looked questioningly at her, as a woman on her own

174

was still regarded as a whore or a free spirit. Either way there was a chance of a pick-up. She coldly ignored all advances, and waited to catch her target alone.

When the man he was with went to the toilet, she moved through the crowd towards him. He was standing at the bar, holding a pint of bitter. She deliberately jogged his arm, and the beer splashed onto her jacket and skirt.

'You clumsy oaf,' she hissed at him.

'I'm sorry, but it was your own fault,' he smiled sweetly. 'You should look where you are going.'

'Kiss my arse,' she snapped.

'Anytime?'

'Oh, you'd like that would you?' she snarled. 'Then how about my toe up your backside?'

'It would be a pleasure.' He grinned.

Her eyes flashed angrily, and she fumbled in her handbag to push a small address card under his nose.

'Six-thirty tonight, if you dare,' she growled. 'Be late, and you'll pay with the skin off your bum.'

She stalked away, and prayed that she hadn't overdone it. At six-thirty, she and Christine sat in the small flat that had been hired by Lord C. for the occasion. They held their breath. There came a knock at the door.

'Come in,' called Jacqui.

The target walked into the room. He looked less confident than he had in the pub. Perhaps he was surprised to see two of them.

'Just stand where you are,' she instructed, 'and keep quiet.'

He was a man in his thirties, of medium height and slim build, and really quite handsome in a boyish way. The two women sat on the sofa talking, and completely ignored him for ten minutes. He appeared happy to be treated that way – perhaps he was anticipating the sexual delights to come. Suddenly, Jacqui rose, whipping her skirt up to her waist.

'Come here, prick,' she snapped, 'and lick my arse.'

Christine watched him move forward. She could see he was excited. There were several men in her past she would have liked to have treated like that.

'Kneel, useless prick,' ordered Jacqui.

When he was on his knees before her, she turned, and jerked down her knickers to present her bare behind to him. She bent her body forward, so her keister stuck out prettily towards him. He kissed the rounded cheeks of her comely rear.

'What do you think you are doing, you dozy prick,' she growled. 'Lick my arsehole out, and do it properly.'

She felt him part the cheeks of her behind, and bury his face in the cleft between them. His tongue located her small brown anus, and she was surprised by the thrill when he licked around it: pushing his tongue into the tightly guarded orifice and nibbling at the puckered rim. After a while she was aware of his tongue straying towards her vagina, and felt a huge wet lick the length of her fleshy labia.

'Stop that,' she scolded. 'How dare you touch me there without my permission. You'll be punished for that. I want you naked in thirty seconds.'

He stood naked against the wall. His cock was half aroused by the sight of the two women sitting laughing at him, but when they stood up and began to remove their clothes, his John Thomas shot up to its full height. Jacqui could see he couldn't believe his luck: two ravishing young women standing naked before him and one of them swinging a strap.

'On your knees, prick,' Jacqui ordered, 'and crawl. You're going to suck my cunt until I'm satisfied, and to help you do it your worthless butt's going to be thrashed.'

Christine raised the strap, and cracked it down across the man's slim haunches, while he anxiously and willingly buried his face between Jacqui's legs. Christine had a strong right arm, developed by years of tennis, but she was tired before Jacqui called a halt. She looked at the slob; his butt shone red like a beacon, and his mouth and chin were dripping with the mucus he'd sucked from Jacqui's pouting quim. He looked a dishevelled article of manhood to both girls, and neither felt the slightest sexual interest in him, but the game had to go on.

Christine moved around to his head and, grabbing a handful of his hair, dragged his face between her open legs. Jacqui by now held an enormous rubber dildo. She greased the shaft and, sitting astride his back, forced it into his arsehole. He started to protest, but stopped short when Christine pushed his face back into her dank muff. Jacqui felt like throwing up. She'd really had enough for one day, and could see Christine wasn't enjoying the meal the man was making of her fanny. She took his clothes, and tossed them out into the corridor.

'That's just a sample of what happens to useless pricks.' She smiled sweetly. 'If you want more, you'll be back here at six-thirty tomorrow.'

He didn't turn up. Whether they'd been too rough, or one dose of humiliation from the same girls was enough they'd never know. Whatever the reason, they had only half succeeded in their task. A member of Central Intelligence had been seduced, but they were unable to say they had been in a position to compromise his work.

* * *

Tanya explained that the third target would be more difficult to get at. A senior official working in Northumberland Avenue, he had the use of a War Department vehicle to drive to work every day from his home in Hertfordshire. It appeared the only way for an accidental meeting to take place would be on the road.

A plan was hatched whereby three girls would act like hitch-hikers. It was decided they would be in uniform to allay any suspicion they might be on the game, which is how Ingrid and Madeleine came to be standing on the Great North Road just outside London. It wasn't expected he'd stop for them, but it would plant an idea in his head, perhaps to fantasise what might happen if he was alone with a young female hitch-hiker in his car. Meik was conveniently thumbing a lift about a mile further up the road, and as he'd been given time to assimilate the idea – and as she was alone – he stopped.

'I'm only going about fifteen miles up the road,' he said.

'That's fine, thanks,' Meik replied, throwing her kitbag into the back of the car, and sliding into the passenger's seat beside him.

'Where are you going?' he asked.

'Doncaster.'

'You'll be lucky to get there tonight.'

'It doesn't matter,' she grinned, 'I've got a forty-eight, and all I really want is a couple of days away from camp.'

'Don't you like the services?'

'S'okay, but you get browned off locked up with all those bloody women.'

'I don't think I would.'

'You wouldn't last a week,' she laughed. 'They'd shag you to death.'

'You're kidding?'

'I'm not,' she retorted. 'You'd be surprised how sex mad a load of women can be.'

'So, I suppose you're off to see the boyfriend?'

'I haven't got one. I've only been in England just over a year, and I was going to look up an aunt in Doncaster.'

'Where're you from?'

'Singapore.'

'Really. What brings you here?'

'I was studying in London when war broke out.'

'And you joined the WAAFS?'

'Something like that. Do you live near here?'

'I'm going home now.'

'You married?'

'Yes.'

'Happily?'

'So, so.'

'You wouldn't like to put me up at a small hotel nearby, just for the weekend?'

As she spoke she slid her hand into his lap. Her slim young fingers massaged his crotch before expertly unfastening his fly. She heard him draw in his breath.

'You're very forward, young lady,' he muttered.

'I'm not on the game,' she said quickly. 'I don't want your money. Just a bit of comfort, and a bit of sex.'

Her fingers were inside his trousers, gently caressing the tip of his awakening knob. She took the helmet between her fingers and thumb, and squeezed it like a ripe plum. She felt him shivering, as she fingered his upright penis as if she were playing the clarinet. It swelled to its working proportions, so she leaned towards him and eased it from his trousers.

'Would you like me to toss you off?' she whispered.

'I'd like that,' he muttered after a pause.

179

Her hand was already caressing his eager prong. She squeezed with her supple fingers, stroking and tickling the rampant weapon. She felt him shudder, and saw his hands tighten on the wheel as his prick quivered like a bow in the palm of her hand. She wrapped her fingers around the shaft, and began to pump in earnest. She heard a long low moan, and the car swerved across the white line as his trembling pole swelled fit to burst. She leaned across to put her left hand over the steaming weapon, and he ejaculated into her palm. Slowly, she milked the last few drops into her spunk-spattered palm, and massaged her hands together as if the sperm was some kind of exotic cosmetic cream.

She sat back in the seat appearing so nonchalant, but she was tense with anticipation. Would he bite? Would her hand relief whet his appetite, or would he be satisfied now he had come? She prayed he was highly sexed, and his wife wasn't giving him all he needed.

Suddenly, he pulled off the road. She saw they had stopped in the car park of a country roadhouse. Although it was only five miles from his home, he had never been in the place, and it wasn't the sort of hostelry his friends used. He booked her a room for two nights, and said he'd be back next morning. Her gratitude was so genuinely touching that he thought she must have fallen for him. He wasn't to know it was sheer relief at having hooked him, although perhaps his fifteen years in security should have warned him. She enjoyed the evening in the bar with the locals, where she learned how to play shove-halfpenny and dominoes.

Her target appeared soon after ten o'clock the next morning. He'd told his wife he had to spend most of the day in the office. He tipped the chambermaid, and disappeared with Meik into the bedroom.

'Take your clothes off,' he ordered, almost before they were through the door.

She had dressed in a pretty summer dress, thinking they might go out driving or walking. Instead she was stripping off clothes she had put on less than an hour ago. She slipped off her camiknickers, and stood there naked but for her stockings and narrow suspender belt. She found it difficult being sexy so early in the day; it wasn't her best time. She must think of it as going to work, which was what it was.

'Where is your uniform?' he asked.

'In the wardrobe.'

'Get it for me. I'd like to see you dressed in it.'

She laid the blue uniform on the bed. He was obviously someone who had a thing about girls in uniform. He would have probably never have picked her up if she hadn't been wearing it.

She stood still as he dressed her. He slipped the airforce blue shirt over her head, and carefully fastened all the buttons before tying her tie neatly under her collar. She felt a warm feeling spread over her; she hadn't been dressed since she was a little girl. He held out the blue uniform skirt, and after she'd stepped into it, he pulled it up her long shapely legs. He meticulously tucked her shirt into the waistband, before helping her into the heavy jacket. She watched him fastening all the brass buttons, and pulling the material into shape. He hadn't bothered with her underclothes.

He sat on an upright chair in the middle of the bedroom, and bade her parade for him. She must have walked up and down for more than ten minutes, before he commanded her to remove her jacket. She stood in front of him in shirt-sleeve order.

'Lift your skirt right up to your waist. Now pirouette.'

She turned slowly with skirt raised high, so he could gorge on the naked delights of her shapely backside, her olive-brown thighs, and her curly black pubic hair. He signalled her to come closer, and slid the heavy blue uniform skirt down to the floor. He folded it fastidiously before running his fingers up her stockinged legs, and under the tails of her skirt to touch her inquisitively between the legs. His fingertips brushed her muff, tickling the soft curly hair before exploring between the lips of her vagina to seek her most sensitive clitoris. She parted her legs, and moaned sensuously sinking her quim onto his hand as he patiently fondled her erect clitoris until she was certain it must be red hot. She knew the juices were pouring from her agitated slit, and imagined his hand would be soaked.

Suddenly, he became impatient. He ripped down his trousers and, grabbing her by the thighs, dragged her down onto his lap. His cock was hard and straight. She spread her legs wide, straddling his thighs and the chair, and guided his impatient chopper into her sticky orifice. She sat impaled on his lap, while he buried his face in her throat. She remained still, while he kissed and nuzzled and bit her ears and neck and face.

Then he exploded into a frenzy of action, forcing her to ride his prong as if she was a rodeo showgirl astride a wild mustang. She pumped up and down his piston, and so hectic were their movements that his cock kept slipping out of her. They continued until their thighs ached, and their genitals were dripping wet, only then did he explode inside her. As she felt his pent up sexuality flood her passage, she threw back her head and groaned in the ecstasy of her own climax.

He took her out to lunch, but insisted she stay in uniform. After their meal, he fucked her again, insisting she mount him while still wearing her uniform. When he left in mid afternoon, she realised he hadn't once touched her breasts, which she found strange. He promised to return next day, but she never saw him again.

She returned to base to tell the Colonel that her mission was only half successful. She could see he was despondent. The plans had all gone so smoothly and all three targets had been seduced, yet none of the girls had got near to penetrating into the government offices. Lord C. wondered whether the seduction of three of their senior members would be enough to make SIS take them seriously. He doubted it.

The one girl still in with a chance was Sylvia, and she turned up trumps. As luck would have it Sir Reginald was duty officer over that weekend, which meant he was confined to his office buildings day and night. He was completely infatuated with Sylvia, and there being no bigger fool than an old fool, he jumped at the idea of her visiting him at night.

The Blitz was getting worse by the week, and the Luftwaffe had bombed London every night for the last month. An offshoot was that anyone forced to stay late invariably stayed overnight at their place of work, as once the sirens blew there was little chance of getting anywhere. Sylvia gathered that this often happened at Baker Street, and she planned accordingly.

She arrived with Madeleine and Jeanne just before eight o'clock to find three men other than the duty officer. They all lived out of town, and were staying overnight. The girls soon livened things up, and suggested they all go to a pub. Sir Reginald couldn't leave, so Sylvia stayed with him. The other three were only too pleased to escort the two beautiful women, who had appeared from nowhere. Sir Reginald, however, wasn't pleased.

'They can't stay here,' he grumbled, 'it's strictly against regulations.'

'Where else are they to go?'

'Didn't you say they have a flat in town?'

'They gave up their job and their flat, and are waiting to go into the ATS.'

'What are they doing here then?'

'We were having a farewell party before they enlist,' she explained. 'Come on, don't be such an old crosspatch. If I've been a naughty girl you can spank me.'

'I can't do that here,' he said indignantly.

'Then we'll have to find another way to teach a disobedient little girl a lesson, shan't we?'

He didn't reply. She wound her arms around his neck, and kissed him hard on the lips, her lithe tongue flickering into his mouth like the forked tongue of a serpent. She could feel him relax, and knew she had nearly conquered his doubts.

'I know,' she breathed coquettishly into his ear, 'you could make me take your great big willy up my poor little botty hole.'

She felt his grip tighten on her. He hadn't done that to her; she doubted whether he had ever done it to any girl. To a boy, perhaps, in his public-school days, but never to a girl's sweet arse.

She broke away from him, and slid both hands down the front of his trousers in search of his prick. She cupped her hands under his balls, and felt his chopper begin to rise until it strained against the confining material. She removed her hands and unfastened his belt and waistband, which resulted in his trousers

184

falling to the floor. She lifted his shirt with a girlish giggle, and peered at his rampant member.

'See,' she murmured, 'John Thomas is itching to be let in the back way. He's a lecherous old dick, isn't he?'

She turned, and bent forward across a nearby desk, flipping up the back of her silk dress.

'Take my knickers down, and fuck me up the arse. Teach a naughty girl she must be obedient.'

'Please, Sylvia, be quiet,' he snapped.

Her stomach turned over. She thought she had gone too far, but she felt his tool between the cheeks of her bum, the tip straining at her tight brown orifice. He had made no attempt at foreplay, and she realised by her babbling she had either annoyed him, or aroused him to a cruel passion. He stabbed at her anus, gradually invading her. She yelped, and stifled a scream. She arched her back, and parted her legs further.

In spite of her continual wriggling, however, he seemed no nearer climax. She gripped the desk and closed her eyes, until she became aware of an easy, sensual sensation to the piston strokes within her. Moisture from her rectal passage had lubricated his chopper. Just as she was beginning to enjoy being sodomised, he came with an almighty rush. Hot spunk flooded her bowels. She felt him move away from her.

'Oh, my poor bottom,' she whimpered.

He smiled, because he'd never bummed a woman before. She smiled, because in a few hours it would be game, set and match to the girls of Lord C.'s circus.

It was almost midnight before the others returned, and the bombs were already falling like confetti. They had found a pub where the landlord was an old soldier

185

who'd spent two years in the trenches in the last lot, and swore the only way Hitler would close his pub was a direct hit.

The raid seemed to be south of the river, but the sky was red with the flames of burning buildings, and the crump of exploding bombs rasped the ears. The three men were too drunk to notice it. They found a gramophone, and Madeleine sang to the melodic strains of Benny Goodman's clarinet. They listened to her thin voice crooning 'The Very Thought of You', then shouted for something more lively. Soon the party became rowdy, and they began to barrack the singer.

'Get 'em off,' screamed the youngest and drunkest of the party. 'Get 'em bloody off.'

Jeanne moved towards Madeleine, who had climbed onto a table as if it was a stage, and reached up under the full-skirted dress. She yanked down Madeleine's flimsy knickers, and she crossed to the young man. To shouts of delight she jammed them down over his head. Taking the cue, Madeleine began to strip. Tantalisingly, she played with the buttons down the front of her dress, before opening it briefly like a female flasher. She went into a burlesque routine, using her unbuttoned dress like a fan dancer uses a fan. She finished by displaying herself gloriously naked, and made no objection when one of the men dragged her from the room. The festivities were over, the game all but won.

Madeleine's lips encircled the man's cock, sucking delightfully until his spunk shot down her throat. After that he slept.

Jeanne was on her back on the carpet, her legs wrapped around her punter's back, but she soon discovered he was a victim of brewer's droop, and used her hand to slake his lust.

Sylvia took Sir Reginald to the camp bed reserved

for the duty officer; the youngest and drunkest slept like a baby. The men snored peacefully, while Madeleine and Jeanne explored the building, gaining access to every nook and cranny, so that it could be said without doubt they had penetrated security.

Lord C. had been speaking to the director of Central Intelligence for more than an hour. At times their discussions had become quite heated.

'And as a result of all this larking about, George,' said the director, 'you expect me to recognise your girls as intelligence agents?'

'If they can seduce senior members of your organisation, and have free run of your offices,' Lord C. replied, 'then they could do the same to our enemies.'

'They didn't obtain any special information.'

'They didn't try.'

'You realise that if I whispered the existence of your little circus to the press, there'd be an almighty outcry. The vociferous minority would raise Cain. There would be questions in the House. Churchill would have to deny all knowledge.'

'And if I told the great man of this fiasco, your department would be cleared out quicker than Harrod's at sale time.'

'All right, I'll play ball. Your girls will be code-named C's Circus, but only the top echelon in British Intelligence will know your real identity and aims. If it ever gets out, we'll all be thrown in the Tower.'

'Thank you, sir,' smiled Lord C. 'I'm obliged.'

'You're a scoundrel, George. You always were.'

Liverpool

It was a little more than a week later that Lord C. was summoned to the director's office again. This time the circumstances were entirely different.

'A situation has arisen where I think I can use your girls,' announced the director.

'Good, they'll be glad to be on the move.'

'My agents believe they have discovered a Nazi secret agent living in Liverpool. He must have been placed in this country before the war, as a sleeper. We have no idea if he has been activated, or still awaits orders from Berlin.'

'How did you find out about him?'

'Bits and pieces of information from different sources, but that's not your worry. I don't want to pull him in: I want him watched. If he's active, I want to know what he's up to. If he's still sleeping, I want someone there to keep tabs on him, so when he's contacted by Nazi intelligence we'll be in a position to scuttle their operation.'

'I understand,' nodded Lord C.

'To put him under constant surveillance would be difficult and expensive, and probably prove unsatisfactory. However, if one of your girls could move in with him, that would solve the problem,' explained the director. 'Do you think that's possible?'

'Why not?' said Lord C. 'It sounds the sort of mission that's tailor-made for us.'

'He runs some sort of small factory in Liverpool,' grunted the director. 'My people will give you all the details.'

'I'll get straight onto it,' said Lord C. He stood up to leave. 'Thanks for the opportunity.'

'Just make certain those man-eaters of yours don't cock it up.'

'They won't, sir.'

It was decided that Ingrid and Meik would be assigned to this first mission. Ingrid spoke English with a gutteral accent, which suggested she originated from northern Europe, and that, together with her Nordic appearance, would make it possible to believe she had Nazi sympathies. Meik was in a position to pretend she was a colonial who had suffered under the yoke of British imperialism, thus assuming a deep-rooted hatred of the English.

Nigel drove them to Liverpool. They parked across the road from their target's house to catch a glimpse of the man. They had been told his name was Paul Ames. He lived in a semi-detached house built at the beginning of the 1930s, when the middle class flocked from the inner cities to the green and leafy suburbs of the larger industrial towns. He was a nondescript man in his forties, with a hatchet face and wispy brown hair – the sort of man who merged into the background, and no one ever remembered seeing. It was a perfect portrait of a spy.

The following day Ingrid caught the bus to the factory, which was little more than a conglomeration of tin-roofed huts behind a sprawling housing estate. The place was as disreputable inside as it looked from outside. She was shown to the manager's office by a surly woman.

She knocked at the door.

'Come in.'

The man behind the desk was enormous. He sat hunched forward, and his heavy shoulders and deep chest, together with the great jowls of his face and protruding eyes, made him look like a huge toad.

'You'll be the girl looking for a job?'

'Yes, sir.'

He leaned across the desk, and held out a flabby hand. It was damp and sweaty, and she could smell his BO from the other side of the desk. She'd never seen a more repulsive man.

'It's Ingrid, isn't it?'

'Yes, sir.'

'Have you worked in a factory before?'

'No, sir.'

'No matter, there's nothing to it. You'll soon learn.' He grinned. 'We pay well over the odds.'

'I need the job, sir.'

'And you shall have it, my dear. You only have to ask politely, and be nice to me.'

'I'm not sure what you mean.'

'Do you go to the movies?'

'Yes, sir.'

'Imagine you are a young actress looking for a job, and I'm a big director. Do you know what a casting couch is?'

'Yes.' She hesitated.

'Now you've got the idea.'

'You want to make love to me?'

'I wouldn't put it quite like that,' he guffawed. 'I just want to shag your arse off.'

Ingrid managed to look both shocked and indignant.

It was a good bit of acting. She lowered her head, making certain her eyes didn't meet his.

'All right,' she whispered tearfully, 'if I must.'

He lumbered over to the door, and locked it. From a nearby cupboard, he dragged an old mattress and threw it into the middle of the room. The exertion made him break out into a heavy sweat.

'Take your clothes off, girlie.'

He stood watching her, panting like a grampas. She wore a threadbare button-through dress, and cheap camiknickers. She stepped out of them, and kicked off her high-heeled shoes. She stood before him, gloriously naked. His mouth dropped open like a goldfish, as he goggled at her beauty.

'Gawd, you're pretty,' he muttered.

It was a compliment indeed, for he was the sort of man who paid little heed to beauty. To him, a woman was sex. He was living proof of the adage: you don't look at the mantelpiece when you poke the fire. His interest in women began and ended between their legs.

Ingrid was forced to watch him undress. She felt revulsion. The fat was layered in great rolls over his belly and chest as he stood grunting and panting like some prehistoric monster. She lay on her back on the hair mattress, and shut her eyes. He knelt over her, his huge belly hanging down to flop onto the cool flesh of her thighs. She shuddered. His mouth closed over her breast, and he masticated the tender globe like a toothless man chewing a steak. She could feel his saliva running down her yielding boobs onto her chest, and she wanted to vomit.

He collapsed onto her, his fat smothering her shapely body. She gasped for breath, as his drivelling mouth closed over hers. She fought desperately to free her lips. She could understand why whores would happily fuck like rattlesnakes, but refused to let their punters kiss them. She got her mouth free, but he slobbered over her throat and neck. She fought off a wild desire to bite him.

When she felt her legs being levered apart, she quickly became aware that there was nothing flabby about his cock. It was like a rod of iron stabbing painfully at the lips of her unwilling pussy. She wanted to massage herself, to make her vagina ready to receive him, but she was buried under acres of flab like a pie dish covered by too much pastry. She raised her knees and parted her legs, swinging them up either side of the mountain of flesh covering her. She struggled to get a grip around his hips with her long legs, but it was like trying to grip a barrel of lard. With her legs raised, however, she was able to slide a hand into her crotch.

She located the helmet of his prong, and gripped it between her slim fingers. She manoeuvred the tip to touch her labia, and used the pulsating stick to massage herself. She fought to relax, but it wasn't easy beneath so much male flesh. Slowly, she felt her slit relaxing, and guessed she would be moist enough to receive him without hurt. She planted it at the entrance of her dainty orifice, and removed her hand.

He stabbed into her as if he was drilling for oil. His desperate writhing lasted several minutes, before she felt his prick tremble and squirt its charge of warm spunk into her uterus. As he climaxed, so his whole body shook like an enormous bowl of jelly.

When he rolled off her, she was dripping with sweat. She had never been so disgusted.

'And that, little girl,' he sighed, 'is what I call a fuck.'

She began to dress, but he grabbed her camiknickers and refused to give them back. She knew everyone in the factory would know she was nude beneath the thin dress, and inexplicably felt as embarrassed as a shy young maiden. As she left his office, he held up her underwear.

'You can come and get them any time you feel randy. You don't have to make an appointment. I'm always willing to pleasure my prettier female staff.'

He'd have to wait a long time, she thought. When she walked onto the factory floor, the hooter had just gone for teabreak. A couple of women grabbed her, and put a big bowl of evil-looking liquid into her arms.

'Take it to the bloke at the end of the line,' they instructed. 'Be careful. If you spill it he'll have your guts for garters.'

She walked in the direction she was told, aware of several dozens of pairs of eyes watching her. It was so unnaturally quiet, it made her nervous. The foul liquid swilled in the shallow bowl. She stepped onto a grating to be met with a gush of warm air. It shot up from the grating like a hurricane, and blew her skirts high above her waist. She stood still, terrified of spilling the liquid, and yet blushing at the thought of showing her private parts to the assembled workforce. Instantly, her ears rang to the sound of crude laughter and whistles and catcalls. Out of the corner of her eye she saw Mr Ames arriving. It was her opportunity. She dropped the bowl, and clasped her skirts around her legs.

'Swine,' she screamed in a loud voice laden with a German accent, 'only English pigs would do such rude things to girls.'

The noise stopped abruptly. She felt she could cut the silence with a knife. Something had to give. A voice began to chant, 'Der Fuhrer's face'. It was taken up by the others.

'She sounds like a bloody Jerry.'

'What's she doin' 'ere?'

'English swine are we?'

'I know what we'll do . . .'

The last voice was obviously respected, because silence fell again. It came from an oldish man with a mean face and a bitter smile.

'We'll decorate her arse with swastikas,' she shouted, 'the Nazi-loving whore.'

She was grabbed by a dozen willing hands. To raucous laughter her clothes were dragged up to her shoulders, and a big black swastika was daubed on each cheek of her behind. When they let her go, she ran sobbing towards the offices, straight into the arms of Mr Ames. He comforted her, holding her at arm's length as if he couldn't quite bring himself to hug her.

'Have you done factory work before?'

'No, sir.'

'I thought not,' he sighed. 'How were you employed?'

'I've been in service in Sweden, sir,' she sniffed, 'ever since I left school.'

'I'm in need of a housekeeper. Would you like to come and look after me?'

'Oh, thank you, sir.'

It had gone like clockwork. She had seen the opportunity, and it had worked. Nigel had bribed Ames's housekeeper to quit with the promise of a better job. It hadn't been difficult. She had been relieved to go. Ingrid hadn't been in the house many hours when she realised why.

After his evening meal, Ames disappeared into his study, which was kept permanently locked. She was sitting on the toilet when she had a strange feeling she was being watched. She shrugged it off. She mustn't start imagining things like an adolescent girl. Again, when in the bathroom she had the same feeling.

To put her mind at rest she went to her bedroom, and began searching. Sure enough, there was a small peephole in the ceiling: Mr Ames was a voyeur.

That night she angled a mirror so she could see the peephole while lying on her bed. She undressed and, throwing back the bedclothes, stretched out on the bed. Her magnificent blonde hair spread over the pillow; the ivory sheen of her white skin shimmered under the electric light. Glancing in the mirror, she noticed an eye had arrived at the peephole: he was watching her.

She decided to give him a show beyond his wildest dreams. She began to move her hands sensuously over her body, squeezing her full breasts and pinching the nipples, stroking her flat stomach and thighs, and running her fingertips down the inside of her long legs. As she caressed herself, so she began to moan. Gradually, she increased the tempo; her erotic sighs turned to elated panting as she caressed her ravishing female body with frantic haste. She threw her legs apart to display the jewel that nestled in its surround of delicate foliage. She could imagine Ames gorging on the delectations she was presenting to him. She stroked the fleshy inrolled folds of her succulent fig and, inserting her fingers, pulled the lips wide apart to display the erotic red gateway to her nirvana.

Holding her cunt lips apart with the fingers of her right hand, she slid her left hand along the length of her pink slit until her fingertips rested on her dainty clitoris. Easing back its hood, she fingered it sensually until it stood erect like a little red soldier. She masturbated for his entertainment, writhing and wriggling her body, and groaning to simulate the greatest orgasm the world had ever seen. She finished by throwing her legs high in the air, and forcing her fingers deep into her twat.

What a finale, she thought smugly. She could imagine him wanking for dear life in the rafters above. Tomorrow she must buy a cucumber from the market to star in her next show.

Over the next few days Ingrid tried surreptitiously to give him the impression that her outburst at the factory had been her real feelings. He caught her listening avidly to Lord Haw-Haw, and often heard her muttering to herself in German how she detested the British. On the sixth day he asked her to accompany him the next morning.

On that day he drove her to the docks to a hostel for seamen. The warden was a big, ugly brute, who took one look at Ingrid and eyed up a young boy behind her. If this was the thieves' kitchen she had been sent to find out about, she was going to get no help from him.

'You'll be more use working here,' said Ames. 'The seamen will appreciate you, and you'll be doing more for the war effort than cleaning my house.'

He didn't wait for her to argue. She wondered why he had dumped her here. He must have a good reason to deprive himself of the nightly shows she put on. As a dedicated voyeur he couldn't have had things better for him. Perhaps the hostel was mixed up with his covert activities. That is, if SIS was correct, and he really was a spy. She could only keep her eyes open.

The hostel was right on the waterfront, and had four dormitories sleeping a total of thirty men. In addition, there was a large canteen, open to merchant and naval personnel.

The following day Ingrid contacted Meik, and suggested she tried for a job at the hostel too as two pairs of eyes were better than one. Meik arrived for interview with the warden looking like a waif from the docks of Calcutta. She wore a threadbare dress a size too small for her, and open-toed sandals. She looked decidedly grubby.

'You look as if you've been through a tough time,' said the warden.

'I have,' snapped Meik, 'ever since I came to this damn country.'

'Why did you come?'

'My father brought me from Bombay to make a fortune in the sahib's country. He was sure it flowed with milk and honey.'

'What happened?'

'The war happened. He was killed at sea fighting for the sahibs, and I have had to sell my body to keep alive.'

'So, you aren't in love with England?'

'I hate it. I can't wait for the war to end, so I can go back East.'

'OK, you can have a job,' he grunted. 'Get one of the girls to fix you up with a few clothes.'

As far as the rest of the staff were concerned, the two new girls became firm friends. They were both hard workers, and kept themselves to themselves, so nobody worried them. Strangely, they both seemed cynical of the British, but as a dozen different nationalities used the hostel, no one cared.

It was during the second week that the warden approached Meik. She had recently had a slanging match with a Scottish seaman, and had spat in his face. She thought she was to be reprimanded.

197

'How do you think the war is going?' he asked conversationally.

'Not fast enough,' she snapped. 'I thought the Nazis would have invaded, and it would all be over by now.'

'You can be put in jail for talk like that.'

'The bloody British wouldn't need an excuse.'

'If there was a chance to work against them, would you take it?'

'What's in it for me?'

'Twenty pounds.'

Her eyes lit up.

She was told to find out from a young seaman the time of sailing and destination of his ship, plus anything he might know about the convoy they would be joining.

The seaman was pointed out to her at breakfast. He was little more than a boy, nineteen at the most, with enormous rough hands and a clumsy rolling gait. She gave him the eye all day, making it obvious to the thickest male that she was available. At tea time he caught her alone.

'Fancy going to the flicks later on?'

'Why not?' she smiled. 'My stars said I was going to meet a handsome seafarer.'

'Gaw'n, what else did they say?'

'That he'll take me in the one an' nines. I ain't no cheap little tart, y'know.'

'I didn't think you were.'

'Well, that's all right then.'

They sat in the back row. The lights had hardly dimmed before he slipped his arm around her slim shoulders, and his hand had cupped her ample breast. He was a fast worker, she thought, but had she known, she would have realised they were both acting out of character. He smiled to himself. He was onto a good thing. It was the first time he'd dare slip an arm around a girl's shoulder so quickly. Normally, he waited ages before daring to act. The warden had told him the girl was suspected of being a Nazi sympathiser, and of passing information to the enemy. The little tramp. He had been given false information about shipping to pass to her. He was a patriotic lad, and pleased to be of service to his country. He had been told she would be eager to offer sex for the information, so he couldn't really lose.

He began furtively to pull her blouse out from the waistband of her skirt, and work his fingers beneath until he could touch her soft young breasts. She wore no bra. The touch of the warm tender flesh sent a charge of electricity through his body. He dared to squeeze a dainty upright nipple between his fingers. She leaned closer to him, making the blood pump through his veins in sexual anticipation. The warden was right; she wouldn't resist any advance until she'd got the information she wanted. He was going to enjoy himself tonight.

She was surprised when she felt his hand move beneath her skirt. He didn't look a Lothario, but he was certainly a bit of a wolf. One hand was already fondling her bare titty and now, after leaning over to kiss her lips, he was stealthily busy with his other hand under her skirt. She gave the hand a little slap. She mustn't appear too eager – she couldn't be taken for an out-and-out slut.

The hand persisted at intervals, until she decided to allow him a step further. She felt his fingertips explore her stocking tops before moving upwards onto the soft flesh of her thigh. She eased her legs apart to allow the hand to slip into her crotch, and his fingers to reach their goal. She shivered and gripped his arm, as one finger crept between the moist folds of her slit. She gasped audibly, as he fumbled among her pubic hairs and pushed two fingers into her quim. She was about to reach over and touch his throbbing cock, when the picture moved to a sudden end. He quickly removed his hand from under her skirt. She took his wrist, and guided his fingers to his mouth. He sucked her mucus from them; when the lights came up she saw him blush.

When he guided her out of the cinema it was dark. There wasn't a pin-hole of light to be seen in the blackout, but the moonlight was sufficient to make out shapes. In spite of the cool night air he was boiling hot. He ran a finger under his collar where the sweat had formed. He could feel his cock rampant in his trousers, and his belly knotted with the want of her. He'd explored her hot wet crack for over an hour. His fingers had caressed her thighs and belly and breasts, and even delved into her small cute navel. Now, he itched to insert his zealous prong into her glutinous cave of love.

He pushed her into a shop doorway, and crushed her to him. His open mouth sought her lips, and his tongue darted into her wet mouth. He felt her draw her head back, and suck avidly at his lower lip. He reached down to yank up the hem of her skirt. She halted him, and he watched in amazement as she whipped off her knickers, and stuffed them in her handbag.

He unbuttoned his trousers, allowing his tool to jump free like a jack-in-the-box. She had her skirt raised high, and stood with legs apart waiting for him. He bent his knees, and slipped his throbbing cock between her thighs. His cock, which had been raring to go for over an hour in the cinema, was screaming out to climax. He couldn't hold himself back. He flooded her with a long moan of ecstatic relief. Immediately he felt guilty for coming too soon.

He was about to excuse himself when he felt her lips gently kiss his. He understood that the evening was far from over. She hadn't mentioned shipping or convoy movements. He smiled. She would have to seduce him again, unless the warden was wrong and she wasn't a spy.

She linked an arm through his, and guided him back to the hostel: it was time to get down to work.

The lights were off in the kitchen, when they arrived. She found a bowl of dripping in the larder, and began to cut two slices of bread. He came up behind her as she picked up the knife from the draining board. She found herself bent forward over the sink, and was forced to grab the taps. He certainly was an enterprising young man. Only ten minutes ago she had been treated to a knee-trembler in a shop doorway; now she was to be poked over the kitchen sink. She felt the back of her skirt jerked up as he pushed her further forward over the sink. He grunted in frustrated agitation as he fumbled with his fly.

Soon she was aware of his anxious knob nudging against her haunches, demanding entrance to her grotto once again. She was saved the embarrassment of having her knickers torn off, as they were still in her handbag. She spread her legs, with the patient sigh of a good wife about to satisfy an oversexed husband. She arched her back, and raised her backside to give John Thomas a better sight of the goalposts. It wasn't exactly a comfortable position she'd been forced to adopt. The rim of the sink dug into her ribs, and her boobs hung down into the basin. She gripped the taps for dear life, as her head hung down between them and her jet-black hair fell forward into the plug-hole.

His weapon was poised at her gateway, and slowly he began to rotate it around the perimeter of her vulva, tickling and teasing the lips of her orifice. Any other time she would have screamed with joy, but all she wanted of him was his conclusion. He jabbed into her, and she felt herself fill. He drove into her until his testicles slapped against her backside, and there he remained. He was deliberately holding himself still inside her, so obviously trying to make up for his swift emission in the shop doorway. She rotated her butt, grinding at the swollen pecker trapped in her gum-drenched fanny. She closed her legs tightly, allowing her cunt muscles to grip the greedy prick inside her in a velvet vice. She clung onto the taps, and used her arms to lever her body in lateral movements. She knew she had defeated him, for she felt his agitated weapon pumping inside her lubricated passage. She groaned, moaned and gasped, urging him to pump faster and faster.

As he came, he withdrew to spatter her back with his load of spunk. She wailed like a wild animal, as she felt him rubbing the semen into the flesh of her back and buttocks.

She gave him a make-do supper of bread and dripping, and cocoa. They sat talking, and when she prompted him he gave her the information she wanted without a qualm. As she bathed, she decided it had been too easy. The whole evening had gone too smoothly. He had assumed too much for a first date, and he wasn't that sort of lad. She was sure he'd been told she was available because she wanted information from him. She must give that same information back to the warden. If she changed it, they would know she was a British agent. If her reasoning was incorrect, however, the result would be catastrophic, as genuine information would be passed to the Nazi U-boats.

There was no time to get in touch with Lord C., as the warden had demanded she report to him tonight. She spoke to Ingrid, who agreed with her. Fortunately, she took the right decision.

As the warden handed over her £20, he was pleased to think he had the use of such a pretty girl for such a trifling sum. Mr Ames had asked him to test Ingrid too, as he was certain she was anti-British. He wasn't so sure about her. There was something he didn't quite trust about Ingrid, in spite of her blonde beauty and her overt hatred of anything British.

Unlike Meik, Ingrid hadn't really settled in at the hostel. She didn't feel at home, and she knew she was intensely disliked by the warden and his disgusting boyfriend. While he was distantly polite to the other girls, the warden was invariably rude to her, perhaps because she was uneasy in the presence of homosexuals.

The boyfriend was a hundred times worse – a dreadful posturing she-male who wore long dyed hair and make-up, and had grown over-developed breasts. The other girls flattered him, and laughed with him to his face. It was all Ingrid could do to be civil to him, and he hated her for it. When he did a grotesque drag act on the small stage in the canteen, the audience clapped and cheered, but she nearly threw up. He must have seen her look of disgust, for afterwards he was coldly distant. Two days later he was in the cellar attending to the beer, when she passed the trapdoor.

'Ingrid,' he called, 'I need help with a barrel. Would you come down please?'

She descended the steps into the cellar, and when

she turned she saw him confront her with the look of Lucifer.

'I hate you,' he screamed, grabbing her full breasts and twisting them painfully, 'I hate you because you're female, and you flaunt your beauty at me.'

'I can't help being a woman.'

'You scorn me, because I'm not,' he yelled in blind anger.

'I don't,' she objected, genuinely frightened of the snarling monster in front of her.

'I'd give anything to have the body you have,' he shrieked dementedly. 'You don't deserve it. I'm going to punish you.'

She made to move away from him, but he swung at her savagely, striking her on the point of the jaw.

'Help,' she shrieked, 'help me.'

Her shouts ended in a high squeal as he hit her again and again as she fell. It was the warden who saved her. He arrived at her side, and bodily threw his lover against the wall of the cellar.

'You madman,' he yelled at the youth, 'you'll get us all hung.'

She whimpered as she was helped to her feet. She found herself clinging to her rescuer for a few seconds until she recovered her confidence. She knew she mustn't make too much of it.

Three days later they heard from Lord C. It seemed the SIS intended to eliminate the hostel, as it was nothing more than a thorn in their side. Mr Ames was the fish they wanted to fry, so the two girls were instructed to stay close to him.

The following night the hostel was burnt to the ground. The sole casualties were the warden and his lover, who were found dead in their bed. The fire service informed the police they had good reason to suspect arson. Nothing was done about it.

Ingrid went to Mr Ames, and asked whether she could return to being his housekeeper. When he agreed, she asked whether her friend Meik could be given a job in the factory, and share her room in his house. He knew of Meik's activities in the hostel, and realised he might have work for two co-operative girls when Berlin contacted him. He gave his permission for Meik to stay the night, but said she must see the factory manager for a job.

Ingrid sighed: poor Meik would have to suffer that twenty-stone oaf, and his dreadful casting couch.

When she took Meik to her old room, they saw an enormous double-headed dildo lying on the bed. It had obviously been put there for their use. Mr Ames wanted a show from them; otherwise they could kiss goodbye to their jobs and accommodation.

After supper they bathed together, giggling like two adolescent girls as they soaped and rinsed each other. It was like acting for a camera, and the idea of being watched excited Meik. She began to overact, and Ingrid had to warn her. By now she was an old hand at preening before a voyeur. She had come to realise that all her movements must be natural. She must act as if she had no idea she was being watched. She presumed that was how a voyeur got his kicks. She realised she should have explained it to Meik, who was still dramatically overacting. She helped her out of the bath and, wrapping her in a large towel, began vigorously rubbing her, while taking the opportunity to whisper another warning in her ear.

In the bedroom Meik immediately took the rubber dildo and, standing with feet wide apart and knees bent, she forced it slowly up into her vagina. The look of contented pleasure on her face made Ingrid gently kiss and caress her olive-brown body. Pushing Meik's hand away from the dildo she began working it inside her friend's cunt with long sensuous strokes. Meik gasped in simulated ecstasy as she rubbed her own breasts with an urgent passion. Meik sank down onto the hand that held the dildo, and whinnied.

Next, Ingrid knelt on the bed, and Meik took her from behind. Suddenly, with the skill of an acrobat, Meik swung her leg over Ingrid's back, and they were kneeling back to back, bum to bum with the dildo still embedded inside their love boxes. It was a spectacular finale for their friendly neighbourhood voyeur.

The result was that Mr Ames informed the two girls that they were welcome to stay. He was certain that when the time came they would be worth their gullible weight in gold. He would use them and dispose of them without a twinge of conscience. Until then, he would wait patiently for his orders from the Fatherland.

Lord C. informed the director that his two girls were in place, ready to inform him of any activity on the part of Mr Ames. The director informed his department that he had two agents positioned to watch and report on the Nazi sleeper in Liverpool. They would know immediately he was activated, so there should be no further danger from that quarter.

The agents within his department asked among themselves who was watching the sleeper. No one knew, and the director's reputation grew. He was a crafty old bird, they whispered. The director was as good as his word: the girls of C's Circus were being kept a closely guarded secret.

Paris

The old Handley-Page aircraft rumbled through the sky like an ancient charabanc. It was a beautiful autumn day, without a cloud in sight, but the wind that rushed into the belly of the aircraft was decidedly chilly. It was certainly cold to Jeanne's bare legs, as she lay on her back in the shuddering fuselage. The pile of canvas sacks beneath her gave little relief from the shaking and rattling of the worn-out aeroplane, and the young man covering her gave no protection against the cold air whistling about her naked thighs.

She decided this Sky-Screw Club wasn't all it was cracked up to be. She had a liking for the young man she was screwing, otherwise she would never have fallen in with this silly nonsense, which she knew they had invented just for Madeleine and her. They'd only been at the RAF station for a few days, but it was proving terrific fun, and they both adored the RAF lads who flew the planes.

The girls were on a two-week course to learn parachute jumping, and the flight was very unofficial – a sort of Sunday afternoon jaunt. It was only the second time the girls had been up, and they jumped at the chance. As for the Sky-Screw Club, well, why not? Life was short, and it wasn't every girl who'd performed in the back of an RAF plane.

Jeanne tightened her legs around the young pilot's back, and wound her arms around his neck beneath the thick rolled collar of his flying jacket. She wore a man's flying jacket too. They had given her the smallest size they had, but it hung on her like a horse blanket. It made the top half of her as warm as toast, in contrast to the chilly wind below. He lay perfectly still on top of her, but she could feel his hard cock quivering inside her salacious vagina.

He was a thoughtful lover, even in the surroundings of their lovemaking. He kissed her on the lips, his tongue probing inside her open mouth. His kisses were long and passionate, in the manner of the great lovers of the silver screen. She forgot her icy cold limbs, and snuggled close to him. She realised she was enjoying this strange interlude, thousands of feet above the ground.

The juddering, rolling motion of the aircraft was enough to stimulate his cock, which filled her adorable tunnel of love. She began to move her bottom to the rhythm of the engine, and felt him answer in short quick thrusts that titillated the walls of her vagina. She lowered her legs and crossed them beneath him, trapping his prick within her and milking him as a milkmaid might a cow's udder. She whinnied, nibbling his neck, as she climaxed. Her erotic threshing beneath him triggered his own orgasm. She felt his trembling staff drive in and out of her, as he clutched at her and gasped at the ecstasy of his relief. His sperm flooded into her, but she continued to hold him prisoner between her crossed legs. He was happy to lie inert on her until the cold numbness of their thighs forced them to dress.

She looked at him. She doubted whether he was twenty-one. A Battle of Britain hero who had been shot down and badly hurt, and now unfit to fly Spitfires, he had wangled a posting to a training squadron rather than be grounded.

'Am I a full member of the Sky-Screw Club now?' she asked wickedly.

'You certainly are,' he replied. 'Fully qualified to copulate over five thousand feet.'

'That'll come in handy,' she grinned.

Madeleine was sitting beside the co-pilot who was flying the aircraft. He was a much older man, an ex-RFC officer who had flown SE5s in the last war, but was considered too old to fly anything other than training aircraft now. Madeleine liked him. He fitted in with the younger wilder men, but retained a quiet maturity which she respected.

'Am I to become a member of your club too?' she asked.

'Nothing I'd enjoy more,' he grinned, 'but it's cold and uncomfortable back there. Let's cheat, and wait until we're back on terra firma, shall we?'

'I suppose you've done it all before?'

'No, but I've often dreamed of a pretty girl sitting beside me when I'm flying . . .'

'Go on.'

'I don't like to say,' he laughed, 'it's rude.'

'Giving you head?'

As she spoke she leaned across to the pilot's seat, lowering her head towards his lap. In seconds her nimble fingers had unfastened his fly buttons, and eased his semi-rampant weapon free of the rough material. He sat motionless, flying the plane as if she didn't exist. She moved her slim delicate fingers along the shaft of his John Thomas, gently massaging the foreskin and tantalising the helmet with pressure from her long nails. It stood proudly erect, quivering like a flagpole in a high wind, as she closed her warm satin lips over the trembling knob. With an infinite care born of experience, she slid her lips slowly down his shaft until the whole tool was enclosed in her wet, welcoming mouth.

She moved her tongue like quicksilver over the throbbing length, and sucked so divinely she dragged a low ecstatic moan from deep down in his soul. Patiently, she tongued him, as the long minutes ticked by and the fantasies of past years were fulfilled. As she contentedly sucked like a small girl on a dummy, she wondered whether he had dreamed of this between dogfights above the trenches of Flanders.

Her reverie ended when she became aware of her big dummy swelling and pulsating in her mouth. She sucked avidly, and it discharged its cargo of warm spunk into the back of her throat. She gulped it down greedily. When she glanced up he was still looking steadfastly ahead, as if she didn't exist. She licked the last drops of sperm from the tip of his limp knob, and tucked it back in his trousers where it belonged.

Another girl might have been angry at his indifference, but she realised he was reliving a hundred fantasies inside his head, and she was now the face in every one of them.

The young pilot returned, and Madeleine went to Jeanne in the bowels of the aircraft.

The two girls had been selected for the second mission by Lord C. Just over a week ago they had been called to his office and told about it.

Information had trickled through from occupied Paris that someone was endeavouring to amalgamate the many small resistance groups into one united force.

If this was possible, it would help the Special Operations Executive, which would effectively have use of a small army in occupied territory. The Director, however, feared that the man could be working for the Nazis, or for his own ends. Nothing was known about him, because he was a newcomer to Paris.

Lord C. had been approached to send two girls, who might worm their way into the bed of this newcomer or his aides, and discover where their allegiance lay. Until that was established the new resistance movement couldn't be trusted with British agents or supplies.

It would take three weeks to contact their known sympathisers within the city to arrange plans for the two girls to be received. In the meanwhile they would learn parachute jumping in case they were required to drop behind enemy lines.

After the plane had landed, Madeleine strode towards the showers reserved for the girls. As she stood beneath the spray of hot water, and began soaping her body, she saw the co-pilot enter. She turned to meet him.

'Now, about becoming a member of our exclusive club,' he smiled. 'Can you imagine we are five thousand feet up?'

'Floating on air, you mean?'

'I certainly could be, with the help of your bountiful body.'

'Be my guest.'

He joined her under the warm spray and, falling to his knees, buried his face into her wet stomach. She clasped the back of his head, and opened wide her legs to feel the stubble of his chin rub against her soft muff of pubic hair. It was like sandpaper moving against her flesh, but when it rasped against the top folds of her tender labia, she winced and drew back.

He lowered his face, so that his lips were on the level of her delicious crack. The outer folds of her pocket hung partly open, and she felt his tongue burrow into her moist interior as it searched for her adorable clitoris. He tongued her a dozen times along the complete length of her luscious slit, each time pausing to caress her clitoris with his lips.

She tossed back her head, and bent her knees to sink further down onto his mouth. She was in raptures of delight as her sensitive clitoris was teased and pinched between his teeth. The water poured in torrents over them, gushing down her parted thighs, between the open lips of her vagina and into his mouth. He was about to insert his fingers into her, when she urged him upwards. She was hot for him. It wasn't his fingers she wanted. When he stood, she grabbed at his prong and guided the tip to the entrance of her grotto. With a sigh of combined greed and lust they took each other.

A fortnight later they were in the same plane flying over the channel, heading for a large isolated field outside Paris. The night was dark as there was little moonlight. The fast-moving clouds were low in the sky, and helped hide them from ground defences. Madeleine fancied she could hear her heart beating above the roar of the engines.

Suddenly the pilot spotted the lone beacon flickering as dimly as a Toc H lamp. Fearful of overshooting, he had Madeleine bundled out before she realised what was happening. Floating down in the cool still night she saw the outline of Jeanne's parachute swimming in the slipstream of the aircraft.

It was the last time she would see her for sometime. She was preparing herself for her landing when she heard the shooting. Her stomach lurched. It could only be the Nazis. Oh God, she was floating down gracefully into the hands of the enemy. She had no more time to think as she hit the ground and rolled over. As she fought to rid herself of the chute, she saw two figures running towards her. She thanked the Lord they weren't in uniform.

She was grabbed, and bundled towards a clump of trees, and all she could think about was the need to hide the chute.

There were half a dozen men hiding in the bushes, and already one was sprawled out dead. She saw two others were forcing open the container that housed her wireless. When they saw it they cursed, and senselessly riddled it with bullets. Whatever it was they were expecting, it certainly wasn't a wireless. A voice shouted instructions for them to get out. She was forced to run betwen two men towards a van, but as they rushed across open ground several shots rang out. Two men dropped wounded. One of the men holding her shot their ambusher. As they scrambled into the van, one man moved to return to the wounded.

'We'll have to leave them,' shouted the voice again. 'Chicot, see to them.'

The tall man, who had shot the gunman, left her side and disappeared into the darkness. She flinched when two shots rang out. The van bumped over rough ground, and in the back it was pitch black. She had no idea where she was, or who these men were. Just about everything had gone wrong.

About twenty minutes later they stopped at an isolated farmhouse, and she was bundled into the big kitchen.

'Search him,' ordered the same voice, 'take anything of value. Then, take him out and shoot him.'

She felt hands searching her heavy overalls, and

heard a grunt of satisfaction when they found her pistol. She thought there was a slight chance they might not kill her if they saw she was a woman. She unstrapped her helmet at the chin, and quickly pulled it off. As the light from the lamp flooded the room, so she shook out her long black hair.

'*Mon Dieu*, a woman . . .'

They questioned her roughly, but she would only say she was a British servicewoman dropped to contact the resistance. They seemed uninterested. She wondered who the hell they were.

'She's no use to us,' announced the man who'd done all the talking. 'Chicot, take her out and get rid of her.'

'No.'

All eyes turned on the man they called Chicot. It was obvious he was the cold-blooded killer of the group. He was a man to be respected or feared: no one argued with him.

'OK, have it your own way. Take her in the other room and look after her. It's you who'll answer to Papa.'

Chicot shrugged, and pushed her through the door into the living room. A fire burnt brightly in the big grate, and the flickering flames lit the room with a soft glow. Chicot was a young man, maybe twenty, who wore a well-cut lounge suit, and a pork pie trilby on the back of his head. He was tall and slim, with muscles like whipcord, but he was different from the ordinary run of men. Mentally, he was retarded; his mind was that of a child of eight. Physically, he was the nearest thing to an albino she had ever seen. His skin was chalk white, his hair colourless, and his eyes an ice-cold blue. He was a young man of phenomenal strength and uncertain temper, with no fear in him.

She unfastened the thick overalls they'd given her

for the drop, and stepped out of them. She revealed herself dressed in a cheap but pretty rayon dress, and as she preened she watched him carefully. She realised he was her only ally, her one chance of survival. She had to have his protection. She took him by the hand, and shyly led him to the big sofa in front of the fire. He sat and watched her, as she combed her long hair and smoothed her dress.

'You're pretty,' he murmured.

It was what she wanted to hear. She sat beside him; and winding her arms around his neck, she kissed him on the lips. He was as unmoved as a rock. His lips didn't part for her tongue, and his body remained rigid. She knew better than to question her own sexual expertise. It was him. He was shy, and completely inexperienced. If he'd had a woman it would have been in a whorehouse. She coquettishly took off his hat, and ran her fingers through his thin silky hair. His cold blue eyes never left her face, and it was difficult to remember there was the mind of a child behind them. She rested her head on his shoulder and cuddled up to him, as an adolescent girl would smooch with her first love.

'Can I be your girl?' she breathed in his ear.

'I don't know. I've never had a girl.'

'Don't you like girls?'

'I like the girls at Madame Liski's.'

She guessed it was a brothel he used in Paris, and she suddenly realised who these men were – they were Parisienne gangsters. It all slotted into place. She wondered what they were doing out here, and who the people were they were fighting.

She moved her hand down into Chicot's lap, where she felt his member standing to attention in his trousers. With teasing fingers she began to undress him. He remained motionless, allowing her to disrobe him. She felt it difficult to concentrate on sexual nuances as she felt more like a mother undressing a child.

Realising her life probably depended on this one fuck, she stood and stripped off her clothes with more finesse than Gypsy Rose Lee had ever achieved. His eyes were still as cold as those of a prowling shark, but he was breathing quickly, and his upright cock was pulsing fit to burst. She ran her fingertips down his shoulders and chest, as she knelt between his legs. She allowed her fingers gently to caress his balls, as she bent forward to tongue his belly with long luscious licks. Sitting back on her haunches, she moved her fingertips seductively down his legs while salaciously kissing the end of his quivering knob with bewitching butterfly kisses.

Hardly pausing, she shifted her position so her soft delectable bubbies hung over his pulsating prong, and then she lowered them so they contacted the tip of his pole. She cupped her ample globes, crushing his agitated staff between their velvet softness.

Her seduction was contrived to be one of continual movement, as she knew a child's mind was stimulated by ever-changing sensations. Returning her mouth to his prick, she sucked sweetly until she felt it swell in her throat. She released it from between her lips as she didn't want him coming yet: she had some way to go. Standing on the sofa, one foot either side of his body, she positioned her open crotch against his face, praying he would want to gorge on her sex, or at least inspect her pussy. She felt him grasp her buttocks and pull her to him, before landing a great slobbery kiss on the lips of her cunt.

Unable to control the game from her precarious

position, she squatted down over his lap until her open quim lips teased the tip of his throbbing weapon. With one long deliberate thrust she impaled herself.

Now, it was his turn. He must roger her as if she was his girl, and not some tart he'd met in a knocking shop. She clasped her hands around his neck, and rocked him, urging him to fall with her from the sofa onto the floor. She was about to admit defeat, when he grabbed her in his arms and rolled forward on top of her onto the threadbare carpet. She held on for dear life; her arms and legs wound around his body, as she moaned and whispered words of love. All the time she squeezed his swollen prick with the walls of her vagina, and answered every thrust he made within her compliant love box.

She was far too nervous to come, but faked an orgasm which moved him to unleash a torrent of sperm inside her. She hugged him closer, and at the zenith of his passion she whispered the fatal words in his ear.

'Am I your girl now?'

'Yes,' he gasped.

'For ever and ever?'

He didn't answer, and she wasn't going to push him. She kissed him fiercely on the lips, and he answered her, but when she felt the pressure from his mouth ease, she rolled from under him. Cajoling him onto his back, she knelt over him, gulping his limp dick in her mouth. Greedily, she licked it free of his sperm and her love juices. He watched her making a great show of swallowing their intermingled fluids, and then she tongued his testicles, his stomach and the inside of his thighs. She prayed she was pleasing him, but she had no way of knowing, as he didn't show his feelings.

That was how the others caught them: her kneeling over him in the act of fellatio. Neither Madeleine nor

Chicot had heard the door open.

'Chicot,' a voice called, 'you bastard. Good for you, my friend.'

'Piss off,' Chicot replied without moving a muscle.

The door closed. When the two of them had dressed, he led her back to the big kitchen.

She tried to question him, but without much success. They had come from Paris, because they'd been told of the drop and believed it was the British dropping arms to the resistance. Such a haul would be invaluable to them. They were staying here until dawn, because of the curfew, and no, he had no idea who had ambushed them. She dared not ask more. In the kitchen, the leader told Chicot that the girl was of no use to them, and they'd decided to kill her. Chicot looked at them without emotion.

'No,' he said.

'What do you mean, Chicot. We say she dies?'

'She's my girl.'

Madeleine heaved a great sigh of relief. She'd succeeded. She was still in with a chance. She heard the man, who'd seen them from the doorway, laugh.

'So the tramp let you screw her. What're you gonna do, marry the whore?'

Chicot moved like lightning. His slim powerful body sprang towards the man, and hit him a perfectly timed blow on the jaw. It was like watching a tightly coiled spring unwind. The man staggered like a felled ox. As he did so, she saw another man reach towards his inside pocket, but before she could shout a warning a gun had appeared in Chicot's hand as if by magic. She had seen the Beretta nestling in the shoulder holster when she undressed him, and was certainly glad he was wearing it.

'That's enough,' snapped the leader, 'if you want to

take her with you, that's your affair. But you answer to Papa when we get to Paris.'

Chicot nodded, and she gripped his arm tightly.

Jeanne landed in the middle of the confusion. Several men seized her as she hit the ground, and the chute and harness were ripped from her.

'Where's the rest of the drop?' they screamed at her.

She had no idea what they meant, and the bullets flying about added to the mayhem. She could make out more than a dozen men advancing towards a small copse at the edge of the field. It was where the fighting was taking place. She was dragged along with them, but when they arrived the enemy had fled.

She watched the men picking up their wounded, and searching the enemy dead. She was marched to an old rambling farmhouse where they hid in the cellars. Soon the Nazis arrived to search the area, no doubt attracted by the shooting. Not a word was spoken until they left. She wondered who the two feuding groups were, and who held her prisoner. What a cock-up, she thought. All that training to land in the middle of a private war. She wondered who was responsible.

Dawn had broken when they all sat around the big kitchen table, and were given bread and wine. The men had been surprised to find she was female, and although they were civil it was very obvious they had no need of her.

'What shall we do with her?'

'Sell her to a brothel. Rich Parisiennes would pay well for tits like hers.'

They all looked at her, and laughed dirtily.

'Who are you?' she asked.

'Who were you expecting?'

'The resistance.'

'We are the comrades of the resistance.'

'Then you were expecting me. Why are you treating me as a prisoner?'

'We are members of the communist party. We were expecting a consignment of arms to be dropped.'

'London didn't tell you that, did they?'

'No, we heard it elsewhere.'

'You heard it wrong. My friend and I were to be taken to the Paris resistance.'

'Your friend will be taken to Paris, but not to the resistance. She is in the hands of thieves and gangsters.'

'And me? What is going to happen to me?'

'Your case will go before the committee.'

By mid morning all the men had gone. A lorry had arrived to take them back to their work in the factories of Paris. Jeanne was locked in an outhouse with little more than a bed of straw.

It was late afternoon when the lorry returned, and she caught sight of the driver's face. It was Roland. Her heart lurched. She knew Roland from her Sorbonne days. He had been in the same year as Pierre. They had been compatriots in left-wing politics, and she'd hated him as much as she'd loved Pierre. Roland had pursued her relentlessly. He had taken every opportunity to touch her, proposition her, leer up her skirt or down her blouse. He lusted after her, and he made it plain, yet Pierre had never really believed her. Now, she was in his hands. He could tell her captors who she was, but she knew what he'd demand in return.

'Roland,' she called from the barred window.

'Great heavens, Jeanne. What are you doing here?'

She waited while he got the key to her prison, and

when he returned he brought a bottle of wine with him. She outlined her life since the death of Pierre, while he listened intently. She knew his lust for her hadn't changed, for he sat close to her and touched her at every opportunity.

'Will you tell them who I am?'

'Of course I will, Jeanne,' he leered at her, 'I don't want you hurt in any way.'

'But you have a condition?'

'You know I have, and you know what it is?'

'Yes,' she sighed, 'and I agree. You've always made it clear you wanted me.'

'Now, it's different. I want you to want me.'

'I don't understand?'

'I want to be lusted after by you. I want you to screw me,' he babbled, 'and I want you to talk dirty to me while you do it.'

She could have hit him. She'd always detested the little creep, and now she had to treat him as if he were her grand passion. She just couldn't bring herself to do it. Then, she remembered Holmsley Manor and the comtesse, and she became calm and collected. Hadn't she been trained for this very situation? He thought he was humiliating her by forcing her to take the initiative, but in reality he was giving her control. She literally tore the shirt off his back, and ripped the fly buttons from his trousers in a demented frenzy of exaggerated passion.

'I want you, Roland,' she breathed, 'I want you to screw me. I want you to fuck me till it hurts.'

She ripped down his trousers, and saw her sudden action had taken him unawares. He seemed nervous of her. It was as if the gentle purring cat had turned into a tigress. She clawed at the hair on his naked chest, and bit deep into his shoulders. He drew back in pained

221

surprise at the impact of her sharp teeth into his flesh, and cried out in anguish. She had drawn blood.

She stood back from him, and stripped off her sweater to reveal her huge delectable breasts. They hung unblemished, like two magnificent ripe pumpkins in a greengrocer's window. The twin globes trembled like white blancmange as she shook them before his bedazzled eyes. She let her skirt fall to her feet, before she slipped her thumbs inside her knickers and slowly eased them down onto her hips. She watched his eyes staring at the beguiling tangle of soft thatch that peeped above the cotton material.

'Do you want to see my sweet pussy?'

With a delicate flip of her fingers she divested herself of that last piece of clothing as she stepped daintily out of her knickers to pounce on him again. She took his head between her palms, and pulled his face towards her resplendent boobs. She pushed his face firmly into the soft warm flesh, and rocked her body so those delicious melons rubbed delightfully against his cheeks.

'Pussy's shy. She's hiding from you.'

She pulled away from him, still holding his head between her palms, and then she kissed him. It was a long wet kiss, during which her tongue probed the back of his throat. She drew away.

'Pussy wants you to play with her,' she crooned.

She pushed him back onto the bed of straw, and knelt over him. Her open crotch was above his face, and he was staring up into her.

'Isn't she cute, don't you want to kiss her?'

She crushed her quim down onto his face, grinding her hot crotch into his nose and face. She felt him open his mouth to devour her, and knew the exertions had made her wet. He sucked the moisture from her. His nose was stuck between the folds of her twat, and he was pulling at her inner lips with his teeth. Her tone changed.

'Suck me,' she demanded breathlessly, 'lick my cunt. Taste my sex.'

She raised her thighs a little, so he could tongue her whole quim and the muff of pubic hair that surrounded that delectable playground.

'Oh, Roland,' she gasped. 'Haven't you always wanted to kiss me there? Haven't you thirsted for my love juices?'

She felt his lips discover her erect clitoris, and fondle and tease it until erotic palpitations seemed to engulf her whole body. Suddenly, his hands slipped beneath her thighs, and his fingers pulled the folds of her slit so far apart that he could look right up into her glistening red tunnel.

'Now,' she screamed, 'fuck me now.'

She slid down his body in one smooth movement, and took his prick in her mouth before he realised what was happening. His staff was rock hard, and ready for action. She sucked it into her mouth twice and felt his body tremble.

'It's ready for me, isn't it?' she purred. 'It wants to poke me, doesn't it?'

She squatted on her haunches above his thighs. Her quim lips were directly above his quivering pole, and she lowered herself just enough to touch him. The effect was electric. She could feel his need to be inside her.

'You've dreamed of this moment, haven't you Roland?' she crooned. 'Say you want to screw me. Tell me you'd rather be inside me than any other woman in the world?'

He let out a low moan, and raised his thighs in an

effort to penetrate her. She teased him, holding the tip of his cock between the folds of her fig.

'If you want me,' she murmured sweetly, 'you'll have to take me.'

He pushed her backwards, so she rolled laughing onto her back with her legs high in the air. Impatiently, he pounced upon her, pinning her shoulders to the straw pallet, and searching for the entrance to her love grotto. She knew she was wet and relaxed to receive him, and he was quickly rooted within her.

'Now come,' she urged, 'shoot your load inside me. I want your spunk. Come.'

She squeezed his hips with her legs, and moved her buttocks in rhythm with the cock driving inside her. Gradually, she brought him to a climax. It had taken longer than she'd wanted, and she knew he'd been deliberately holding back. She felt his semen squirt into her, and she rolled from under him.

'Now, take me to the committee, and tell them who I am.'

'They'll probably want you to stay with us.'

'I might as well. I've no way of finding what happened to my friend.'

'Then I can see you again?'

'Why not?' she said, but she thought differently.

The committee members were surprised when Roland told them who she was. Pierre was something of a martyr to them. He had been murdered for his political principles, and they were more than pleased to welcome his girlfriend among them. She decided she would stay with the group until she had the opportunity to look for Madeleine. After all, she would be fighting Nazis.

★　★　★

In Paris, Madeleine was taken by Chicot to see Papa. Papa was a man nearing sixty, who looked much older. His deeply lined face, hooded grey eyes and bald head gave him the look of an old pirate, which about summed him up. He had mellowed with age, however, and thought the world of Chicot, as she was about to discover.

He dismissed Chicot, and turned to her.

'Chicot tells me you're his girl?'

'That's right.'

'Are you?'

'Yes.'

'You mean that truly? I won't have him hurt.'

'I wouldn't hurt him.'

'If you're lying I'll have you flogged.'

He asked her about herself, and she told him of her life in Belgium and how she'd escaped to England. He asked her why she was in France, and she told him she was an agent hoping to contact the resistance.

'There is no resistance, only small bands of amateurs.'

'I was sent to meet the man who is to knit them into one combined force.'

'Who is that?'

'I know him as St Pannes.'

'Pannes is a rogue. It was he who told me the British were making an arms drop.'

'Why would he do that?'

'Money. I gave him a lot of francs.'

'I must warn London he's an imposter, but I have no wireless. Your men destroyed it in temper.'

'I can get you the use of a wireless, and an operator,' he said. When you have sent your message, you must kill Pannes. How were you to contact him?'

'Through a woman whose address I have.'

'Chicot will go with you, and when you've killed the rogue I will search for a man to lead the resistance.'

'Why should you help me?'

'Because I hate the Bosche, and you are Chicot's woman.'

'You love Chicot, don't you?'

'He is my son.'

'Then why can't the two of you lead the resistance?'

'I am an outlaw, a gangster. The people of Paris wouldn't trust me. Why should they?'

Three days later RSS Maldon monitored a message with the call signs corresponding to British SIS. No one was able to decode it until it reached the director. On receipt of it he immediately phoned Lord C. to inform him St Pannes was an imposter and a rogue, who had been killed.

Madeleine had done all she could. Now, she could only stay with Chicot, and try to persuade Papa to take up arms against the Nazis. She grieved for Jeanne, who she felt certain must have been killed.

Marseilles

The siren had already gone, and there would be no more trains out of London that night. Jacqui hurried off the station concourse on the arm of the man she'd been with all day. He had had to come to London on business, and she'd accompanied him for a day out.

They stumbled down the maze of back streets bordering the railway yards. Whole blocks of houses were in ruins from the bombing.

She could hear the malevolent uneven drone of the Heinkels and the Dorniers above. Searchlights stabbed upwards, sweeping the sky in search of a target. One caught a plane in its beam, and others swept towards the aircraft like spiders to a fly. The grunt of anti-aircraft fire drowned the noise of the bombers, and suddenly the sky was illuminated by chandeliers of flares that hung in the air like brilliant fireflies.

No sooner had the flares died down than the bombs began. Jacqui and her companion began to run. A series of blinding flashes accompanied by claps of thunder sounded very close. The two of them fell to the ground against the wall of a Methodist chapel. She buried her head in her arms, and felt his body covering hers.

A few days ago Lord C. had informed her that she had been chosen to help this man on a mission. He was to be dispatched to Vichy France and Marseilles, where he would endeavour to set up an anti-Nazi movement. Churchill was certain that the Nazis would occupy Vichy sooner or later, and he wanted to be ready for them.

The man had been introduced as Michael Mallson, an American working in Britain, who had been a successful spy in the Spanish Civil War. Jacqui had taken an immediate liking to him. Dressed in an old sports coat and baggy flannels, he reminded her of an old journalist flame she knew in New York. She felt his hand creep beneath her, and cup her breast over her heavy overcoat. She suddenly remembered he'd told her he had a strange desire to make love during an air raid. The feeling had apparently swept over him during a raid on Madrid, and it had never been satisfied.

A mighty crash shook the buildings around them, and bits of brick flew everywhere. She felt the ground shake below her, as if it would open and swallow them. The hot wind of blast wailed above them, and dust filled the air.

'It's no night to be outside,' he yelled, pulling her to her feet. 'Let's find a shelter. There should be Andersons behind some of these houses.'

She stumbled after him through the terrible red glow. The ground was uneven and covered with rubble. When she caught up she found him kneeling by the entrance of a deserted Anderson.

'I'll go down first. These things can get flooded.'

He disappeared from view. She saw the shelter was in the small back garden of someone's bombed-out house. She waited for a while, sweating like a pig under her heavy overcoat. Then she climbed down into the small rectangular pit.

The ceiling was formed by curved corrugated iron sheets covered with earth. The owners had put duck-boards on the floor, and covered them with old carpeting. She saw the outline of an upright kitchen chair. She laughed aloud, and perhaps a trifle hysteri-cally.

She felt his arms go around her, and he gently rocked her. She regained control of herself, and as he unfast-ened the buttons of her coat she became aware she was unbelievably horny. She knew, intuitively, he was feeling that way too. The danger and terror and proximity to death accelerated the adrenalin, and when it was over the sheer relief at having survived was an even greater elation. It gave way to an incredible heightening of sexual awareness. A real lust pounded through her veins.

She felt him sit on the chair, and pull her towards him. He fumbled to bare himself while she wriggled her skirt up beneath her overcoat. Lustily, she strad-dled his lap, as he kissed her with an animal passion and his tongue searched deep into her mouth. Urgent-ly, she pushed aside the crotch of her camiknickers, and guided his prick to the entrance of her anxious tube. He grasped her shoulders, and roughly pulled her down onto him. She howled, as his swollen John Thomas penetrated deep into her sticky honey-pot. It was a moment of pure sensual joy.

The ground shook like an earthquake when a bomb blew apart the very foundations of the nearby chapel, but they were oblivious to anything except each other. Such was the depth of their sensuality that they fought each other to orgasm to relieve the tension within themselves. Their howls came in unison, as they climaxed as one.

He hugged her body like a great bear, and she

gripped his pego with the walls of her palpitating quim. She gasped. His ejaculation was like an explosion; never had she experienced such lust so quickly satisfied.

He found a single bunk covered by a damp hair mattress. They covered it with their coats, and stretched out. The bombing had moved to the other side of the river. She slithered over him to face his feet, and took his long tool in her mouth. She wanted him again.

The first time had slaked her lust: but now, she wanted a long lingering coupling to rid her of the terrible itch she felt for him. The raid still continued, and the second wave of planes were droning overhead.

She straddled her legs over his head, and hoisting her skirts sat on his face. Then, leaning forward over him, she took his weapon into her mouth. They sucked at each other's sex, as greedily as piglets at a sow's teats. Within minutes they were both aroused to a pitch where they had to copulate again.

He bade her put her coat on, and she watched him throw the mattress onto the parapet of the shelter. He guided her to the exit, where the mattress covered the bare earth. She thought he was about to help her out of the shelter, when she realised what he had in mind. If she leaned forward over the mattress he could take her from behind, and they could both peer out into the night sky above. She yanked her coat and skirt up over her buttocks, and stretched her body over the mattress so that her head and shoulders were out in the cool night air. Finally, she felt his warm flesh against the bare skin of her bottom. She moaned, as he parted the wet folds of her impatient slit in readiness to impale her. He drove his iron weapon into her slippery passage centimere by centimetre, holding back the speed of his penetration to tease her into thrusting back onto him.

When he was rooted deep within her, she pushed back onto him. He fucked her with slow stimulating strokes, using the full length of his prong for each and every stroke. His hands cupped her gorgeous boobs, as he kissed her neck and shoulders and hair.

The third wave of bombers had come and gone, and the raid now seemed to be centred over the docks. The two of them gazed up silently into the terror of the night, and she was glad she was giving him the fuck he'd craved during an air raid. She wondered whether he had deliberately made them miss the last train for that very reason.

The long slow strokes of his cock made her purr like a kitten, but when they changed to quick driving thrusts she began to snarl like a she-cat. He squeezed her tits, and screamed into the night as he came inside her.

It wasn't a perfect ending, as she hadn't orgasmed. Perhaps it was her own fault for looking into the night sky, and wondering about the people who had been killed and injured while they'd made love. Anyway, Lord C. would be pleased. He had instructed her to get to know Michael Mallson, and she'd certainly done that.

Plans changed when the director had correlated the information he had gathered from the Marseilles area. He told Lord C. that the most influential man by far was the Duke de Nicolanne. He owned great tracts of land on the riviera outside the city, including many villages. He held sway over hundreds of countryfolk, and had connections in the towns through business and commerce. It was understood he was a popular man, who would be the perfect figurehead for any resistance organisation.

Lord C. knew the duke, the two men having met in

brothels and gaming houses between the wars. The duke had been more secretive about his sexual adventures, and didn't have the reputation of Lord C. However, Lord C. knew him for what he was: a lecher and a libertine. He also knew that the one woman capable of enlisting his aid was the Comtesse de Beccelonne.

It was decided that Tanya and Jacqui would proceed immediately to the south of France, via Switzerland. The cover story to be that they had been residing in Geneva since the outbreak of war; and rather than return to occupied France they had decided to live in Vichy. Jacqui would travel as secretary-companion, and would supervise the small chateau the comtesse would lease on the riviera. Tanya would introduce herself to the duke, and if she could persuade him to lend his aid to forming a resistance group, Michael Mallson would be sent to organise it.

Tanya wasn't keen to leave England, but if she must, she couldn't better the riviera. A week later the two women were flown to Zurich, via Stockholm. They stayed at Geneva for a month to perfect their cover story, and travelled on by train to Marseilles.

A few days later they found a country house for lease on the duke's estates. Little more than a week passed before Tanya was invited to take coffee with him.

When she arrived she found the local police chief had chosen the same morning to visit the duke. They talked trivialities, and when the police chief rose to go he offered Tanya a lift. She had no reason to refuse, and the duke didn't attempt to detain her.

She was a bit frustrated, but there would be other opportunities. From the moment she'd arrived the duke had watched her closely, and there was a strangeness about his scrutiny which she couldn't interpret. It was as if he knew her, and she had a strange feeling she had seen him before.

He was an old man of over seventy, with a mop of untidy white hair that hung lankly onto his shoulders. His thin frame was bent at the shoulders, and his nose was hooked in the shape of a beak. She was reminded of a huge vulture hovering over its prey.

He shook her hand with cold arthritic fingers, and invited her to dine with him later in the week. The police chief drove her in his big official Mercedes to a nearby medieval castle, where he stopped and offered to show her around. She had little interest in that direction, but he was striding up the hill before she could refuse. He appeared to be something of a historian, as he babbled on endlessly. She paid him scant attention, until he stopped at the foot of a flight of stone steps leading to a balcony.

'Let me show you something interesting,' he said, 'which I learned myself only recently.'

He took her hand, and led her up the stone steps to a small balcony overlooking the courtyard, where workmen were busy preparing for a local festival. The balcony was only big enough for one to stand comfortably, and was solid masonry up to waist level.

'This was built in the fifteenth century by a particularly egotistical nobleman, who loved to stand and preen before his serfs. You can see nothing strange about it, can you?'

'No,' she replied without interest.

He slid back a stone below the balcony to reveal a space big enough to house one small person.

'If you step inside you will see narrow steps leading up to the balcony,' he explained. 'You will find you can slide back a part of the stone floor of the balcony, enough to wriggle your body through.'

'For what reason?' she asked. 'It appears pointless, doesn't it? Why bother to have secret steps coming up into a balcony?'

'Depending upon the nobleman's taste,' he continued, 'a young girl or boy was hidden under the balcony, and when the nobleman was speaking or preening before the adoring crowds, so she or he would pop up between the great man's legs.'

'To what purpose?' she asked innocently.

'To pleasure him.' He grinned. 'I suppose he felt enormous power looking down on his people, and to be brought to sexual climax at that time would add spice to the occasion.'

She said nothing, but she knew the man was sexually excited. She had an uneasy feeling he was leading her in a direction she wouldn't want to go. If he thought she was going to squeeze into that space, and play with his balls, he was sadly mistaken.

'I know why you're here,' he said quietly.

Her heart missed a beat. How could he? She fought to keep her voice even.

'Why?'

'To supply the duke with an endless stream of young women.'

'I've no idea what you're talking about,' she answered coolly, but inwardly she heaved a sigh of relief.

'I've known for sometime that he employs young women at inflated wages, and expects them to meet his sexual demands.'

'What makes you think I'm his pimp?' she asked angrily.

He shrugged his shoulders, and climbed onto the balcony to gaze down onto the busy scene below.

'Don't worry, your secret's safe with me,' he drawled complacently.

She saw there was no point in arguing, especially as he was a man to keep on the right side of. She realised he might be very useful in the future, so if he wanted a blow-job she would be wise to oblige him. She wriggled into the space below the balcony and pushed open the ceiling, so she could mount the narrow steps. She rose like a phoenix from the floor of the balcony, until her head was just below the parapet on the level of his crotch. She knocked her head on the masonry, as she reached up under his uniform jacket with both hands to heave down his trousers. He hung on desperately, but she soon had them around his ankles. She knew he wanted her to extract John Thomas through his fly, as he would feel vulnerable with his trousers down, but he couldn't have it all his own way.

She lifted his lifeless chopper with one hand, and began to fondle his testicles with the other. His prick remained limp. She allowed her fingers to creep between his legs, and explore the cleft of his arse. His member still hung soft and lifeless. She rubbed his anus with her index finger, inserting the tip into his anal channel. As she stabbed at his sphincter, so his pestle jerked into life. She started to massage the inert member until the blood began to pump, and it swelled to working proportions. Satisfied it was stiff enough to suck, she popped it into her mouth.

He stood smiling at the crowd, waving to anybody who looked up, while she commenced to gam him. It wasn't easy. She was standing in a space too small for a grown woman, and she couldn't draw her head back without banging it on the masonry. She was forced to hold his hips to control his movements, to ensure his prick moved in and out of her mouth without choking her.

She fondled the helmet between her luscious lips,

but as he became aroused he tried to force his whole cock down her throat. There was no escape. She gobbled his whole tool into her mouth, and sucked for dear life. By expert use of her tongue and teeth, she manipulated him towards orgasm.

From the corner of her eye, she could see his fists tightening on the parapet. His body trembled. She sucked like a dream, and prepared to feel the rush of his spunk into her throat, but instead he withdrew and ejaculated all over her pretty face. She shut her eyes as the warm globlets of sperm spattered over her cheeks, nose and forehead. She would rather have swallowed it. He squatted down on his haunches, and rubbed his semen into her face with apparent glee. When he had completed his task, she sucked each of his fingertips in turn. It was a small enough price to pay to ensure he was on their side.

'Play your cards right,' she whispered sexily, 'and one day I might show you my birthmark!'

It was exactly a week later that the duke held his dinner party. Tanya was accompanied by Jacqui, and found the police chief, the local mayor and the Nazi representative for the district had also been invited. The final place at the table was taken by the duke's housekeeper, a stern-looking woman dressed in black. The meal went well, and if there were any food shortages in Vichy they certainly hadn't reached the duke's kitchen. Tanya and Jacqui enjoyed the spread, but their companions certainly weren't the ones they would have chosen.

The meal over, the duke suggested they have coffee at the table. A pleasant young waitress served them. She was a well-built girl with the bloom of youth and healthy country living on her cheeks. It was when she served Jacqui that the accident happened. Hot coffee poured onto Jacqui's bare shoulder, and spilt onto her gown. She shrieked in pained surprise. Tanya and the mayor went to help, and the housekeeper beckoned another maid to take Jacqui to the bathroom.

'The girl will be punished,' said the duke.

'No, please. It was an accident,' pleaded Jacqui as she was escorted from the room. The duke waited until the door had closed behind her.

'See she's punished,' he snapped at his housekeeper.

The woman disappeared with the guilty maid into the adjoining room.

'What will happen to her?' asked the mayor.

'She will be beaten,' replied the duke.

'Soundly, I trust?' leered the Nazi.

'Certainly, but don't take my word for it. See for yourself.'

The duke crossed the room, and pressed a button in the wall. The long mirror covering that wall became transparent, and they could look into the adjoining room. The girl was being fastened over a tall stool. It resembled a bar stool, and had rungs all the way up.

Her ankles and wrists had been secured to the rungs on either side of the stool, and her stomach was pressed to the seat. It left her backside well positioned to receive punishment. The girl's knickers had been removed, and the housekeeper flipped up the skirt of the flimsy uniform.

Tanya glanced at the faces of the four men. They were all watching enthralled.

She saw the housekeeper take up a long leather strap that must have been three feet in length. The woman swung it casually several times before flailing it across the young girl's bare arse. The girl's head jerked upwards, her long hair flew loose about her face, and her mouth opened to emit a piercing scream. It was a soundless picture, and it was strange to watch the girl's contortions without hearing the sound of leather on bare flesh, or the squeal which accompanied it.

Every time the strap landed full across the girl's prettily curved bum, her white skin was striped red. The hidden audience were able to see the plump fleshy buttocks quiver under each stroke, and watch the pink hue deepen.

Tanya stole another glance at the four men, as the young girl's bottom suffered under the strap. The duke's eyes shone the brightest, followed by the Nazi's and the police chief's. Only the mayor seemed uneasy, although his eyes were firmly fixed on the girl's squirming derrière.

The three men left after the thrashing ended. When they had gone, the duke turned to Tanya and Jacqui.

'Why are you ladies here?' he asked.

'I explained we have been living in Switzerland and . . .'

'No,' interrupted the duke, 'I am well aware the Comtesse de Beccelonne has lived in London for many years.'

'You know of me?' asked a surprised Tanya.

'We'll come to that later. What are you doing here, and what do you want of me?'

'We understand you are a patriot who hates Adolf Hitler's Third Reich. Is that correct?'

'That is so, but we are not threatened here in Vichy.'

'Not at present, but you know it's only a matter of time before the Nazis decide to occupy this part of France.'

'I know,' he said sadly.

'We are here to organise an anti-Nazi group, so we are ready when they come.'

'A secret resistance army?'

'Yes,' replied Tanya, 'and we need your help.'

'I'm an old man. How can I help?'

'Your word that you are supporting us will be sufficient to get most of your people to be sympathetic to our cause.'

'I'll visit you tomorrow, and give you my answer,' he replied. 'It's so unlike the British to plan ahead. They really are taking the war seriously.'

'An American suggested it,' said Jacqui.

'I'm not surprised,' he chuckled.

True to his word the duke arrived at Tanya's home the following afternoon. Away from his own environment he looked frailer than ever.

'I agree to help you all I can,' he announced, 'but there is a proviso. I am a cynical old man, and patriotism is no longer everything.'

'What is it you want of us?' asked Tanya.

'You, my dear.'

She wasn't surprised. Lord C. had told her the duke was an old libertine, and hinted he would ask for her favours.

'I shall be honoured,' she smiled.

'You don't remember me, do you?'

'Should I?'

'Cast your mind back to Paris in 1921, to the Coco Club.'

'Where I was a hostess, and a singer.'

'You refused my request, even though I offered you a fortune.'

'My God,' she exclaimed. 'You're the man who wanted my arse.'

'And I still want it.'

'Is that the condition?' she asked softly.

'It is.'

239

She recalled the incident now. She should have recognised him. She had slept with him when she was drunk, and the next night he'd wanted to bugger her. She'd refused, and he'd offered a fabulous amount of money. The other girls had said she was crazy, that he could have driven a train up their arse for a sum like that.

She remembered telling George the story. She had no idea he knew the duke. No wonder George had insisted she was the one to tempt him. He would guess the old goat would still want her arse, the arse that had escaped him all those years ago.

When Tanya arrived at the château two days later, everything had been prepared for her sodomisation. She was stripped by the housekeeper, and taken to the enema room. It was like a large bathroom, but furnished with little else other than a shower and a deep sink. The walls and floor were tiled, and the instruments of ritual enema were laid out on wall shelves.

The housekeeper bade her mount a chair with stirrups, and she was given an enema. The duke appeared as she was squatting over an open toilet, straining to rid her bowels of the last of the soapy water. He sat down in the viewing room, and watched intently as she was given a second enema.

She felt the housekeeper position her to the duke's satisfaction, and then she relaxed. The water gushed from her arsehole and she heard the duke clap his appreciation. She had to discharge the remainder of the water from her bowels in short sharp bursts. The relief from expelling it gave her a certain satisfaction.

After the duke left, she was dried and perfumed by the housekeeper. She was instructed to prepare herself for the duke's pleasure, and was led into a room where a dress was laid out for her. It looked vaguely familiar. She realised it was a replica of the dress she used to wear all those years ago at the Coco Club. She dressed in it, and pirouetted before a long mirror. The short flared skirt circled her. She laughed. It took her back to the memories of her youth. She put on the high heeled shoes left for her, and smoothed down the dress.

After the initial impact of sharply defined memories from her past, she recalled how hard life had been at that time. She saw what an impression she must have made on the duke. In a few hours they had been together he must have become infatuated with her. She now knew she had to satisfy the lecherous old sod, so when he entered the room she paraded for him, showing herself off in the dress he had remembered so well.

'I'm sorry for what I did all those years ago,' she said, 'I should never have refused you. If only I'd known how much you desired my bottom, I would have bent over for you.'

'Would you?'

'I'm sure I would. I wasn't an uncaring young girl.'

'You were beautiful. I wanted to possess you totally. I asked entrance to your forbidden place, and you refused me. The more I offered, the more adamant you became.'

'I was mistaken. I should have known you genuinely desired me. I was blind. I thought you only wanted to degrade me.'

'Perhaps I did,' he sighed. 'It's a long time ago, but the memory lingers.'

'And now you have me.'

'Yes, I have. And I shall satisfy my lust on you, but it cannot be the same.'

'It can. It must,' she cried. 'Come, my bottom is as

you remember. Perhaps more curvaceous, more seductive. It is yours, to do with what you wish. Isn't that what you've dreamed of all these years?'

'Unfortunately those days have long one. I'm impotent.'

Oh Christ, she thought. All that talk for nothing. Still, if he couldn't screw her, he obviously had something in mind, probably something in the shape of a dildo.

He commanded her to kneel on the bench before him, and she felt her skirt whipped up to expose her most private parts. She lowered her head, so that her forehead rested on the plush surface of the bench. She had her naked butt raised high for his attention. He leaned forward, and placed his lips against the circle of her anus, and kissed the adorable puckered little hole.

He licked and nibbled at the rim that circled the opening into her secret rear orifice. She could feel his tongue probing at her tightly guarded anus with little stabs, as he began to suck avidly at her opening as if to gain entrance for his darting tongue. She moaned and whimpered erotically to encourage him, as he slobbered over her keister. It tickled, but it did little else for her.

She felt him begin to finger her. He had oiled his hand, and his index finger was poised to penetrate her sphincter. The tight ring of muscles surrendered without a fight, as his greased digit entered into her anal channel. She gasped. It was a dainty sigh, and it seemed to excite him.

He massaged the walls just inside the entrance of her anus with his greasy fingers, probing deep inside her. She felt him thrust and jab, but accepted everything until at last the duke withdrew in exhaustion.

* * *

The next day Tanya and Jacqui sent word to London that they were ready to go ahead. A week later Michael Mallson arrived.

Jacqui was sleeping by the pool when Mallson saw her. It was a warm autumn day, and he'd walked the dusty road from the village. He stripped off his clothes, and dived in. A couple of lazy strokes took him to the other side, and he turned on his back to float quietly in the sunshine.

'Hi,' he called.

Jacqui opened her eyes. She had been expecting him, but not naked in the pool. The blood rushed to her head. It had been so boring waiting for him to arrive. She whipped off her two-piece, and dived in towards him. He gripped her when she surfaced, and they kissed hungrily. It was a long passionate embrace, which stiffened his wand so that it pressed against her belly. She reached down with a laugh, and took it in her hand as if it was a basking trout.

Together they coupled beneath the water.

A few days later, Michael, Tanya and Jacqui called at the château to speak to the duke. The comtesse suggested Michael be given some sort of official post supervising his vast estates, and the duke agreed. He was an old man, and he didn't need the hassle, but he was a patriot and proud to be helping. He would give them everything they wanted.

Washington

It was early November, and the director had travelled down to Holmsley Manor for the weekend. He sat down to dinner with Lord C., Christine and Sylvia, who were the only girls left at the manor. The main course had been rabbit pie, which had gone down really well, and they sat talking over a glass of port.

'I have no immediate mission for either of you girls, but I do have a hunch I'd like to play,' said the director.

'Let's hear it,' grunted Lord C. 'Anything to get these last two off my hands.'

'Now, that's not true,' interrupted Sylvia, 'I don't know what he'll do when we've gone.'

'This is only an assignment for one,' explained the director, 'so poor George will still have one of you to see him through the long winter nights.'

'Never mind me,' growled Lord C. 'Let's hear the gen.'

'The one thing that Churchill wants above all others is the support of the USA. Anything to move the Americans along that road would be fine by him.

'I can't imagine how we can help there.'

'Christine is a well-known tennis player with the opportunity to mix freely with society over there,' said the director. 'Not only could she give us the prevailing opinions of politicians, but there is a possibility she could alter them.'

'How?' queried Christine unbelievingly.

'At present the USA is divided into the pro-British, who want to help us all they can, and isolationists who want to be seen to be strictly neutral. Many of them are borderline, and their allegiance could be easily swayed.'

'By sex, you mean?' suggested Sylvia.

'Possibly.'

'It's too big a job. It would take an army of *femmes fatales* to make any impression,' grunted Lord C.

'It's only a hunch,' answered the director. 'I want to send over one girl to test the temperature of the water. If nothing comes of it, no matter.'

'OK,' cried Christine, 'when do I go?'

Sylvia was rather quiet for the remainder of the evening, during which the brandy flowed freely. It was after midnight when the director retired, and he was climbing into his pyjamas when there came a gentle knock at the door. It was Sylvia.

'Can I come in?' she whispered.

He opened the door. She was dressed in a powder-blue silk nightdress, and her blonde hair was loose about her shoulders. She smiled at him saucily.

'When was the last time you had a young lady in your bedroom?'

She knew the director was unmarried, and a bit of a fuddy duddy in his personal life, but she'd seen him popping her whenever he thought she wasn't looking. He wasn't exactly a lecherous old devil, but she was certain he wouldn't turn down an opportunity if it arose.

He was a tall man; she reached up, and put her arms around his neck.

245

'I want to go to America,' she pouted.

'Why?'

'I've always wanted to. Ever since I was a little girl.'

'You're still a little girl.'

'Have you seen my tits lately?'

He laughed. If she wanted to go, there was no reason why she shouldn't. If anything came up in Europe, she could be recalled.

'All right, you can go.'

'Just like that. Don't you want anything in return?'

He didn't reply. Not because he wasn't that sort of man; he was just plain tongue-tied. His experience of young women was strictly during working hours.

'Tell me if you want me to go back to my own room,' she crooned.

She reached up on tiptoe, and kissed him full on the mouth. His whole body stiffened. She wondered whether it was shyness, fright or just old age.

She gave him a moment to relax before she inserted her small pink tongue between his lips. As her lithe tongue explored his mouth, she rubbed her lovely young body against his bony frame. Within minutes she had him breathing heavily.

Falling to her knees she unfastened the cord of his pyjamas. As they slipped down his thin legs, so she covered his half-aroused penis with her sensuous red lips. She heard a gurgling rattle gather in the back of his throat, as she ran her cute lips down the whole shaft, while sucking so sweetly he would have willingly died at that moment. Other than bordello women, only one young female had ever granted him fellatio, and she had insisted on bathing him in antiseptic first. She pushed him backwards, so he sat down on the edge of the bed. She didn't want the old boy collapsing on the floor. He didn't appear in very good shape, although his prong was hard and straight between her open lips. She fondled and caressed it daintily with her sensual tongue, until he grasped her head between his hands. She realised he was nearing climax, but didn't want him coming until she'd given him a decent fuck.

In spite of all his influence and power, she bet he hadn't been inside a woman for a very long time.

She jerked herself upright, and allowed her nightdress to fall to the floor. She stood naked before him. After admiring her nakedness for several minutes, he reached up his bony fingers to touch her softly rounded breasts. She let him knead their malleable plumpness, and squeeze her two pertly erect nipples while his eyes glazed over with memories. In fact he'd been transported to another dimension, where he could look down at himself being pleasured by this adorable young woman. She urged him to lie on the bed, and mounted him.

His upright tool slipped easily between the open lips of her willing orifice. It was as if they were an old married couple. She rode him with a quiet respect, as if he was that old faithful heading for the last round up. He reached up and, taking her shoulders, pulled her down onto him. He held her closely, and when she tried to wag her tail, he clasped her firm young buttocks until she was still.

They lay motionless for an age, his pego buried in her warm inviting cavern. Instinctively, she knew she had made him unbelievably content, and she loved herself for it. She kissed him tenderly.

Christine remained downstairs with Lord C. She poured them both another brandy, and when she'd finished her glass she was quite tipsy. She had reached a stage where most drunks wanted to sing, but Christine didn't sing, she showed off. She had always been the most dreadful exhibitionist.

'I'm going to masturbate,' she announced gaily. 'Do you want to watch?'

'I'd love to,' the colonel smiled.

She took his hand and led him to her bedroom, where she stripped awkwardly to a honky tonk gramophone record. Yet, whatever way she took her clothes off, the result was magnificent. When she drew herself up to her full height she was like an amazon, but with two perfectly noble breasts.

She sat at her dressing table rubbing cold cream into those gorgeous bubbies, as Lord C. watched her reflection in the mirror. To finish, she outlined each pert nipple with lipstick to make them appear a bright carmine red.

By her side she had placed a bowl of warm water, and swinging around she spread her legs, and began soaping her crotch with tantalising little motions of her slim fingers. She paused long enough for him to admire her wet bush, its soapy pubic hair sticking in bunches to the damp skin. The pink lips of her luscious slit hung partly open, and gave the appearance of a conch surrounded by seaweed.

He watched her take a hairdrier, and play the warm current of air onto her soaking muff. The soft hair began to dry, and to curl, and soon her dainty muff was dancing like grass in the wind.

She lay on the bed to masturbate. Her agile fingertips caressed the length of the outer folds of her vagina, occasionally darting inside to titillate the moist entrance of her lush orifice. But it was her clitoris that her fingers sought. Easing back its hood she rubbed it erotically until it was proudly erect. It stood red and throbbing, and as Lord C. watched enthralled, she grimaced and moaned for his entertainment. Her fingers worked on herself like lightning as she masturbated, and she came with a series of gasps leading up to a blood-curdling scream.

She was most certainly a full-blooded extrovert and exhibitionist. She threw her legs back provocatively and, grabbing her ankles, she held them high above her head. Her moist quim was totally exposed. She couldn't have offered herself more overtly. Her twat was like an open door. Watching her antics exhilarated the colonel, and he straddled her without warning.

'You know what you are, m'gal? You're an oversexed exhibitionist.'

'Is that what I am?' she laughed. 'I thought I was just a girl who wanted a good screw. What do you call a girl who likes to masturbate in front of a man?'

'Freud would have a word for it.'

He eased her derrière to the edge of the bed, and standing on the floor, positioned himself to plunge his pulsing rod into her ripe fig. She was so wet and sticky that each long stroke inside her glutinous twat was accompanied by a distinct slurp. He increased his rhythm, plunging into her with the regularity of a clockwork motor. It couldn't last long. They approached climax together.

He curved his back in a supreme effort to get even further inside her. She strove to part her legs even wider, so he could burrow to the very boundaries of her throbbing tunnel.

She came with a series of delightful little ladylike screams, so different from the rutting sow she had been trying to imitate. He gasped with a deep-felt satisfaction, as he flooded her with sperm, which mingled with her own freely flowing quim juices. It was a fitting end to her time at the manor.

Christine and Sylvia arrived in New York by seaplane from Lisbon. It had been an uneventful trip. When they landed they found the country bubbling with the aftermath of a presidential election campaign. Franklin D. Roosevelt had been elected for a third term. He had fought his campaign by promising not to take the nation into the European war, but he was sympathetic to Britain.

Since the fall of France many Americans wanted to give Britain aid, realising the Atlantic wasn't an absolute barrier against Nazism. Roosevelt would now try to get a Lease Lend Bill passed to help near-bankrupt Britain. Although more than sixty per cent of the nation wanted to send aid, the American First Committee was fiercely isolationist, and it was both powerful and influential.

The two girls moved to Washington to be at the heart of the game of politics, and within a month were party-going with the rich and famous.

Sylvia was lusted after by a southern senator, and she played him along without allowing him any favours. It was when she learned he was to speak about the controversial Lease Lend Bill at a big social gathering that she saw the opportunity to go to work.

It wasn't difficult wangling an invitation from him, but she found it awkward introducing a political subject into their conversation, as she had taken the role of an empty-headed dizzy blonde.

'What are you going to say about lease lend tonight?' she asked.

'Now, that's something you don't have to worry your pretty head about.'

'I'd really like to know,' she cooed.

'Great heavens, what for?'

'I'm British, remember?'

'So you are. It's important to your folks back home, isn't it? You're a sweet kid to worry about them.'

He irritated her, but she smiled sweetly like the dumb blonde she was supposed to be.

'Don't worry, I'm going to make a case for both sides, but I'm coming down for aid.'

'How strong?'

'Well, to be honest I daren't be too strong. A lot of my people are isolationists.'

'You're going to lose out on the chance of being a rallying point in a campaign the president supports?'

'Just listen to you, little girl,' he chortled. 'No, it's too big a chance to take.'

'My country is taking a bigger one. We are standing alone now, fighting for freedom.'

'I've heard it all before,' he murmured, 'but coming from you, it makes me feel a bit of a shit.'

'Be brave, and I'll reward my knight with my favours.'

'You mean that, girlie?'

'I do, sir. Your wish will be my command.'

'I'd be a fool to turn down an offer like that, wouldn't I?'

'I think so,' she smiled. 'I'll be listening, and afterwards I'll be waiting for you – or not.'

She listened to his after-dinner speech with bated breath, and smiled when he came out strongly on the side of the Bill. There was still a long way to go, but she reckoned she had already repaid her transatlantic fare.

Much later he joined her at a table at the rear of the bar.

'Satisfied, missie?'

'You're a darling, and a brilliant politician.'

'Less of the smarm. What do I get to do?'

'Whatever you want. I don't go back on my word.'

'I've a young niece. She's just coming up to her sixteenth birthday. She's a sweet kid with the loveliest butt,' he said, 'and she's high spirited like an unbroken filly.'

'And you'd like to break her in?'

'Jeese, wouldn't I? I've dreamed of spanking that sweet butt, and taking her panties down to give her the balling of her young life.'

'Shall I call you uncle?'

'Would you?'

'Why not, if that's your pleasure?' she crooned. 'My hotel room, tomorrow afternoon.'

The following morning she shopped for the sort of clothes an average American teenage girl would wear.

When he arrived she was dressed in a white sweater, a short pleated kilt and ankle socks. He took one look at her, and his eyes sparkled with unbridled lechery. She watched him pull an upright chair into the centre of the room, and take his jacket off with slow deliberation.

'What are you going to do, uncle?' she asked anxiously.

'You've been a sassy young pup for too long,' he growled, 'and now I'm gonna slap your butt.'

'You can't do that.'

'And when your ass is good and sore,' he grunted, 'you're gonna get humped.'

'But uncle,' she squealed, 'I'm a virgin.'

'And if I find you're telling lies, you'll get another whipping.'

'Uncle . . .'

He grabbed her arm, and dragged her protesting towards the chair where he was sitting. Whining like a spoilt girl-child, she nervously stretched her young body over his lap.

He positioned her impatiently. Her palms were flat on the carpet, as he settled her tummy and thighs comfortably across his knees. Her gorgeous long legs reached straight out, with only her toes touching the floor. He seemed to be satisfied, while she was very conscious of her behind raised in such a juvenile and vulnerable manner for spanking. It was bloody undignified, and she felt ashamed for herself, until he commenced to slap her comely derrière, and she forgot her dignity.

He warmed up with half a dozen half-hearted swipes at her kilted fundament. She hissed in indignation, but it didn't really hurt. Once her kilt had been whipped up onto her shoulder blades, he began to skelp her knickered bottom in earnest. She wriggled and bawled, as the palm of his hand lambasted her poor bum.

'Stop, uncle. Please stop,' she shrieked.

He stopped long enough to grab the waistband of her brief white knickers, and yank them down to her dimpled knees.

'Wilful little girls get their knickers taken down,' he snapped.

'No,' she shrilled. 'You mustn't.'

Her protests went unnoticed as he commenced spanking her bare posterior. She kicked her legs, but he pushed them down again. She writhed and squirmed, as the slaps landed on her tender white flesh.

'Stand up,' he barked, 'and get those panties off.'

She did as she was bid. She stood facing him, quietly snivelling and wiping the tears from her eyes with her fingers. She felt just like a young adolescent who had been punished.

'Turn around,' he ordered, 'feet apart. Bend over. Palms of your hands on the ground. I want that saucy red ass high in the air, girl. You're gonna get screwed like you've never been.'

'No, uncle,' she wailed, 'You mustn't fuck me.'

She fell forward on to her hands, and he immediately moved forward between her legs. She could feel his anxious pecker nudging at the gates of her quim. She was surprised when she felt the tip of his quivering prong slip easily between her cunt lips into her ripe fig. The spanking had left her moist, and ready for intercourse.

He stabbed into her with indecent haste like a young man with his first prostitute. His rampant weapon travelled her slippery tunnel of love until his balls swung against her stomach.

The torment of his thighs pushing against her anguished derrière made her sob. As she began to cry, he began to work his tool frantically inside her glutinous honey-pot. She gasped and wailed, as the storm of orgasm gathered inside her, and when she climaxed she whinnied like a mare on heat. He shouted gleefully at his success, and threw her on to the bed to continue humping her in the missionary position. It was a long fuck, and when he finally came she was exhausted.

When they contacted Lord C. he was thrilled with Sylvia's achievements, and suggested they continue along that path. A little research revealed the names of other politicians who were sitting on the fence. The number quickly reduced when it came to finding out those who might be susceptible to female charms. One name was a distinct possibility, and he was a well-known tennis fanatic. Christine was the obvious choice to net him.

She had been accepted to play in a local tournament in Philadelphia, and the British embassy had been instructed to make certain he had been invited as a VIP. Although her game was rusty, Christine played sufficiently well to reach the semi-finals. Her brief white shorts, extra tight tennis top and loosely tied golden hair were enough to gain the attention of a certain congressman, and he went out of his way to seek her out during the grand ball following the final.

'You're a fine tennis player, Christine.'

'Thank you.'

'May I call you Christine?'

'Please do.'

She decided to take the bull by the horns. After all if he walked away she would have trouble getting to know him again: and more importantly they were alone.

'You did well to get in the semis,' he continued. 'I'm a great tennis fan. I saw you play at Forest Hills in 1938.'

'I know you too. Aren't you the senator who is campaigning for lease lend?'

'Well, not exactly.'

'I could have sworn . . .'

'No, I'm still very much on the fence,' he smiled. 'You've been listening to tittle-tattle.'

'But you are coming down on that side.'

'Why?' he asked. 'Have you a vested interest?'

'I've just come from Europe. There's a war going on over there.'

'You're Australian.'

'We're fighting the same war.'

'I'm sorry. Of course you are.'

'So is the US of A going to lend a hand?'

'I think it will work out that way.'

'With a little help from people like you?'

'You're a persistent young lady.'

'I've been in that war, senator. I've heard the guns. It makes a difference.'

'Hey, steady up. I'm on your side.'

'Well, come out and say so.'

He suddenly looked peeved, and a trifle sullen. She thought she'd gone too far.

'I'm sorry to talk like that,' she murmured, 'but I'm prepared to put myself on the line. I'll do anything which will help persuade you. Anything.'

'Now, that's an offer I'll find hard to refuse,' he grinned. 'You'll be hearing from me.'

After a fortnight had gone by she had given up hope of ever hearing from him again. She began to fish around for another politician to contact.

It was approaching Christmas, and she'd just returned from an orgy of shopping, when the phone rang. The senator wanted to take advantage of her offer, and suggested she meet him at the airport that evening. He was off to New Orleans to stay with his regular tennis partner, who held an influential post at the US Treasury.

Both men were waiting for her at the airport, and they flew to New Orleans via St Louis.

Washington was bitter cold when they left, but New Orleans was bathed in winter sunshine. On the plane the senator told her the score. The treasury man was a southerner, who had a hideaway just outside New Orleans which he used for tennis and poker. She thought the tennis would be straightforward, but guessed she would be on the receiving end of the poker. The following morning she wore her smartest tennis outfit. She needn't have bothered.

'How about if you play a set against us in turn,' asked the senator. 'Only thing is we'd kind of like it if you were nude.'

'You want me to take my clothes off?'

'That's about the size of it.'

'All of them?'

'Yup.'

'Can I wear my plimsolls?'

'I don't see why not.'

'Thanks a million,' she muttered.

She played the treasury man, while the senator watched. She was very conscious that he was watching her, and not the tennis – watching her naked athleticism.

She nearly lost the first set, but gradually managed to push her nakedness to the back of her mind and concentrate to win 8-6. Against the senator it was easier, and she defeated him 6-3. They gave her no respite, as they forced her to play two more sets without rest. She fought to win them both. She was damned if she was going to be beaten, as well as humiliated.

She was exhausted by the end of the last set, and the perspiration soaked her as if she had been in a swimming pool rather than a tennis court. She had been well over two hours on court, and she reckoned they must be more familiar with her naked body than she was.

She went to get a towel to wipe herself, and was dying for a shower. Instead she was led to the centre of the court, and made to bend forward over the net. The senator had taken off his shorts, and was standing behind her. The treasury man was on the other side of the net, and held her shoulders to make certain she stayed bent double over the net. She became aware of a stiff John Thomas trying to nudge his way between her thighs, so she parted her legs obligingly. The senator's knob moved across the smooth white skin of her open thighs, and was soon covered with sweat which trickled from her body. Only when he was satisfied it was moist with her sweat, did he position the tip at the entrance to her exquisite love grotto.

As the tip of his weapon nuzzled gently against the outer folds of her moist vagina, the senator could feel the heat of her body. The exercise and the hot sun had made her cunt-lips as warm as toast, and he wondered whether the temperature inside her grotto was any higher. He sank into her with one smooth thrust. Once he was deep inside her, he held her motionless.

She hung over the net, impaled from the rear, looking through her own shapely legs at his hairy ones, while her golden hair cascaded on to the grass. She couldn't see the treasury man standing at her head, but could sense he was still there.

'Don't just stand there like a spare prick at a wedding,' she cried. 'Pop it in my mouth, and I'll suck you off.'

He took her up on her offer, and lifted her so she could hold him around the waist. His dick was positioned under her nose, and she wasn't surprised to see it was as hard as iron. Maybe it was the idea of her giving him head, or listening to her talk dirty, or watching her being taken from behind. Whatever the reason he was raring to go, and she circled the helmet of his agitated knob with her soft wet lips.

Sucking sweetly, she felt the other prick begin to move inside her tube. As the tempo of the penis inside her steaming hot cunt increased, so she sucked the second cock in rhythm. The senator grasped her shoulders, and leaned his whole weight on her back. She was forced to brace her legs, and desperately hold on to the man she was gobbling.

The senator commenced to ride her like a racehorse in a desperate finish, as his palpitating knob stabbed in and out of her glutinous hole sixteen to the dozen. She wanted to urge him to ease off, but her mouth was full of cock.

As the senator approached orgasm, he jerked his bursting prick out of her, and shot his load all over her back.

Now the piston had been moved from between her legs, she could gobble the dick in her mouth with a gentle expertise. She sucked and licked the whole length of his quivering shaft, until he ached for her to drag his orgasm from him. Teasingly, she fingered his testicles, as he groaned in the ecstasy of his gathering storm. Her mouth went right down on him, as she felt his wand trembling on her tongue. He clasped her head between outstretched palms, and cupping her face in his crotch he urged her to receive his sperm in her mouth. Thus, she was surprised when at the moment of ejaculation he withdrew from her lips, and spunked all over her face and hair.

Her back ached, and when she stood erect she found pain in every muscle. She had forgotten she had just played four strenuous sets of tennis. She must present a pretty sight, she thought, her body glistening with a mixture of sweat and semen.

There was a garden hose on the patio, and they hosed each other down like horses after a punishing race. She felt cooler, as they towelled themselves dry. They had even used the hose on her like a huge douche to flush out her vagina with rushes of cold water. The senator switched on the radio to catch the end of a news summary.

'. . . and the senator made it clear in his speech yesterday afternoon that he would be supporting the president in his efforts to introduce a system of lease lend to aid the British in their heroic fight against the Nazis.'

'You see,' he smiled, 'I keep my word.'

She knew he had already decided where his allegiance lay before he met her, but maybe she had got him to jump off the fence earlier than he'd planned. It was certain that the more who supported the president, the more would be likely to line up behind them.

She wondered whether her father knew she was a spy. She wondered if he'd be proud, or just condemn the methods she was using. She smiled to herself. What a way to fight a war.

Epilogue

Lord C. was lonely. All the girls had flown the nest, and he was alone. It had begun as a bit of a joke. An old lecher with an impudent idea which would give him access to sexy young women. Women who, at his word, would take part in any kind of debauchery.

Gradually, he had seen that his licentious fantasies had a substance which could make them reality. They really could be used to assist the covert security services in their wartime role.

He had used many personal contacts to get his scheme off the ground, and had received the blessings of many at the very top. Now he was the controller of C's Circus, and his female operatives were working in the four corners of the globe.

He wasn't certain where he could go from here. He had people to see, and plans to discuss. Perhaps there would be another intake of girls. He certainly missed them around. He missed their bouncing breasts, and their wicked smiles. Most of all, he missed them in his bed.

There was a knock at the door. It would be his new driver, assigned to him by HQ Western Command.

'Come in,' he called wearily.

A young woman in ATS uniform entered – a good-looking young woman with attributes which were bursting to get out of her uniform. She smiled at him, and her sultry brown eyes seemed to hold a promise. She snapped to attention.

'Corporal Hawkes reporting for duty, sir.'

'I couldn't possibly call you that. What's your first name?'

'Betty, sir.'

'I was about to have tea. Would you care to join me?'

'I'd love to sir,' she smiled prettily.

On the tea tray she noticed a large cucumber.

HELP US TO PLAN THE FUTURE OF EROTIC FICTION –

– and no stamp required!

The Nexus Library is Britain's largest and fastest-growing collection of erotic fiction. We'd like your help to make it even bigger and better.

Like many of our books, the questionnaire below is completely anonymous, so don't feel shy about telling us what you really think. We want to know what kind of people our readers are – we want to know what you like about Nexus books, what you dislike, and what changes you'd like to see.

Just answer the questions on the following pages in the spaces provided; if more than one person would like to take part, please feel free to photocopy the questionnaire. Then tear the pages from the book and send them in an envelope to the address at the end of the questionnaire. No stamp is required.

THE NEXUS QUESTIONNAIRE

SECTION ONE: ABOUT YOU

1.1 Sex *(yes, of course, but try to be serious for just a moment)*
    Male ☐   Female ☐

1.2 Age
    under 21 ☐   21 – 30 ☐
    31 – 40 ☐   41 – 50 ☐
    51 – 60 ☐   over 60 ☐

1.3 At what age did you leave full-time education?
    still in education ☐   16 or younger ☐
    17 – 19 ☐   20 or older ☐

1.4 Occupation _____

1.5 Annual household income
    under £10,000 ☐   £10–£20,000 ☐
    £20–£30,000 ☐   £30–£40,000 ☐
    over £40,000 ☐

1.6 Where do you live?
Please write in the county in which you live (for example Hampshire), or the city if you live in a large metropolitan area (for example Manchester) _____

SECTION TWO : ABOUT BUYING NEXUS BOOKS

2.1 How did you acquire this book?
I bought it myself ☐   My partner bought it ☐
I borrowed it/found it ☐

2.2 If this book was bought ...
... in which town or city? _____
... in what sort of shop: High Street bookshop ☐
local newsagent ☐
at a railway station ☐
at an airport ☐
at motorway services ☐
other: _____

2.3 Have you ever had difficulty finding Nexus books on sale?
Yes ☐   No ☐
If you have had difficulty in buying Nexus books, where would you like to be able to buy them?
... in which town or city _____
... in what sort of shop from list in previous question _____

2.4 Have you ever been reluctant to buy a Nexus book because of the sexual nature of the cover picture?
Yes ☐   No ☐

2.5 Please tick which of the following statements you agree with:
I find some Nexus cover pictures offensive/ too blatant ☐

I would be less embarassed about buying Nexus books if the cover pictures were less blatant ☐

I think that in general the pictures on Nexus books are about right ☐

I think Nexus cover pictures should be as sexy as possible ☐

SECTION THREE: ABOUT NEXUS BOOKS

3.1   How many Nexus books do you own? _____

3.2   Roughly how many Nexus books have you read? _____

3.3   What are your three favourite Nexus books?
        First choice   _____
        Second Choice   _____
        Third Choice   _____

3.4   What are your three favourite Nexus cover pictures?
        First choice   _____
        Second choice   _____
        Third choice   _____

SECTION FOUR: ABOUT YOUR IDEAL EROTIC NOVEL

We want to publish books you want to read − so this is your chance to tell us exactly what your ideal erotic novel would be like.

4.1   Using a scale of 1 to 5 (1 = no interest at all, 5 = your ideal), please rate the following possible settings for an erotic novel:
        Medieval/barbarian/sword 'n' sorcery   ☐
        Renaissance/Elizabethan/Restoration   ☐
        Victorian/Edwardian   ☐
        1920s & 1930s − the Jazz Age   ☐
        Present day   ☐
        Future/Science Fiction   ☐

4.2   Using the same scale of 1 to 5, please rate the following styles in which an erotic novel could be written:
        Realistic, down to earth, set in real life   ☐
        Escapist fantasy, but just about believable   ☐
        Completely unreal, impressionistic, dreamlike ☐

4.3   Would you prefer your ideal erotic novel to be written from the viewpoint of the main male characters or the main female characters?
        Male   ☐   Female   ☐

4.4   Is there one particular setting or subject matter that your ideal erotic novel would contain?
        _____

SECTION FIVE: LAST WORDS

5.1   What do you like best about Nexus books?

_____

_____

5.2   What do you most dislike about Nexus books?

_____

_____

5.3   In what way, if any, would you like to change Nexus covers?

_____

_____

5.4   Here's a space for any other comments:

_____

_____

_____

_____

_____

_____

_____

_____

Thank you for completing this questionnaire. Now tear it out of the book – carefully! – put it in an envelope and send it to:

Nexus Books
FREEPOST
London
W10 5BR

No stamp is required.